PUFFIN BOOKS

green jasper

Books are to be returned on or before
the last date below

Books by K. M. Grant

BLOOD RED HORSE
GREEN JASPER

green jasper

K. M. GRANT

PUFFIN

PUFFIN BOOKS

Published by the Penguin Group
Penguin Books Ltd, 80 Strand, London WC2R 0RL, England
Penguin Group (USA) Inc., 375 Hudson Street, New York, New York 10014, USA
Penguin Group (Canada), 10 Alcorn Avenue, Toronto, Ontario, Canada M4V 3B2
(a division of Pearson Penguin Canada Inc.)
Penguin Ireland, 25 St Stephen's Green, Dublin 2, Ireland
(a division of Penguin Books Ltd)
Penguin Group (Australia), 250 Camberwell Road,
Camberwell, Victoria 3124, Australia (a division of Pearson Australia Group Pty Ltd)
Penguin Books India Pvt Ltd, 11 Community Centre,
Panchsheel Park, New Delhi – 110 017, India
Penguin Group (NZ), cnr Airborne and Rosedale Roads, Albany,
Auckland 1310, New Zealand (a division of Pearson New Zealand Ltd)
Penguin Books (South Africa) (Pty) Ltd, 24 Sturdee Avenue,
Rosebank, Johannesburg 2196, South Africa

Penguin Books Ltd, Registered Offices: 80 Strand, London WC2R 0RL, England

www.penguin.com

First published 2005
1

Copyright © K. M. Grant, 2005
All rights reserved

The moral right of the author has been asserted

Set in 11/13.75 pt Adobe Sabon
Typeset by Rowland Phototypesetting Ltd, Bury St Edmunds, Suffolk
Made and printed in England by Clays Ltd, St Ives plc

British Library Cataloguing in Publication Data
A CIP catalogue record for this book is available from the British Library

ISBN 0–141–31737–X

for my father and my mother
tenez le vraye

Prologue

Through chilly winter sunshine, a young man galloped at speed along a track roughly following the curves of the river Danube. He rode at speed not because he was afraid, although he was in a foreign land and his dark features made him an object of curiosity in the Austrian villages through which he passed: he rode at speed because it eased the turmoil in his heart. Not yet twenty-one, his world had just been shattered for the second time. Saladin, the Saracen leader who had adopted him as a son after the death of his parents, had fallen ill and felt in his bones that his time on earth would be measured in months, not years. When he died, so the young man's security and hopes would die too. Saladin had told the young man as much before urging him, with what strength the bilious fever that blackened his blood allowed, not to wait until the end, but to take a horse now, find a ship and flee from Palestine. 'I have been listening to the chatter of the emirs through the ears of their servants,' he said. 'You are not safe here. I wanted you for my heir, Kamil, but I am no longer strong enough to insist. The emirs are jealous of all you achieved during the crusade just past and I can no longer protect you. Go, my precious son, and may Allah go with you.'

1

Kamil had been appalled. Why should the jealousy of old men who preferred plotting to fighting cause him to leave behind everything familiar? His lean face hardened like rock. 'I do not fear the emirs,' he said, but Saladin had caught his arm and, with a supreme effort, raised himself a fraction from his bed.

'I have a task for you, Kamil, the last I shall ever demand,' he whispered. 'Go to Richard, whom they call the Lionheart. Tell him the war between us is over. Tell him, if he values what is right, to stay in his own country and never come to the Holy Land again. He will listen to you. Now, embrace me once, then go. I command it.'

Kamil's embrace had been full of resentment but the habit of obedience was strong. Nevertheless, three months later, as he rode along the river in search of the English king, he still felt angry. By fleeing, he was condemned always to live among enemies. In the Christian West he was despised for his Muslim religion. In the Muslim East he was hated for being the sultan's favourite. He cursed Saladin, then felt overwhelmed with guilt at the memory of his sulky farewell because he knew that he would never again see the man who had been more than a father to him; never again feel the warmth of his approval; never again beat him at chess in the cool of the evening. Kamil leant forward and urged his mount to go faster, but the horse was already doing his best. The young man shut his eyes and, just for a moment, tried to pretend that this grey plodder was the luminous red horse he had briefly captured from the Christians the previous year. But it was no good. All he had left of the best horse he had ever known were memories and the thick braid of russet mane-hair that now swung gently from the belt at his waist. The grey stumbled and Kamil's eyes were jolted open just in time to see a fox slope across the track and disappear into the frosted undergrowth. He allowed the grey to fall back into an easy canter and his heart ached.

From the very top of a castle built so high above the river that it could make even the bravest man dizzy, Richard the Lionheart, Duke of Normandy and Aquitaine and King of England, stared out over the forest and the distant hills. In other circumstances, his practised eye would have been searching for any signs of quarry for the hunt. But there was no hunting in these lands, for Richard, captured by treachery on his way back from crusade, was held against his will. He climbed the weary steps to the top of the castle several times daily, not to spy, but because it was the only exercise he was allowed and he was fearful of growing fat during his enforced inactivity. He would not give his enemies that satisfaction. Leaning over the parapet, he followed the arc of an eagle as it flew across the setting sun. He did not spend time envying its freedom, for he knew, with unflagging certainty, that God would not desert one like himself who had fought on His behalf. One day he would be free and his revenge would be deadly.

Nevertheless, as he watched the eagle hover, Richard missed the tense folded weight of one of his own hawks on his arm and squinted down, trying to see what had caught the creature's eye. He was patient, and eventually something glinted through the leaves far below. He stood perfectly still, able to tell by the rhythm of the glint – flash, flash, flash – that it was a rider. He leant further forward but as the rider came closer, also realized with disappointment that it was not a Frankish or an English knight. It was clear from the fluid and easy way the man sat that he was a stranger to heavy armour and a stiff saddle. *Why*, thought Richard, narrowing his eyes to slits, *he may be dressed like a German man of business, but the man's a Saracen*. He waited until he was sure that the rider was going to beg for entrance to the castle, then hurried down the steps and into the small rooms that comprised his prison quarters.

Kamil had learnt at the Italian coast that Richard was a captive in Austria and at first he had been glad, for it seemed to spell the end of Saladin's mission. But, on further enquiry, it seemed that the king, like an animal in the zoo, was publicly displayed by his captors to any Christian dignitary who asked to see him. Whether this same privilege would apply to a Muslim, nobody could say, but Kamil felt honour bound to make an attempt. He met no resistance, and when he was eventually shown into the king's presence, although he knew it was customary, he did not bow. 'I am come from my master, Saladin,' he said. 'He believes he will die soon.'

Richard moved forward at once and fell to his knees. This was not what Kamil expected. 'I should be grateful for the deliverance,' Richard said, crossing himself as Kamil stood unbending, 'but we were worthy enemies, your master and I.' He prayed in silence as the rooks cawed outside, but got up before the recent creeping stiffness in his knees would have obliged him to use a chair as a prop.

'This is how I now live,' he said, gesturing at his rooms, his eyes never leaving Kamil's face. 'I am surrounded by Christian traitors. My captors barter with me as if I were a slab of meat. My own brother, John, plots to take my

English crown and all my French lands. There is nobody left I can trust.'

Kamil's expression remained blank.

'We are not strangers, you and I,' Richard continued carefully. 'We met in Palestine as enemies but do you not agree that honour makes a bond between us?' When Kamil made no movement, Richard chose to take that for assent. 'In memory of the suffering your master and I shared during the crusade and in the name of your God and mine, I want you now to do something for me, something I can trust to no other, since among my own people I do not know who is still loyal and who is not. Will you accept such a charge? Enemies we may be, but I think we can strike a bargain.'

Kamil could see the small muscle in Richard's cheek working through his beard. It was the only sign of weakness the king exhibited and it prompted the young man to break his silence. 'You trust a Muslim before any Christian? Your own people must be traitors indeed.'

'Not all of them. Those two young knights, Gavin de Granville and his brother, Will Ravensgarth, whose red horse you seemed so taken with, they are to be trusted. I wish to send a letter to them to prove that I am still alive and will return. Will you take such a letter to England? I think they will be happy to receive it. And I dare say the red horse will be pleased to see you. There was something of a bond between you, was there not?'

Richard watched Kamil blink and a shiver pass through him. It was cold, but both men knew it was not the cold that caused it.

Kamil drew back. 'I know nothing of England,' he said icily.

'Oh,' said Richard, keeping his voice light. 'It is a

small sort of place. I have never been particularly fond of it, even though I was born there. But the de Granvilles are fine people and I know I can put my faith in them. I believe they live somewhere south-west of the port of Whitby. A clever man like you could easily find them.' He walked with a soldier's swift and economical gait to a table and sat down. Pushing quantities of ruined parchment out of the way, he took a clean vellum and a quill, speaking as he wrote. 'I don't think either of those de Granville boys can read, and if you can't either –' he looked up but Kamil gave nothing away – 'I dare say some old monk will do it for a shilling or so.'

The quill scratched. Richard rolled the parchment, lit a taper and, with a disarming smile, attached his seal.

Afterwards, Kamil realized that, just as he had never delivered Saladin's plea, so he had never actually agreed to carry out Richard's task. Nevertheless, the following day he found himself riding westwards, travelling swiftly through the German empire and heading for the Flemish coast with the letter flattened against his breast. He hardly rested until he reached Bruges, for he seldom felt safe, but in Bruges he took a room for the night and allowed himself to sleep. His sleep was deep but full of disturbance, for he seemed to hear Saladin's voice, not berating him for being a poor messenger, but repeating the red horse's name. *Hosanna! Hosanna!* The echo sounded like a clarion and suddenly the red horse was there, his sweet breath cool on Kamil's cheek. Still sleeping, Kamil blindly stretched out his hand to touch the horse's familiar star, that distinctive patch of white on his forehead, the only white mark in that deep-red coat, but it faded just as he reached it. The young man woke with a cry, clutching at nothing. And suddenly he was sure that Saladin was at death's door. That was the reason his voice had seemed so clear. His allotted time span was drawing rapidly to an end, and his last thoughts were of his adopted son.

Kamil lay sleepless now, half wanting to throw Richard's letter away and return home, despite the sultan's warnings. However, he did not. He had come too far. Instead, the next morning, he went down to the waterside and made enquiries about a passage to England.

1

Hartslove, Valentine's Day 1193

'If you don't sit still, Miss Ellie, wedding day or no wedding day, I'll be tempted to box your ears.'

High up in the keep of Hartslove Castle, a fat old nurse was braiding Eleanor de Barre's smooth hanks of auburn hair and threading them through with gold. It was early afternoon, but the candles were lit because it was snowing lightly and darkness had already begun to fall. Lurking by the door, two smaller girls, identically dressed in long red tunics, were staring at the bride.

Ellie coloured slightly. 'It's only hair,' she said defiantly, and made a face into the tin disc that hung on the wall. Old Nurse opened her mouth, but something in Ellie's face made her shut it again.

One of the smaller girls moved forward to help, but the other looked mutinous and kicked the door with the edge of her foot. *Bang, bang, bang.* The girl knew it irritated Ellie, but she didn't care. Marissa cared about very little, except her twin sister, Marie, and not always about her. It was just over a fortnight since they had been brought to Hartslove Castle in a cart and dumped, so it seemed to Marissa, because, after their father was killed on crusade, Gavin de Granville was the only person who would agree to take them in. It was his duty, so she had heard him say. Fourteen-year-old girls could not be left to fend for themselves. Duty!

She kicked the door harder. *Bang, bang, BANG.* If she were to be considered a duty, she was going to make the duty a hard one. Now Gavin was to marry this Ellie, who clearly resented having two children foisted on to her and scarcely bothered to conceal the fact.

Bang, BANG, BANG! Not that Marissa was jealous of Ellie. Who on earth could really want to marry a knight with one arm, even if he had lost his arm heroically on crusade? Ellie was welcome to Gavin. Yes, she was welcome to him, particularly since that got her out of the way of Gavin's younger brother, Will.

At the thought of Will, Marissa temporarily suspended the banging and, quite without thinking, smoothed her own hair. Old Nurse threw her a glance, which was a mistake since Marissa immediately dropped her hands and began banging again. Will had been nice to them, when, that is, he could be dragged away from that red horse, with whom he seemed unhealthily obsessed. Horses were just animals – animals Marissa hated. She kicked the door harder than ever.

Will had only stayed a day before going off to take possession of lands in the west given to him by King Richard, along with the title Earl of Ravensgarth. After he had gone, Marissa had written, in the careful hand her mother had taught her before she died, 'Marissa, Countess of Ravensgarth' on a vellum piece, leaving it purposefully out for Ellie to see. She knew Ellie had burnt it, pushing every piece into the flames with a poker. This gave Marissa particular pleasure. Ellie was marrying Gavin. She couldn't have Will too. *BANG, BANG, BANG* and a smile of triumph.

Irritated beyond endurance, Ellie turned round, causing Old Nurse to huff like a hippopotamus as her neat handiwork was whipped out of her hands. 'Why don't you both go and find some mistletoe or something to thread through the dogs' collars?' Ellie tried to make it a suggestion rather than an order. 'You'll find piles of greenery in the great hall. The dogs should look nice today as well as us.'

Marissa gave an insolent stare, which Ellie, forgetting herself entirely, returned in kind. 'Come, Marie,' Marissa glared at Old Nurse. 'They don't want us here.' Then, giving the door a final kick, she stamped unevenly down the stone steps.

Marissa had been lame for about three years, and when the sleeve of her dress fell back, it revealed that she also had two red and unsightly marks on her left forearm. Just before the twins' father, Sir Hugh de Neville, left on crusade, he had come to visit the steward's house in which his children were lodging. He was riding a new Spanish stallion purchased for the journey and while Marie smiled and nodded but kept her distance, for she was nervous of all animals except kittens, Marissa had been thrilled, desperate to show her father how brave she was. At that time, horses held no fears for her. She had laughed with delight when Sir Hugh tossed her into the saddle in front of him and rode around the water meadows. If he went a little fast, Marissa was not going to complain. She basked in his adulation while Marie was ignored.

But the evening before Sir Hugh was to depart, Marissa had gone back into the stables to give the stallion an apple. The horse was restive but she fearlessly climbed on to the manger and held out her hand. He backed away and stamped his foot. Marissa leant a little further, then lost her balance and, clutching wildly at the animal's tethering rope, fell into the straw. Terrified and angry, the stallion reared and plunged down to attack. By the time his teeth buried themselves in Marissa's arm and his weight had crushed her leg, the child was almost unconscious, and when the stable boys finally severed the rope and beat the stallion off, Marissa was given up for dead.

She was not dead, however. Flung roughly on to a bed by her father, she came to just long enough to hear his diatribe about her stupidity and how the horse, the most expensive animal he had ever bought, had injured his knee. He had not the money, he said, to pay for a surgeon for his daughter as well as medicines for his Spanish stallion and he was clear which creature was the more important. He could not replace his horse, but Marissa was a girl – a twin girl at that – so her loss would be no loss. As Marie cowered behind a chair, too frightened of her father to plead on her sister's behalf, the steward was told to leave Marissa to die. Without a further word, Hugh stormed off, cursing the day his daughters had been born. It was the last time they ever saw him.

Since then, great, hovering hooves and bared teeth featured almost nightly in Marissa's dreams, and every day she cursed firstly her father, then the steward, who had spent much of his own gold on a surgeon, then the steward's wife who had nursed her so carefully. She cursed Marie, whose gentle hands had eased her fever with cold cloths and tears. She cursed the local apothecary, who had taught her to swim so that her leg might not wither through lack of exercise, and, most of all, Marissa cursed herself.

Marie could hear curses echoing in the stairway now and had Marissa not been adamant that Ellie was to know nothing of the accident, Marie would have explained everything so that Ellie could understand. But Marissa had made her promise and, anyway, this was not the time. Marie could see that Ellie wanted to be rid of her too, so she just said shyly, 'I think you look beautiful. Please don't mind Marissa.' Then she fled.

Ellie turned back to her mirror and felt ashamed. It was not the twins' fault that they were here. 'Everything is changed,' she said to Old Nurse plaintively. 'It wasn't supposed to be like this.' And she burst into tears.

Old Nurse shifted her great weight, clucking with dismay. She patted Ellie's shoulder then settled her fat knees a little wider apart and picked up the hank of hair once again. 'There, dearie,' she said. 'There. Not on your wedding day. There's all the guests down in the hall and Master Will will be here soon. He'll want to see you happy. With Hosanna in his old stable for at least a night or two, it will seem quite like old times, or at least the best that can be done.'

Ellie stopped crying. Old Nurse was right. It was the best that could be done. She wiped her eyes and looked out through the glassless window. She would concentrate on how pretty the snow was, with each flake landing serenely in its allotted place; just as she was filling her allotted place by marrying Gavin, for whom she had been earmarked from childhood when his father, Sir Thomas de Granville, had taken her in; just as Gavin in his turn was taking in Marissa and Marie.

What's more, Ellie told herself, *I'm really very lucky. Gavin needs me and there is no reason at all why we should not be happy. No reason at all.* She repeated these sentiments several times as Old Nurse's fingers, though rough and podgy, bound up the glossy wedding plait surprisingly deftly and immediately transformed an impish girl into an elegant young woman.

'I wish Sir Thomas could see you now,' Old Nurse murmured, dabbing her eyes on her apron. 'I don't know why he had to die on crusade when so many wicked people survived. Mistress Cranby's husband got himself home and I know for certain that he is a thief.' She made a loud harrumphing noise and took a swig from a small stoppered pot. 'Now, my sweet, are you ready?'

But Ellie felt far from ready. 'Just a few more moments,' she begged, and, as Old Nurse lowered herself, puffing, on to a chair, suddenly ran over and plumped herself on to the old lady's lap. There was always comfort to be found in Old Nurse's familiar lumpy softness and she needed it very much now.

Sighing, Old Nurse enfolded Ellie in her great arms and began to rock and sing in a low, cavernous voice that ebbed and flowed like a full tide. Ellie leant her head against the welcoming shoulder and shut her eyes, forgetting, for the moment, about the wedding and remembering only her childhood, when Will and she had been inseparable playmates and marriage to Gavin was something for a future still far off. She remembered the day Hosanna arrived at Hartslove and how exciting it had been. That time seemed to have passed before she had ever properly appreciated it, for, all too soon, the Hartslove horses and men had left to fight the dreaded Saracens on crusade. Ellie shuddered slightly and Old Nurse held her tighter. But Ellie knew that not all Saracens were wicked. After all, one of them had saved Hosanna's life. Old Nurse felt Ellie relax a little.

Hosanna. It was impossible to be sad when thinking about him. The horse had some quality that made you feel that the world was a good place. Ellie couldn't say quite what this quality was. Nobody could. But everybody recognized it. When Hosanna was at Hartslove, tempers were a little better and smiles a little wider. Ellie smiled now, rather wistfully, at the round face of the woman who had tended all her childish illnesses and injuries. *Dear Old Nurse*, she thought, and planted a spontaneous kiss on the old lady's appley cheek. Tasting tears, Ellie felt a lump rise in her own throat and she slid to the floor. It was time for them both to be strong.

'Come on,' she said as cheerfully as she could. 'Time to put on my necklace,' and she reached over to pick up the small box that contained carefully threaded ovals of deep green jasper, her wedding present from Gavin.

'Red jasper for love, white for gentleness, but green for faith,' he had said. 'I had a hard time deciding, but in the end I chose green, Ellie, because we must keep faith with each other, and also because green goes with your hair.'

Ellie tried not to remember that their laughter had been very uncomfortable, since neither could quite get used to thinking of the other as bride or groom and, holding the necklace up to catch the light, she also tried not to dwell on the fact that, since his return from crusade, Gavin was only occasionally the energetic tease of old, a shadow of the vigorous, impetuous knight who had once delighted in making Ellie giggle and driving Will mad. The terrible wound he had suffered had changed him. *It would have changed anybody*, Ellie thought, *but surely it does not mean that we cannot be content together?*

As Old Nurse fastened the necklace, the girl tried her

best to recapture the feeling that had overwhelmed her when she had first seen Gavin, broken in spirit and body, crossing the drawbridge as he returned from the war. At that moment she had known, with absolute certainty, that she alone could make his life whole again. The feeling had been so strong that all doubts and all worries over his injury had been pushed to one side. She had tried to explain the feeling to Will but he had not wanted to listen. In fact, he had acted very strangely ever since.

'I must have faith,' the girl whispered as she felt the ovals warm against her skin. 'Gavin's right. That's the key to everything.' In the candlelight, the green jasper glowed.

A tremendous hubbub arose from the courtyard and Ellie peered out. 'Will's here!' she exclaimed. 'Look, Old Nurse. Oh, look! He has got Hal to braid golden threads into Hosanna's mane and tail. We are a matching pair!'

Old Nurse grunted. 'Earl or no earl,' she grumbled, 'he is late. Now, Miss Ellie, or "my lady" as I shall have to get used to calling you, I am going downstairs to see what those good-for-nothing servants have done about the wedding dinner. Master Gavin likes his venison rare. If I leave it to the idiot meat cook it will be roasted to a crisp. And then there's the mulled wine and the honey. If you don't need me any more, I'll be off.'

Ellie spun round. 'I'll always need you, Old Nurse,' she burst out. Then, recovering her composure, she smiled and slowly circled. 'How do I look – I mean, really?'

Old Nurse scanned her up and down. 'You look perfect, dearie, just perfect,' she said, and Ellie flew back into her arms.

'Wish me luck, Old Nurse,' she whispered as they held tightly on to each other. 'Wish me luck and promise never, ever to call me "my lady".'

'You'll always be Miss Ellie to me.' The nurse's voice was muffled. 'Now, we'd both better get downstairs.'

They embraced again, after which Old Nurse straightened Ellie's dress, smoothed her hair for a final time and chivvied her out of the door.

At the turn of the steps leading down from Ellie's chamber they parted. Ellie made as if to go straight into the great hall but, once the nurse was out of sight, she paused for a moment. She could hear the babble of voices, nearly all male, within.

Suddenly she picked up her skirts and descended further until she emerged from a small door opening straight into the courtyard. The air was bitter and the hoof marks that Will's party had made on their arrival were already turning crusty. The snow was still falling quite gently, but a heavy sky threatened worse to come.

Ellie strained her eyes towards the stables. At first she could make out nothing, then, as torches flared one after the other all over the castle, she saw Hosanna, red as a flame himself, framed in the doorway of the long block of stalls. Will's squire, Hal, had thrown a heavy, embroidered blanket over him and hooked the reins on a spike while he took Will's second horse, Dargent, inside. Hosanna stamped his foot, impatient for his supper.

'Hosanna!' Ellie called. Oblivious to what the snow might do to her gold wedding slippers, she slithered across to greet him properly. Hosanna whickered gently as she approached, and put his nose into her hand.

Ellie laughed. 'Hello to you too!' she said, and touched the star between his eyes. 'I haven't got anything, dear Hosanna,' she went on. 'Sacramenta, your greedy mother, had all my titbits earlier today.' As she stroked his ears, he bent his neck round her and Ellie leant against him, savouring the warmth. 'Everything will be all right, won't it?' she murmured into his thick mane. She stood for a moment, then patted him and began to walk slowly back into the hall. As she turned, Hosanna was looking at her and in his deep, liquid eyes, the green stones of her necklace were reflected back at her.

Inside the hall, the air was pungent with spices, wood-smoke and wet dog. Trestles were laid across the width of the room, with steaming wine jugs and great trenchers of bread stacked up on top of them. Men were drinking freely and watching the cooks and pantry boys bringing in custards and tarts. The actual marriage ceremony would only take a few moments and they were very glad. The dinner was what they had really come for and their mouths were already beginning to water.

Gavin was standing by the huge hearth, surrounded by his favourite wolfhounds, his empty sleeve tucked into his belt. Marissa and Marie had not decorated the dogs' collars. Instead, Marie was helping the servants and Marissa was sitting, swinging her legs and tossing her hair. Ellie knew from the tilt of Gavin's dark head and from Marissa's high-pitched laughter that he was indulging her and she felt two small pangs, one of pride that this handsome man was to be her husband and one of jealousy that he was paying attention to another girl. She hurried forward.

Actually, Gavin was less interested in Marissa than in catching the words of an old man, Sir Percy Manderlay, who had been one of his father's greatest friends, as he waited impatiently for Ellie to appear. He nodded at the men and women still arriving through the solid double doors at the far end of the hall, banging the snow off their boots and throwing their swords into a great pile in the corner, but his eyes were only for his bride. When Ellie approached, although his expression hardly changed, his heart jumped. She looked so poised. He stood back as Sir Percy kissed the girl warmly on both cheeks and scarcely noticed when Marissa, her lip curled, slipped away.

'My dear, you are freezing!' Sir Percy exclaimed, drawing Ellie towards the fire. 'What has that Old Nurse been doing to you? Feeding you ice?'

'I went outside for a moment, Sir Percy,' Ellie explained. 'Do you like my necklace? Gavin gave it to me.'

Sir Percy squinted at Ellie's neck. 'Very pretty indeed,' he said. 'Suits you, that jasper. Now, where's young William? He cut it pretty fine, but he's here now and that's what matters.'

'Are you talking about me?' Will was suddenly beside them, brimming with robust good health, his brown hair tousled and damp from the journey. 'Well, Ellie, you do look something. Did you see Hosanna's mane? Hal spent hours doing it.'

Ellie beamed but Will backed away. He was speaking quite fast and, although he grasped Gavin's arm, he did not look his brother directly in the eye. 'Congratulations on your wedding day, Gavin.'

'I'm very glad to see you, Will,' Gavin replied.

'Sorry to be so late,' Will rushed on. 'The roads are awful and we could only travel slowly. The snow is really bad further to the west. Hope we haven't kept you waiting.'

Ellie opened her mouth, but was given no chance to speak. 'I have brought you a present.' Will was like a torrent in full flood. 'It's nothing, really. Hope you like it, though.'

With that he thrust a small parcel wrapped in silk into Ellie's hands and vanished into the crowd where she could hear him laughing very loudly at somebody's joke. She looked at the parcel. Gavin was watching.

'Open it,' he said. Ellie obeyed. Inside she found a small ruby horse's head set into a gold bar on which a craftsman had inscribed one word: Hosanna. 'Oh! How beautiful,' she whispered.

Gavin took the brooch. 'What is that word?' His lips tightened because he had to ask. Neither he nor Will had ever learnt to read.

'It says "Hosanna",' said Ellie. 'Look, here is the H–'

'This is not a schoolroom, Ellie,' Gavin said shortly.

Ellie looked mortified. 'Of course not.'

'Here,' Gavin was quickly ashamed of his ill humour. 'You should wear the brooch today. Let's fasten it to your bodice.' Ellie moved closer to him. He fumbled with the clasp and she helped him. They managed between them, and Gavin let his hand drop back to his side.

'Ellie –' he began to say. But she interrupted him.

'I still prefer this.' She put her hand into the folds of her dress and brought out a small, rather battered-looking wooden dog. Some of the tension eased from Gavin's face. When Ellie was small, he had given her the dog and since then it had been something of a talisman between them, marking the various phases when they had been either childhood friends or enemies.

He took the dog briefly, then handed it back. 'I can

20

still remember that day by the moat with – what was the dog's name?'

'Diligent.'

'That's it. Diligent. I still don't know what got into me, having this carved.'

They were both silent.

'It all seems ages ago, Ellie. Another life. A different life.'

'Yes,' she agreed, touching her green jasper necklace. 'But now we have our life together. It is what your father wanted.'

'But is it what you want?' Gavin's eyes grew troubled. 'My arm will not grow again, you know. There will be no miracle.'

'Gavin,' Ellie said, looking straight at him. 'In the three weeks since you have been back, have I given you any reason to doubt that I want to marry you?'

'No – but three weeks is hardly a lifetime.' He paused. 'I know how fond you are of Will . . .' His voice trailed away.

'Of course I am fond of Will,' said Ellie gently. 'I am very fond of Will. But in as much as I want to marry anybody, I want to marry you. Please, Gavin. Please try to believe me.'

He inclined his head, but did not seem convinced. Without thinking, Ellie put up her hand, wanting to touch his cheek, but he turned away at just the wrong moment and Ellie was left feeling foolish. Catching her gesture in the corner of his eye, Gavin immediately turned back, but it was too late. Ruefully, he raised his eyebrows and his expression was so comical that Ellie felt a sudden uprush of hope. Everything *would* be all right.

21

'Shall we do the deed?' Gavin asked more easily. His eyes were still anxious, but his voice was now half mocking, half serious, just as Ellie loved.

'Better not keep the guests waiting for dinner,' she replied. He took her arm and helped her through the throng and up on to the dais, to be greeted by Brother Ranulf, who was to bless them.

He squeezed her hand, then took a deep breath. 'My friends,' he shouted. 'My friends.' Nobody took any notice.

He turned to Ellie. 'Shout "DINNER!",' she suggested. Gavin raised his eyebrows again but in the end, to Gavin's minor discomfort, it was Will who called the gathering to order.

'Fellow knights, pray silence for the Count of Hartslove,' he demanded in the new deep voice he had developed in the years he had been away on crusade. There was silence at once. Will now had the authority of a knight twice his age.

'My friends,' Gavin said, nodding to his brother but not smiling. 'You are invited to feast here today to mark the wedding of Eleanor Theodora de Barre to me, made Lord de Granville, Count of Hartslove, by King Richard, and master here since the death of my father. We were betrothed before my father, my brother and some of you good people, as well as I myself, left to follow King Richard to Jerusalem. Many did not return. My father was one of those. We do not forget him. But today is a day for rejoicing. Eleanor and I will make our promises, then Brother Ranulf will bless our union. After that, we will feast. You remember the custom here at Hartslove of leaving my late mother's chair empty? Well, we are not going to do away with that. Both my father's and my mother's chairs will sit up here. I have had new chairs made for my wife –' Ellie blushed prettily as rowdy cheers broke out at the back – 'and me. Now, if we are all ready?'

Nobody spoke, so Gavin took Ellie's hand again and they turned to face each other. Old Nurse sniffed loudly.

Gavin began. 'I solemnly declare,' he said, 'that I wish to take you –'

As he spoke there was a slight commotion. Gavin took no notice at first, only raised his voice slightly. 'I wish to take you, Eleanor Theodora de Barre, as my –'

Now the noise was louder. Gavin repeated, 'I wish to take you,' but then had no choice but to stop. He looked apologetically at Ellie and frowned into the body of the hall, his mouth already open to demand a bit of hush.

However, the noise was not coming from the guests. Somebody was attempting to force open the double doors from the outside.

'What the devil?' At that moment about forty knights, heavily armed, broke through and strode in with their swords drawn. The dogs growled, but although their hackles rose, they hesitated.

'Who on earth are you?' Gavin demanded as he moved quickly in front of Ellie.

The leading knight pulled off his helmet and shouted at the dogs by name, his grating voice and darting eyes daring them to attack him. The dogs slunk back, perplexed.

Gavin stepped forward. He could hear Ellie breathing hard behind him as they both recognized the intruder. 'Constable de Scabious,' Gavin said with no hint of welcome. 'I am surprised you show your face here. As someone who betrayed our father's trust in spectacular fashion while we were away, you should know better. Since we have returned, we have heard nothing but ill of you. Unless you come in peace, the king will hear of this and he will not be pleased.' Gavin's eyes, now cool and unflinching, held the constable's for a moment.

Piers de Scabious hesitated, then flourished his sword. At once, the Hartslove knights rushed for the corner where their own weapons were piled, but their way was blocked. In the hubbub, de Scabious smiled, displaying much of his breakfast between his teeth.

'You can forget your swords!' he shouted at the wedding guests, thrusting his head back and forth like a startled turkey, a characteristic that had given Will and Ellie ample scope for mimicry when they were small and the constable ran the castle for Sir Thomas. 'And you, *Master* Gavin, can forget your fine words.' De Scabious could hardly contain himself. 'The king will indeed hear of this. You see, the king is no longer your Richard. Richard is dead. All loyal men now pay homage to John, and as one of those loyal men, I have been charged with giving you these glad tidings. Long live the king!'

There was silence as de Scabious's words sank in, then wild murmurings as men turned to each other with stricken faces. Some knelt and crossed themselves.

'The king is dead!'

'King Richard is dead!'

Gavin banged a tankard hard on the table. The murmuring subsided. 'King Richard dead? How do you know this?'

De Scabious bent his head to one side, tipping his mouth into an oily, lopsided grin. 'The news from abroad is that he died before the New Year in custody of

Duke Leopold of Austria. We have it on good authority. Nobody doubts that it is true. Now the important thing is that we have a new king, King John, the last surviving true son of the late King Henry II of blessed memory. And everybody who is not with him, Master Gavin, is against him.'

'How can John be the new king?' Gavin demanded. 'We all know that Richard named his nephew Arthur as his heir.'

'John has a better claim.' The constable was supremely smug as he repeated what he had been told by John himself. 'Arthur is a child and, besides, has never even been to England. Are you going to disagree?'

Gavin was silent, but Will spoke up. 'Yes,' he said loudly. 'I disagree. We have known since we got back from Palestine that Richard is in prison, but if we are to believe he is dead, we need proof.'

'You can believe it or not,' replied the constable, trying to keep his voice from squeaking against Will's bass. 'It's all the same. But I tell you this – that we are living in John's world now, not Richard's.' He turned back to Gavin and puffed out his chest. 'And on a different but related subject, I must thank you, Master Gavin, for getting such a perfect bride ready for me.'

Gavin's face was ashen. De Scabious pointed his sword towards the dais. 'Miss Eleanor,' he declared, trying to turn his smile from oily to charming. 'I have come for you. King John has given me permission to make you Lady de Scabious as soon as matters can be arranged. You are to be *my* wife, it seems.'

'Get out,' Gavin hissed.

De Scabious wagged his finger and smirked. 'You really can be very rude, Master Gavin. Certainly I will get out when I have got what I came for. Come along, Eleanor. It's very exciting that King John himself wants to come to our wedding.'

Ellie looked straight back at him, not concealing her revulsion and contempt. 'I will not consent,' she said in a clear voice. 'And we are not living in the Dark Ages any more, Constable de Scabious. King or no king, women must consent to marriage these days.'

The constable laughed and clambered clumsily on to the dais. 'Oh,' he said, and his face was so close that Ellie could feel the rankness of his breath, 'I think when you see what John has in store for your precious de Granvilles if you don't consent, you will not keep me waiting long.'

At that Gavin rushed towards him, but de Scabious was ready. Picking his moment with supreme care, he raised his sword and brought it crashing down on the stump of Gavin's missing arm. The pain was so blinding that Gavin dropped to his knees, unable even to cry out, and before he could recover himself, de Scabious kicked him viciously in the ribs.

Ellie screamed and was immediately caught by the constable's serjeant, who pinned her so tightly against him that she could hardly breathe.

Everybody began to shout and bawl, Will's voice booming through, but de Scabious was confident enough to take his time. What could a bunch of unarmed wedding guests do against a group of well-armed knights? Making a great show of mock surprise at Gavin's empty sleeve, he rolled him over with his boot, then raised his sword again.

'NO!' Will was frantic, kicking and shoving. 'NO!'

De Scabious shrugged, lowered the sword and ran the

sharp edge of the blade up and down, from Gavin's right shoulder to his wound, purposefully ruining months of healing. Blood dripped like red tears, and Gavin's eyes darkened with agony and humiliation.

Ellie struggled violently. 'Leave him alone!' she cried.

The constable bowed. 'Miss Ellie wants me to spare you because she feels sorry for you,' he gloated. 'Now, I'm not an unreasonable man. I can find it in my heart to be merciful to a one-armed knight, especially when asked by a lady.'

He put his sword away and dropped a rope round Gavin's left wrist, forcing him to kneel so that he could tie the other end round the table leg. His soldiers applauded. 'There now. That's you dealt with.' De Scabious pushed out his stomach as he enjoyed his petty victory. He ostentatiously shook drops of Gavin's blood from his sword. 'Let the girl go and bring the Old Nurse here,' he told his serjeant. Old Nurse, spluttering and objecting, was rolled forward.

Ellie knelt beside Gavin, pulled the rope from under the table leg and tried to wipe his face. But Gavin would not look at her, and before she could make him, the constable was pushing her down the dais steps. She could feel his sweaty hands through her dress and her skin crawled. He stood her in front of Old Nurse, who he knew well from his time at the castle. He had always hated her. She had a way of looking at him that indicated many things, none of them respectful.

'I want you to pack all Miss Eleanor's things up, ready to load into a wagon,' he said, digging into her fat ribs with his elbow. Old Nurse shook her head and put her hands on her rolling hips. De Scabious made a gesture and a sword was levelled at her throat. 'Now,' de Scabious prodded her again, 'I could slice you up and feed you to a whole pack of hounds, and perhaps I will if you don't do as you are told.'

Ellie tried to stamp on the constable's toes. 'Don't you touch Old Nurse,' she spat. 'Leave her alone.'

De Scabious gave an airy sigh. 'Ah, Miss Eleanor,' he said. 'How wonderful you look when you are angry.' He put out his hand to touch her hair and Ellie bit his wrist. He yelped.

'Drag the nurse upstairs if need be,' he ordered, his voice filled with spite, 'and make her gather the girl's belongings together. Any nonsense and push her down into the meat cellar – if, that is, she'll fit.'

The soldiers sniggered and suddenly they were stripping the tables of food and carrying off swords and armour. Within minutes, the wedding guests were left with nothing but the clothes they stood up in. More terrified of the soldiers than the dogs, Marie ran to Sir Percy and he tucked her behind him.

Will stood absolutely still. He wanted to grab Ellie, whatever the consequences to himself, but he could not do it alone. Gavin could not help for he knelt at the centre of a deepening stain, his head bent towards the floor. Brother Ranulf was praying beside him. Will glanced over at Sir Percy, who nodded. Taking the only chance left, the old man leant down and kicked a burning log into the room, hoping to provide a distraction, but, in a moment, he fell, the serjeant's sword through his heart. Marie, splattered with his blood, cried out, but her cries were drowned by the howls of the dogs.

De Scabious set about collecting what he wanted. Some of the castle servants, used to obeying him when the de Granvilles were away, simply followed his orders and packed waiting carts with Ellie's clothes, chests of treasure and flagons of wine from the cellar.

Like a sulky performing bear, Old Nurse snarled at the three men who had forced her first up, then down the keep steps, but she could do nothing as the treasure wagons rolled away through the thickening snow, leaving, she saw with a sinking heart, a covered wagon with its back open. Ellie kicked and bit as she was hustled into it and one of the soldiers used this as an excuse to nick Old Nurse's throat with a knife. A thin line of blood coloured the creases in her neck. At once Ellie was still.

'Please,' she begged, aghast. 'I'll go quietly.'

At that, Old Nurse pulled herself to her full height. Constable or not, she declared, Ellie could not travel on her own.

De Scabious, to his soldiers' surprise, agreed. 'As the old woman is so keen,' he said, with a grin, 'let's take her with my future wife. After all, Miss Eleanor needs a servant and –' he winked – 'who better than a pork barrel? There will be no thought of escape. Old Nurse will act as a ball and chain for Miss Eleanor Theodora de Barre. So put the girl in first and wedge the fat lady in at the back. Now, my dear,' he addressed Ellie with mock deference, 'if you leap out of the wagon at any point, my soldiers will deal appropriately with your lumpy friend. Do you hear me?'

When everybody the soldiers could find had been herded into the great hall, the doors were swung shut and locked. Will, fighting and roaring, could do nothing to stop it and could only listen in agony as orders were given to fire the place. Burning torches were immediately pitched through the windows. Then de Scabious's soldiers ran to the stables and hustled the horses out before dropping flaming brands into the straw. The animals were too valuable to burn and would, with any luck, follow de Scabious's fleeing entourage long enough to be captured.

Within minutes, where there had been a joyful wedding, there was nothing but the crackle of flames and the thumping of trestles being used as battering rams by the Hartslove prisoners.

But by the time the doors splintered, the castle was well alight and the wagon, with its precious stolen cargo, was already far away.

2

Ellie was quite numb at first, crouching down and trying to balance herself as the wagon lurched wildly along. The wheels skidded over the impacted snow and, veering round corners, they often came close to tipping over completely. Soon they were in the woods and she began to panic. Those flames above the stables. Hosanna. Dargent. Sacramenta. Surely even de Scabious would not have let them perish. She buried her face in her cloak and felt for her necklace, her wooden dog and her ruby brooch. The necklace was still clasped round her neck and the little wooden dog dug into her hip, but the ruby brooch had gone. Its loss seemed like a premonition of disasters yet to come and Ellie began to pray as hard as she could.

Soon, however, the pitching and rolling made even prayer impossible and Ellie's hands were rubbed raw from scrabbling against the rough wooden sides. Icy tree roots rattled the wheels as the wagon toppled from pothole to pothole, and when the horses struggled through the ford, Ellie and Old Nurse, who kept up a running commentary of insults directed at the soldiers behind, were badly splashed.

'Heathens! Villains! Toads!' Old Nurse bawled as

the water rose. 'One-legged newts! Frankish FROGS!'

Once safely on the opposite bank, the horses were whipped up again, but even under the lash could not keep up their crazy gallop and eventually, panting and heaving, they slowed to a trot as Old Nurse's voice finally gave out.

Soon the wagon was shrouded in the foggy black of a miserable winter's night, and Ellie's chilled bones ached. The pace altered dramatically at irregular intervals. Sometimes the horses sweated and strained up hills with the carter bellowing encouragement. Other times he got off his box and shouted from below as the horses slithered and slid down tracks made treacherous by ruts and ditches. Twice more they forded rivers, one shallow and one deep enough for water again to soak Ellie's dress, then finally even the carter was silent and there was only the blowing of the horses, the groaning of the wagon and the eerie hooting of hunting owls.

At the break of dawn, the wagon entered a village and the horses ground to a halt. Ellie and Old Nurse were allowed out, and several curious men from the village stopped to look as new horses were harnessed. 'Is that a woman or a mountain?' they joked, staring at Old Nurse. 'You should harness her up and let the horses ride in the back!'

The serjeant kicked the onlookers away, anxious to be off. 'Hurry up, Gethin, you mumbling slowcoach. There'll be more snow before evening,' he growled at the shambling boy who he and the constable felt they owned because they had found him starving in the gutter after his family had died of fever.

Gethin tightened a last buckle and helped Ellie back into the cart. She reminded him of his dead sister but he

32

was puzzled. He had been told that the raid on Hartslove was to rescue a beautiful lady from wicked people. Yet she seemed unhappy. He tried to pat her, to reassure her, but Ellie shrank from him, and Gethin, to whom speech did not come easily, let her be.

The journey dragged on. Ellie was not frightened for herself. She knew de Scabious would not murder her: her lands made her too valuable for that. If she died, everything she owned would revert to the king, and kings were unpredictable. *No*, she thought, *Prince John is making a bid for the throne and has held me out as a reward for the constable's support. Me, and my lands, of course.* She scowled. She hated her lands. She had never even seen them herself, but they were what everybody wanted. Those stupid great fields, moors, woods and rivers somewhere miles to the south were, after all, the reason why even good Sir Thomas had agreed to take her in after she had been orphaned, and if she had been poor she would never have been betrothed to Gavin.

At the thought of Gavin, Ellie found tears pouring down her face for she knew that the wounds made by de Scabious's sword would be much easier to bear than the memory of being made a public spectacle. De Scabious had done his work well. Ellie hugged her arms round her knees and wondered whether even she would be able to repair the damage.

By noon on the fifth day, the snow eased to an occasional flurry and the sun turned the roads to slush. Exhausted beyond measure, Ellie slept fitfully, with her teeth chattering even as she dozed.

In mid-afternoon, the angle of the wagon woke her and as she slid backwards, she realized with a terrible fright that Old Nurse had gone. Easing the cramp from her legs, she looked out. Old Nurse was walking, or, rather, shuffling, as best she could, dragging one unsteady foot in front of the other. The hill was too steep for the horses to manage with her great weight. As the snow crept above her plump ankles, Ellie thought she had never seen the old lady look so defeated. Even when the soldiers rudely pushed her from behind, she could not so much as grunt. Ellie clenched her fists. She would never forgive de Scabious for this.

But behind Old Nurse was a sight that made the girl gasp. Horses. Dozens of them. The Hartslove herd, just as de Scabious had hoped, was following the wagon. Having scattered in fear of the fire, the animals had eventually come together and instinct kept them moving forward. Right at the front, head held high, was Ellie's mare, Sacramenta. Ellie did not call out, she just stared and stared. Against the snow, the horses' coats shone and the air was smoky with steam. The soldiers ran back with ropes but the horses made fools of them, stretching out their necks inviting capture, then dashing away. Ellie watched, not knowing what to think. But she was glad that the horses were safe and near.

When at last the slope lessened, Old Nurse was allowed to get back into the wagon. She needed a great deal of help and when she was finally wedged between the chests again, she listed heavily to one side. Her boots were soaked and in tatters, her legs chapped and red. Ellie stroked the old lady's head, but kept her own eyes fixed on the chestnut mare daintily picking her way through the mud.

The following day, the whole entourage turned off the main track and began to wind its way slowly through a wood even thicker than usual. The road was barely visible and the Hartslove horses disappeared. Ellie's heart fell. Perhaps they had turned back, put off by the low-hanging branches that whipped the faces of the carthorses like icy wands. When the track began to rise and the forest gave way to tufting grass and open moorland, Ellie looked out for them again, but there was no sign.

Now the road vanished completely and Ellie and Old Nurse were both ordered to walk while Gethin sympathetically nursed the pack animals up the steep climb. They stopped only once and Ellie glanced behind her. A river, thin as a line of mercury, wound through the valley far below and, on the rising land the other side, the untouched snow was dazzling.

Gethin took a deep breath. 'God's view,' he said, but Ellie did not answer.

As they breasted the hill, the track became more pronounced, almost a proper causeway again, and descended into a small, hidden valley. By an untidy clump of wind-stunted bushes, there was a fork in the road, the downward route full of sheep tracks and obviously leading to a village, while the rougher path, which the soldiers took, led upwards on to a small, narrow plateau. Directly ahead, a large square tower appeared. It carried no standard and its curtain wall was beaten into uneven ridges by the weather. Nevertheless, behind the partially derelict keep, a small courtyard was filled with low buildings, all of them newly roofed and showing signs of occupancy. On the far edge of the plateau, the land fell steeply away. Despite the view, the place was very bleak and when Ellie saw a gibbet, from which a scraggy corpse was dangling like a forgotten piece of washing, her skin prickled.

'We call this place Hangem,' said the serjeant with nasty satisfaction as he hustled his charges through double, ironclad gates reinforced with bolts and a heavy metal grille.

The carthorses stumbled to the water trough that flanked the well. Journey's end had not come a moment too soon. The garrison servants stared at Old Nurse and made obscene remarks as they took off the horses' harnesses. The old lady was swaying on her feet, but Ellie straightened her shoulders and touched her necklace for courage.

Gethin gestured towards the steps that led to the tower's first floor. The courtyard had been swept clear of snow and Ellie was suddenly conscious of her filthy clothes and stained shoes. Before anybody moved, however, a wild drumming shattered the calm and, in a moment, led by Sacramenta, around two dozen horses galloped through the still open gates and slithered to a halt, snorting and stamping their feet.

'Watch out!' came a shout. 'There's more!'

Ellie dragged Old Nurse to the wall, calling to the mare, who skittered towards her, blowing and trembling. But even as Ellie reached to clutch her mane, she knew that any plans to leap on and gallop off were hopeless. De Scabious had been right. How could she leave Old Nurse behind? Instead, she urged Sacramenta to flee, but before she could push the mare away, the constable himself appeared. Without his armour, he was a plump, ungainly figure. 'Capture all the horses,' he shrilled. 'And in particular, I want that stallion of William's. Is it there?'

He did not need an answer for at that moment Hosanna swept in, his tail like a fiery river behind him and drops of ice sparkling in his mane. Dargent stuck to his side like a limpet. At Hosanna's instigation, the horses began to turn and head back for the gate, barging the soldiers out of the way, but even above the noise and chaos, de Scabious's voice could be heard rising with excitement as he implored his men to secure the red stallion.

In the melee, archers found ropes and made makeshift lassos. But throwing the loops caused more pandemonium and de Scabious grew purple as Hosanna and Sacramenta surged towards freedom, side by side. 'Get him! Get him!' he howled.

From above the portcullis, one archer thought he had his quarry. He dropped his rope, but just an instant too soon. Instead of lassoing Hosanna, his loop tightened round Sacramenta's neck. As the red horse galloped off, pushing the rest of the Hartslove horses before him, the mare, rearing and plunging, was the only one trapped. De Scabious swore horribly as, too late, the gates swung shut.

Ellie tried to rush to Sacramenta, now dancing and kicking, but de Scabious, leaping about in his fury, shouted at his men to get her and Old Nurse inside. 'See if you can do that at least without a mistake,' he cried, mopping his face and almost crying with vexation.

Ellie found herself carried up the steps and pushed unceremoniously alongside Old Nurse into the tower's larger hall. The door slammed shut behind them but Ellie turned and thumped it, even though she knew it was no use.

Old Nurse tried to calm her. 'Now, dearie,' she said, and then crumpled.

Ellie caught her as she staggered and then really began to panic. She could not survive this without

Old Nurse. Using all her strength, she pulled the old lady towards a bench set in front of the fire and sat her down, relieved to note that as soon as the pressure was taken off her feet, Old Nurse's breathing became less wheezy and the veins above her rheumy eyes sank back into the many crinkles of her forehead. Ellie gently settled her and, as Old Nurse creaked and groaned, looked about.

The hall was small but, in an attempt to make it grander, a minstrels' gallery had been erected at one end. Nothing, however, could disguise the fact that it was a shabby place, with no hangings to cover dirty walls. It was clear that de Scabious had not been here for very long, for, despite the fire and the chairs, the air smelt of neglect. On a table was set a jug of wine – *doubtless*, the girl thought bitterly, *Hartslove wine* – and three tankards. She poured some out for Old Nurse and sat down beside her. They stretched their feet towards the blaze, trying to warm them.

A sudden chill made them both jump. De Scabious bustled in. Ellie saw his look of greedy lust before he managed to transform it into something more polite. He wiped his chin and even bowed a little. 'Welcome, ladies.' His voice reeked of false friendliness. 'I am sorry your arrival was somewhat disrupted but I hope your journey was pleasant. Quarters have been prepared for you and I'm sure you'll find them comfortable. I am glad to see you are making yourselves at home.' He nodded smugly towards Old Nurse's drink. Despite the fire, Ellie shivered. 'You are cold.' The constable was assiduous in his concern and called for furs to be brought. Two nervous girls from the kitchen came and dumped some down, but Ellie left them on the floor.

'Now,' the constable said, rocking on his toes. 'I wish you to remember that you are here for safekeeping. When a king dies abroad and another takes over, there are those in England who – how shall I put it? – hanker for the past, long after such hankerings are good for them. The de Granvilles are such people. Now, Miss Eleanor, if you want to help them adapt or even –' de Scabious paused for dramatic effect – 'survive in the new king's world, you should do the wise thing and marry me.'

'Never,' said Ellie wearily. 'And there is no new king.'

De Scabious gave an affected sigh. 'If you really care about those de Granvilles, you really should consider what I am offering, you know. The new king – and, my dear, there certainly is one – will deal harshly with those who don't recognize his writ and will reward those, like me,' he wiped an imaginary crumb from his surcoat, 'who do. It's quite simple. Even though you are a girl, I thought you might be clever enough to understand.'

Ellie could not stop her mouth from quivering, but her eyes were steady enough.

'Such a pity,' the constable said, still rocking away. 'We who are loyal to our rightful king are a dying breed. I blame the late King Richard myself, and I said as much to King John. All those modern songs about romance and all that simpering poetry about love the supposed "Lionheart" was so keen on! It has addled peoples' brains and made them forget their duty.' To Ellie's horror he sat next to her on the bench. 'The de Granvilles used to be great ones for duty to their king,' he mused. His breath was sticky and foul. 'I should have thought,

Eleanor, that Sir Thomas would have brought you up to do what the king wishes.'

'I am betrothed to Gavin.' Ellie would not give an inch.

'Your betrothal is already broken. John has rendered it null and void so you can quite easily marry me. Girls who don't give consent to what is good for them find themselves with unenviable reputations.'

'How dare you!' exploded Ellie.

'Oh!' said de Scabious. 'What spirit!' He put his hand on her knee and began to enjoy himself, leaning back to display acres of stomach. 'You and I are quite similar really.' His tone was indulgent. 'Both with hot tempers. We will produce fireworks between us.'

Ellie froze and eventually, seeing that he was going to get no further that night, de Scabious got up. 'Go to your rooms now,' he ordered. 'We will speak again in the morning.'

Ellie and Old Nurse found themselves right at the top of the tower directly above the gate. Through a rough window they got a tantalizing view of the road along which they had come. The outline of the gibbet and its sorry cargo was fuzzy under the dusky sky, but Ellie could clearly see that the drop to the ground would mean death if she jumped.

Old Nurse sat heavily on the bed. 'At least we are out of that wagon,' she murmured. 'And we are not in a dungeon. The constable dare not treat you badly if King John has an interest.'

'Richard is my king,' said Ellie, but without much conviction. 'We only have de Scabious's word that he is dead.' She sat down next to the nurse and rested her head in her hands. There was a knock at the door.

'What now?' cried Ellie, jumping up.

It was a team of servants delivering the Hartslove chests along with water and a little supper. 'You should try to eat something,' said Old Nurse, eyeing up the bread and cheese.

'You eat it, Old Nurse,' said Ellie. 'I am not hungry.'

Old Nurse sighed, then set to as Ellie wandered back to the window and looked out. She was close to tears for she had no idea what to do. If King Richard was really dead, then, by resisting de Scabious, she might be making things very bad for Gavin and Will. They would feel they had to stand by her, which would put them in direct opposition to King John. Maybe she should just give her consent and marry the constable. After all, de Scabious must be pretty sure Richard *was* dead otherwise he would not dare to align himself so openly with his brother. And John must know Richard was dead or he would not have given de Scabious permission to interfere between her and Gavin. Richard meted out dire punishments to those who usurped his powers. He *must* be dead for de Scabious to be so bold, and if he were, Ellie had the fate of the de Granvilles in her hands. She closed her eyes and felt the world closing in on her.

3

After burning fiercely for several hours, the intense cold and a blanket of snow eventually helped to put out the fire at Hartslove. The stables and the upper rooms in the castle keep were lost. Much of the needlework, so laboriously undertaken by Gavin and Will's mother, had disintegrated. The roof timbers above the great hall had also been damaged and were left straddling the walls like charred bones. The gatehouse and guardroom escaped the flames, as did the kitchen, the bakery and the brewhouse, together with the servants' quarters of which Sir Thomas had been so proud. Six people, as well as Sir Percy, were dead.

It had taken some time for Gavin to pull himself up from the floor of the dais, but when he had managed, he forced himself straight into the firefighting fray. Dizzy and weak, his eyes black and his wounded arm weeping and hideous, he nevertheless worked without ceasing until he was forced to stop and assess the damage. Will paced up and down in front of him, feeling for the ruby brooch, which he had found by chance almost hidden in the snow. For safekeeping, he had attached it to his undershirt and he could feel it now, sharp and solid against his ribs.

The castle sat in a pall of acrid smoke and the weather showed no signs of letting up. Even the abbey bells, which usually rang clearly across the valley both night and day, were too muffled to make out. The wedding guests and Gavin's household servants were huddled into groups. 'We must send to the monks for whatever horses they can provide,' Will was saying to Gavin. 'Then we must arm and mount everybody who is willing to go after de Scabious.'

Gavin listened in silence, trying to work out what time it was, for the fire and the snow corrupted the light. Eventually he worked out that it must be very late evening.

'If we all go,' Will declared, 'we can beat him. De Scabious is vermin. It is our duty to hunt him down, Gavin. He cannot have got far with Old Nurse inside the wagon.'

However, other voices urged caution. 'I know de Scabious is vermin,' said Alan Shortspur, a well-meaning but pushy young man, the youngest son of a local family, who was hoping to hitch his star to Gavin's and raise himself up in the world. 'But while we are all concerned about Eleanor, we must not forget what de Scabious told us. If our king is now John, we must think before we act.' A furious argument broke out.

Gavin remained silent. It seemed to him that the world was moving in slow motion. He barely heard what was being said because now that he was no longer pumping water, one single image was branded on his mind. Even with his eyes open he could see de Scabious manhandling Ellie, while he, her supposed husband and champion, was collapsed on the floor, one-armed and helpless, an object only of pity and humour. His soul cringed.

'Gavin,' Will's voice seemed to come from far away. 'You, more than anybody, must want to pursue de Scabious. If we get the abbey's horses, in two days at most we can be armed, mounted and ready to go.'

Gavin tried to reply but his mouth was too dry and his wound throbbed as it bled through his shirt. Breathing was difficult with two broken ribs and his left arm ached from overuse. Will's pleading face was blurred. *I must sit down*, Gavin thought, and stumbled over to a bench. He knew his knights felt sorry for him and he wanted to kill them.

'Gavin?' Will's voice insisted. 'Gavin, say something. Ellie is your wife – well, nearly your wife. It is your castle that has been torched. What will you do?'

Gavin tried to think as his father would have thought. Though shamed, he must show that he could still be a leader of men. With an immense effort of will, he concentrated. 'We cannot follow de Scabious right now, Will.' His voice boomed in his ears. 'Even if the abbot gives us every horse he has, we cannot fight with palfreys and ponies. If we knew where de Scabious intended to keep Ellie we could take siege machinery, but we will need warhorses to finish him off in battle. The best thing is to send to Keeper John at the stud while we try to find out exactly what we are up against.'

'But –' Will's voice rose.

'No,' said Gavin. He felt weak as a baby. 'Fury is not helpful. Think, man, think. De Scabious says Richard is dead. Alan Shortspur is right. We must work out what that means for us and for Ellie. We cannot ignore it.' His head felt too heavy to lift, but he tried to address the whole company. 'If we do indeed have a new king, some of you may not want to join in our domestic quarrel, for attacking de Scabious will be seen as an act of grave disobedience to King John. You all know that. You must join us or leave us as you think fit. Neither my brother nor I will hold anything against you.'

'Speak for yourself,' said Will loudly.

Some of the knights began to shuffle and about a dozen slipped away, ignoring the weather. But Will walked very deliberately over to Gavin and stood straight in front of him.

'De Scabious has run off with Ellie,' he said, not caring who heard. 'And at this moment, AT THIS MOMENT, he may be doing God knows what. Our horses have disappeared. De Scabious may also have a good number of those, including . . .' Here Will stopped.

'Including Hosanna,' Gavin finished his sentence for him. 'I know, Will. I know. But we have to think. King John may –'

Will interrupted at once. '*King* John?' His voice was contemptuous. 'Gavin, you don't believe de Scabious, do you?'

Gavin looked at his brother. 'Why would de Scabious lie?' he asked. 'What good would it do him?'

'What is wrong with you?' Will cried, as if explaining something very simple to a dim-witted child. 'He will not be lying, exactly. There are bound to be rumours about Richard since nobody in England has seen him for nearly three years, and we ourselves have not seen him since we left him in the Holy Land five months ago. But don't you see? John has turned a rumour about Richard's death into a test of loyalty to himself, to see what he can get out of it. There is no love lost between Richard and John. We both know that. As for de Scabious – well, he is using the opportunity,

45

through Ellie and her lands, to make himself a great man.'

'And what does de Scabious think will happen to him if – when – Richard returns?' asked Gavin, trying to keep Will's face from continually changing shape.

'Why, he'll just say that he was doing his duty as he saw it and blame everything on John! You know what an oily, creepish man he is. But by then he may have blackmailed Ellie into giving her consent to marry him by telling her that it is the only way to protect you.' Gavin winced but Will showed no mercy. 'And it's worse, Gavin, much worse. If Ellie marries de Scabious and makes him rich, King Richard will be in no position to cross him. He won't even want to. Men like de Scabious are useful. You must be able to see. De Scabious will offer money – Ellie's money – to fund the king's next crusade and you know Richard. The crusade is everything to him. He's not really interested in England and certainly not in our petty squabbles.'

Gavin's brain felt leaden as he tried to follow Will's logic. 'So, whatever happens, whether the king is Richard or John, de Scabious will be the winner?'

Will could not understand his brother at all. It all seemed so clear to him. 'Of course,' he said, growing increasingly agitated. 'But you have missed the real point, Gavin. The real point is that Ellie doesn't *want* to marry de Scabious. She wants to marry you.'

Gavin said nothing. 'Gavin,' Will took his arm and shook it hard. 'Why are you so silent? Can't you hear what I'm saying? It's you Ellie wants to marry, not de Scabious. Do you need to know anything else?'

'Maybe,' Gavin said slowly, 'she would be better off with de Scabious.'

Will was dumbstruck. 'What on earth do you mean?' he asked, when he could bring himself to speak.

The few knights that were left, scenting danger, dispersed. Arguments about women never ended well.

'Look,' Gavin said, gripping the bench to keep himself upright. 'Look. I am a one-armed knight with a ruined castle, who has a position at the court of a dead king.'

Will made a disbelieving sound.

'Will, Richard may be dead. We have no proof either way and I know de Scabious is an odious man, but he has his supporters. I may be Count of Hartslove, but I am not powerful like our father.' He stopped, then steeled himself to say what was really on his mind. 'I am not a catch for a girl like Ellie. The world has changed. Men like de Scabious have taken advantage of our absence on crusade to make sure that they wield real power these days. If Richard is dead, de Scabious will have a place at John's court. If Richard is not dead, even you admit that de Scabious will still come out well. I, on the other hand . . . I can't even . . .' Gavin tailed off.

Will stared at him. 'Are you saying,' he said very deliberately, 'that we should not even attempt to get Ellie back, even though the thought of marrying de Scabious appals her?'

'I am saying,' said Gavin as steadily as he could, 'that we need to think what's best.'

'What's *best*?' Will's voice was stiff with sarcasm. 'I'll tell you what's best! What's best is to think of Ellie. She is alone, except for Old Nurse. We don't know where she is. But we do know that de Scabious is capable of anything and that Ellie would probably rather die than marry him. Never mind about kings or counts or castles. Ellie is more precious than any of them. Surely

47

you, as her betrothed husband, should realize that?'

Roused by his brother's tone, Gavin stood up. 'Will, it is exactly because Ellie is so precious that we can't afford to think like that!' he said. 'The only way women have any freedom is to marry well. Ellie deserves the freedom that a good marriage can bring. I don't doubt that she dislikes Piers de Scabious, but once they have some children, he will leave her well alone just like most other husbands we know. Then she will be able to do much as she pleases and her children will protect her. She will be a great lady. Maybe the best thing we can do for her is to let her go. Or maybe the best thing *I* can do for her.'

Will nodded his head, his hands on his hips, his eyes scorching. 'I see, Gavin, I see,' he said. 'You have lost your courage along with your arm. You can't be bothered to fight for Ellie because you prefer feeling sorry for yourself.'

'How could you possibly understand anything about me any more, Will?' Gavin began to breathe heavily as his temper stuttered to life. 'But one thing you should understand is that I can't afford to be sentimental, especially not over Ellie. De Scabious's stock is rising. Mine is sinking, as will yours if you support a dead Richard against a living John. That should be clear enough even for you.'

'No!' cried Will. 'I don't accept any of what you say. Never mind who is king. Ellie will find her freedom through marrying a man she loves, not through marrying a man whose "stock is rising", as you put it. She loves you. Don't you love her enough to fight for her?'

'I love her more than you could possibly imagine,' said Gavin, every word of Will's rasping his heart. 'But you are wrong about people finding freedom through love alone. I don't believe that can ever happen. People need more than love.'

'More than your type of love,' Will's voice was stinging. 'If Ellie was betrothed to me, I would risk everything. You have never really cared for Ellie, not the way I do!'

Gavin sat down again, his temper subsiding as quickly as it had risen. 'So this is it, Will,' he said quietly. 'You are not really bothered about Richard or John, are you? The fact is, you are in love with Ellie yourself.'

The air cracked with hostility. Something that both had avoided saying, Gavin because he could see no point and Will because he hardly knew the truth of it himself, was now out in the open and could never go unacknowledged again.

Gavin broke the silence. 'It's not a surprise to me that you love Ellie,' he said. 'And what is more, if Ellie were honest, I think she would admit that she loves you back.'

'Ellie doesn't love me,' said Will, almost stamping his foot. 'She loves you. I can tell by the way she looks at you.'

'She thinks she ought to love me,' replied Gavin. 'She tries her best. Sometimes she persuades herself that she does. But it is an effort.'

They stared at each other and it was as if a physical barrier were rising between them. Both were grateful when, from the depths of the castle, the dogs, turfed out of their usual sleeping quarters, set up a melancholy howling and a voice called for somebody to take over at the well.

Grinding his heel hard on some debris underfoot, Will went to answer the summons, but could not resist a parting shot. 'You are failing us, Gavin.' He threw the words over his shoulder. 'Our father would not have been proud.'

Gavin sat a while, then got up and made his way blindly through the wreck of his inheritance.

Outside the bakehouse he stumbled into Marissa and Marie. Marissa, nursing a guilty conscience, was immediately aggressive and stood in his way. 'Will Eleanor be married to that other man by now? And if she is, what will happen to us?' she asked. Gavin stared at her, unable to answer, but Marissa pressed on. 'Marie says the porter is to be punished, perhaps even hung, for letting those men in. But *I* told him to lower the drawbridge,' she said almost proudly. 'It didn't take much doing. He was drunk.'

Marie made a mute gesture of pleading and Gavin saw the terror on her face.

He braced himself to speak. 'The porter is a fool,' he said with a gesture of such weariness and sorrow that Marissa had to look away, 'and we only hang criminals.'

The girl was taken aback. She had expected physical punishment and almost relished the idea. What she had not expected was a look that bit deeper than a belt. 'Damn him,' she muttered as Gavin vanished into the smoke, making his way back towards the great hall. 'And damn his Mistress Perfect, wherever she is.'

When Marie remonstrated, begging her not to cause any more trouble, for the de Granvilles had been so kind to them, Marissa shook her off and wondered whether Will would be so forgiving when he found out.

But Will already knew as much as he needed to about de Scabious's easy entry. The porter was the man who had lowered the drawbridge and Gavin should punish him. All Will cared about was getting Ellie back. Pulling rank over his brother for the first time in his life, he now called the entire Hartslove household to the great hall and addressed them himself while Gavin was forced to sit and watch.

'I have sent my squire on foot to Keeper John,' Will announced. 'He will provide the horses we need to mount an attack on de Scabious. Then a decision must be made. It is also possible that some of the loosed horses will return. Temporary stalls must be erected and the castle reinforced. If the Count of Hartslove does decide to attempt to rescue Ellie . . .' The pause he left stabbed Gavin like a knife. 'If he does, the castle may have to defend itself against the forces of a usurping king until our true king returns. Every man must work to his utmost. Now, let us prepare.'

The knights muttered and Will, having watched them all file out, walked straight past Gavin as if he did not even see him.

4

The waiting for horses was terrible, though there was plenty to do. Will and Gavin avoided each other and when Gavin eventually collapsed with fever and lay, twitching and sweating, with the dogs, Will was relieved. The weather was clearing and once Hal returned with fresh mounts, with Gavin out of the way Will would be able to direct things as he pleased. But where was Hal? Will fretted constantly.

It was a cruel ten days before the squire staggered back in, bedraggled and footsore, to report that the stud was empty and that Keeper John had been forced to flee. Hal had scoured the country in search of mounts, but nobody would lend so much as a donkey to help the Hartslove cause. Piers de Scabious and his King John had been thorough.

Will raged. Hal stood in silence.

It was Gavin who first heard the noise and thought he was hallucinating. 'Will?' he called out, dragging himself upright. 'Will, what's that?'

Will listened for a moment then rushed out. 'Horses!' he cried from the doorway. 'God be praised! The sentry's shouting that it's our horses. I knew it! They're coming back!' He rushed out and up the steps to the battlements.

'Oh, look who's at the front!' he yelled. 'Hosanna is bringing them all home! Lower the drawbridge! Let them in!'

The ground shook as the destriers clattered past, the steam from their flanks forming clouds in the freezing air. Some had minor cuts and bruises and their expressions were wild, but otherwise they seemed unharmed. They made straight for the old stables, but, finding them gone, were happy to be caught and put into the temporary stalls Will had organized. Hal seized both Dargent and Hosanna and his grin nearly split his face.

Hosanna had lost a shoe but golden wedding threads were still hanging like bedraggled spiders' webs down his neck, and when Will rubbed the star between his eyes, he sneezed and shook his head, scattering small droplets of spittle.

'Where have you been?' Will murmured, running his hands over familiar scars. He looked into his horse's eyes, wishing he could see in them where Ellie was. Hosanna did not blink. Will caught his breath and suddenly his expression became very focused.

Making sure both his horses were at the front of the queue for reshoeing, he quietly crossed the courtyard, blessing Hal for keeping both his horses' saddlery not in the stables but tucked away in the bakehouse where the squire sometimes liked to sleep. He slipped inside and found the twins warming their hands on the bread oven. Marie gave him a shy smile but Will did not return it, simply asking if she and her sister could help him carry what he needed over to the other side of the courtyard.

Marissa stepped out of the shadows. 'We may be girls, and poor, not like rich Eleanor,' she said, 'but we are not servants.'

53

'And I don't ask you as servants,' said Will, taken aback. 'You are de Nevilles.' He looked straight at Marissa and she blushed furiously. Before she knew it, her arms were full of leather and steel. Marie carried the blankets. 'Can you manage?' asked Will anxiously. Now that the girls emerged into the light, he could see how thin and dirty they were and felt a little sorry for them. They looked completely lost.

'Of course,' said Marissa. She knew that Will and Gavin had argued and now thought to make something of it to her advantage. 'I am scarred and limp, but I am not a cripple, unlike . . .'

Although every fibre of his being was urging him to hurry, Will stopped dead in his tracks. 'Unlike?'

'Well, you know.'

'No, I don't know.'

Marie tried to intervene. 'Where shall we take all these things?' she ventured.

'Nowhere,' Will said. All his pity vanished. He might find fault with Gavin, but others should not mock. He snatched Marie's bundle and knocked everything Marissa was carrying on to the floor. 'If you had not mentioned your scar and your limp, I doubt I would have noticed either, just as nobody in battle notices that Gavin has only one arm,' he said coldly. 'Your father was a brave man. Your remarks are not worthy of his name.'

Using both arms and holding things between his teeth, he gathered everything up himself. The blankets were rough and Will did not notice the ruby brooch become dislodged and fall to the ground as he strode away. He hurried to put Hosanna's saddle and bridle behind the mounting block, and by the time he collected the horse from the farrier, he had recovered himself again. Marissa was a stupid girl and he would avoid her in future.

'Now then, Hosanna,' he said, smoothing the red mane and forelock as he made his plans. The horse's breath was like balm and as it warmed his face, Will knew exactly what he was going to do. Hosanna bent his head obediently to the bridle and his flank quivered as Will quickly tightened the girth. The day was almost done and he must hurry. Putting on a light hauberk, he tied his helmet to the back of the saddle and made his way across to the gatehouse, leading Hosanna behind him. He was ready. As he tucked himself and the horse into a recess in the wall and prepared to mount, to his intense irritation he suddenly found Marissa beside him again. He glared at her. What on earth did she want now?

Above everything, Marissa wanted Will to think well of her. She had picked up the ruby brooch, which clearly meant a good deal to him, and, instead of keeping it, which was what she wanted to do, had decided to bring it back as a peace offering. But now she was here, she found herself paralysed with fear. Hosanna's head was so close, his teeth just a hair's breadth away. Even wide awake, Marissa's nightmares returned and she found she could not breathe. Her legs began to buckle. Will watched her with increasing fury. The girl was nothing but a pest and he was in such a hurry. But as she sank, floppy as a dead rabbit, there was little he could do except prop her up against Hosanna's shoulder. He looked desperately about for Marie.

Hosanna shifted and slowly turned. Marissa felt him move, shuddered and began to whimper. The horse's whiskers tickled her lips. Now she found her face reflected in wide eyes that seemed to draw her in. She shut her own and made to push him away, but when he lowered his head, she found herself instead touching the white star that so many before her had used as a charm, the soft whirl where the hair grew round instead of straight rubbing soft against her palm. She kept her hand still. Then, very gingerly, as if unable to help herself, her fingers trickled down the horse's long face, down his neck, over one deep scar, then over the deeper indentation that she found near his heart, and she sighed.

Will stared at her, but could wait no longer. Gentler now, he eased her away, made sure she could stand alone and swung himself into the saddle. He was already half swallowed in a crowd of castle servants before the girl remembered why she had come and cried out, 'Will! The brooch!' and held it up.

But it was too late. 'Keep it,' he called to her, and his smile lit her heart. 'Keep it for Ellie!'

She paused for a second, then stuffed the brooch into her belt. *Keep it!* Those words had been unmistakable. She chose not to think any further and slipped out of the recess to where she could hear Will arguing with the porter. She listened for a moment, then hugged herself, knowing what she must do.

The porter was standing, his arms crossed. 'Let down the drawbridge? On whose authority?' He felt within his rights to ask. 'I would be needing the count's permission. I've made one mistake. He will not be so lenient if I make another.'

'I am the Earl of Ravensgarth,' Will's voice was imperious. 'I demand that you let the drawbridge down. Do as I say.'

'Well,' said the porter, his red face beginning to sweat, 'no.'

'Do it.' Hosanna pawed the ground. He no longer looked gentle.

The porter scratched his head. Then all of a sudden, as if of its own accord, the drawbridge began to creak. The porter gave a yowl of horror and rushed to the guardroom door. It was blocked. He shouted about ghosts and witches, but when he had hitched himself up to look through the window, he saw that his ghosts and witches were really a reluctant Marie and a determined Marissa, busy cranking the great chains round and round on their enormous wheel. Well oiled and supple, the machinery was not difficult for the two girls to work, and the drawbridge was soon more than halfway to the ground.

The porter beat his fists against the wall. 'Stop! Stop I tell you!'

Will shouted with delight. 'Hurry!' he urged. 'Hurry, Marissa! If Gavin sees, he will try and stop me.' Even as he spoke, Alan Shortspur came running from the great hall calling again and again that Gavin ordered the drawbridge to be raised at once, for nobody was to either leave or enter without his permission.

Summoning two soldiers to smash their way into the guardhouse, the porter was all ready to obey, but as the door gave way and Marissa and Marie fled up the steps on to the battlements, he was suddenly afflicted by doubts. Who was it best to serve: King Richard's favourite earl or a count with one arm and a doubtful future? The drawbridge hung in mid-air. Hosanna waited. The porter thought quickly. The Count of Hartslove had the power to hang him. The Earl of

Ravensgarth did not. That decided it. He would obey Gavin – for now. 'Going up,' he shouted.

Will hesitated for only a second and in that second, he found Hal on Dargent beside him. He shook his head, but Hal looked straight ahead. 'You are not going anywhere without me,' he said. 'I am your squire. We go together.'

'Hal –'

'If we're going . . .'

'Are you sure?'

'If we're going . . .'

'Hold tight, then.'

They took deep breaths, then, with one accord, pressed their spurs into the horses' flanks.

'Onwards!' shouted Will as they galloped out of the gate. He flung his arm up to salute Marissa. 'You are a de Neville after all!' he yelled, and she waved, feeling for the ruby brooch at her waist.

As the two horses reached the base of the rising drawbridge there was a collective gasp from the crowd. Dargent hesitated slightly before following Hosanna straight up the ramp, both horses' hooves scuffing against the greasy wood. As he reached the crest, Dargent's hocks gave way, but before he could slide backwards Hosanna pressed against him. Now he had no choice but to jump. The crowd gasped as he and Hosanna, every muscle tensed, leapt into the late afternoon sky, arching through the thin air like wingless gods making for heaven. Will and Hal flattened themselves over the horses' necks. Behind them, the shouting stopped and Marissa and Marie clung to each other.

At the top of the arc, Will's blood froze. His mouth was open but no sound emerged. Hanging between the black moat and the fading light, blinded by Hosanna's gold-flecked mane, he thought, *This is what it must feel like just before you die.* Yet he did not feel any fear. It was not possible to feel anything at all, only a kind of timeless suspension. Hosanna's front legs remained curled beneath him. There seemed no reason why he should ever drop.

Then Will felt a rush of wind. Now he had a sense of speed, and fear suddenly gripped him. He could sense the water below, watchful and menacing, just waiting to pull him and Hosanna under. His heart lurched as they began to fall. Slowly, so slowly, impossibly slowly it seemed to Will, Hosanna's shoulders opened. Now he stretched out like a diver, every sinew straining to reach the white drift that marked the slippery safety of the far side. Less than a foot to his right, Dargent was Hosanna's shadow. The landing, when it came, was remarkably smooth. Will's mouth opened wider as Hosanna's front legs almost crumpled and his back quarters folded to propel him forward over the frozen ground. There were several untidy splashes as huge clods of ice-capped earth were tossed backwards by the horses' hooves. Then they were away, galloping towards the wood.

When he could move again, Will glanced over his shoulder. Hal was still crouched over Dargent's neck, his face the colour of marble. Beads of sweat rolled down the horse's flanks. Will felt a primeval surge of naked triumph. He wanted to roar. He *was* one of those ancient gods. With Hosanna, he was invincible. He stood in his stirrups and punched the sky again and again. 'My brave Hosanna!' he crowed, drunk with exhilaration. 'My brave Hosanna!' He whooped at Hal as the horses, once again confident of their footing, increased their speed.

'I have no idea where we are going,' Will shouted. 'But I think Hosanna may.'

Hal eased back in the saddle but still clung to Dargent's mane. His hair was standing straight up on end and, despite his brain telling him over and over, 'We've done it,' his heart remained in his mouth. He could not formulate any words, but, gradually, as his terror subsided, he whispered, 'Thank you.' Dargent twitched his ears then slowed down a little, allowing Hosanna to go in front. The big bay horse liked to set his compass by the red tail in front of him. Hal wiped his face on his sleeve. He hoped his mother, who cooked in the castle, had been watching; then, as he relived the jump, he changed his mind and hoped she had not.

In the Hartslove courtyard, it was several hours before the household stopped shaking their heads in disbelief. Gavin had the two girls brought down from the battlements but once they were standing in front of him, he felt too ill to speak and sent them away. Soon he relapsed into delirium and it was with difficulty that Alan Shortspur got him into bed.

Much later that night, as Marie heard his raving, she crept along to tend to him. His skin was mottled with fever and he did not recognize her, only called again and again for Ellie.

Marissa remained upstairs. She felt sorry for Gavin, but all she could really think about were Will's brown eyes, her ruby brooch and a luminous blood-red horse.

5

Will was right. Hosanna was quite sure of the way to the tower and when the rush of blood generated by the foolhardy leap had died down, he slowed to a canter, then walked and trotted steadily northwards. Will barely held the reins. How good the horse felt. But more than that, Will felt he had something certain to cling to. Hosanna would not lead him astray. *Gavin was wrong*, thought Will as a watery sun came out.

He and Hal slept in barns along the way, speaking to nobody, but listening hard as groups of travelling pedlars speculated about Richard's fate. Many people believed that their king was now John.

If it was not for Ellie's plight, Will thought as Hosanna splashed past some pilgrim monks, *I suppose I would be on my way to Austria today, trying to find out the truth for myself*.

His mind dwelt briefly on Marissa. What had passed between the girl and Hosanna intrigued him. She was pretty too, in an angry kind of way. But she was just a child. When he got back, he would find a quiet horse and teach her to ride.

But soon Will could think of nothing but Ellie and had to resist the urge to spur Hosanna on. Not that there was any need. The horse kept up a steady but relentless pace for Dargent to keep up with, and at dawn on the fourth day they reached the place where the track to the tower split. Here Hosanna stopped and Will patted his neck and dismounted. 'We must be very close,' he said to Hal. 'Take the horses into the wood. I'll follow this track on foot.'

It was late afternoon by the time he returned with the news Hal hoped for. 'I have found a tower,' he said. 'There is nothing else, so it must be where de Scabious hides out. There are hundreds of hoof prints too, so it looks as though the horses followed the wagon all the way here before Hosanna brought them home.' He touched the horse's white star. 'I have looked all round but I can't see any way of getting into the tower unnoticed. I think we'll have to go down into the village. We might find something out there. It is dangerous to be seen, I know, as de Scabious will have spies and the villagers will be suspicious, but we don't have much choice. I am not going back to Hartslove without seeing Ellie. We have left her far too long already.' He remounted. 'If only we had more mounted men and some siege machinery.'

Gavin's warnings sounded an unwelcome echo in his ear. Hal wisely kept his misgivings to himself.

Soon they were through the thickest part of the wood and down on to the valley floor. Where the ground flattened out, the trees had been felled to make a wide clearing. Two strong oaks, however, had been left on their own at the valley head and from them hung three corpses: two men and a boy of about ten. The ropes were stiff with dirty ice and the corpses' faces were waxy in the moonlight. The two young men passed by in silence, averting their gaze. Will did not tell Hal that there was another gibbet outside the tower bearing its own miserable burden.

Fifty yards further on, they could just about make out numerous wooden dwellings clustered close together, with stables and several small barns tucked behind. The left side of the valley was overhung with rocky outcrops that cast a dank shadow, but the right side was less steep and houses were dotted over it. Beyond them, ground was being prepared for tilling.

The horses walked on together and were soon surrounded by noises both friendly and familiar. Cows demanded to be milked and numerous chickens scratched and paddled in the slush. Will knew there were pigs, for Hosanna began to toss his head and snort.

Hal laughed, glad to dispel the horror of the gibbet. Hosanna was always funny about pigs. The horses squelched past a muddy pen in which a couple of oily-coated pack ponies stood nibbling mouldy hay. They looked up but without interest. In the distance, the dull thud of axes could be heard together with the shouts of labourers urging workhorses to pull harder to earn their tea. Beside a quick-running stream, the foundations of a church had been laid and stones were gathered in neat piles, ready for masons to start work.

Before they were accosted by any of the villagers, Will left the path and slid off. 'Let's spread the saddle blanket wide over Hosanna's rump,' he said, 'and splash dirt all down his neck and over his star. Then we'll swap horses. Even with the light fading somebody might recognize him, although he was loose last time he was here. If you ride him behind me, people won't look so hard.'

The simple disguise didn't take long and soon Will was

pushing Dargent back on to the track. The first person they met was a man goading a pair of stubborn plough oxen with a stick. 'No wonder they used to call this Mud Month,' Will said in a conversational way.

'No wonder at all,' came the reply.

As if this were a signal, at once a dozen or so ragged children appeared. They had been throwing stones at each other, but when they saw Will they threw a few at him instead. He dismounted again and offered them a ride. Suddenly they were all shy, but a lift on a smart warhorse was a treat not to be missed and soon Will had quite a following. One small boy asked if he could take Dargent to the door of his house to show his mother.

'Which house?' Will enquired, picking his way carefully between potholes and jumping over puddles. The shadows were deeper now and he was glad that Hal and Hosanna were close to him. The boy pointed to a small, squat house right under the overhanging rock. A candle sputtered in the window. As Dargent approached the door, the small boy called out loudly and it flew open.

'What on earth . . .' exclaimed a thin woman, behind whom Will could see a pile of laundry in front of the fire.

He smiled. 'Your son here has turned into a knight.'

'And who might you be?' the woman asked.

Will ignored the question. 'My squire and I, and our horses, need food and shelter for the night,' he said pleasantly. 'Might we find it here?'

'I can't say,' said the woman. She turned to go inside.

'Mother, look at me!' demanded the boy.

'I see you, Elric,' she said, turning round again, and her face softened. 'But the baby's crying.' She disappeared.

Crestfallen, the little boy allowed Will to help him off as the other children melted away. But in a second he brightened. 'I'll show you where you can put your horses,' he said to Will. 'And I'll fetch my father. We don't have much room in our house, but if your squire and I sleep in the stable, we can manage.' He turned to Hal. 'I hope your horses are used to cows. We will have to put the horses in with them and some of them make a horrible noise.'

'Our horses are used to everything,' said Hal. 'There is not much they haven't seen.'

The little boy took them to a barn on the other side of the village and fetched straw for the horses' beds. Will, meanwhile, was subjected to a barrage of questions. 'Are you crusaders? Have you been in the Holy Land?' Elric's eyes lit up when Will nodded his head. 'That's what I want to be when I grow up, not a rotten farmer, always tilling somebody else's land, but a crusader with a big horse and a suit of armour made from silver.'

Will laughed. 'Would you really like to leave your mother and cross the sea?'

'The sea,' said the little boy dreamily. Then he shook his head. 'I can't imagine what it must be like. They say it is so wide that you can't see the other side. I don't believe them. No bit of water could be so big you couldn't see the other side. But I do want to go to Jerusalem. Once a knight came through here and his squire was one of those Saladins –'

'Saracens,' Hal corrected him as he put the horses' trappings down within easy reach, just in case.

'Whatever,' said the little boy. 'Anyway, a knight came here who had one of THOSE as his squire. He was a boy, only a few years older than me. He had dark skin and was wearing a surcoat of purple and gold. A squire

65

wearing purple and gold! He didn't like it when we stared. Some of the villagers spat at him and he swore in a funny language. Then Constable de Scab–'

Elric broke off as the barn door opened and a group of men entered. He ran over to them. 'Father,' he said. 'These are brave crusaders. They just want to stay the night. This one gave me a ride on his horse. Please, Father, they just need food and shelter. I'm sure they can pay for it.'

Will smiled and stepped forward. 'We are on a journey,' he said, 'and your son is right about one thing, at least. We need food and shelter for the night. May we ask for hospitality?'

The man picked uncertainly at some pockmarks on his broad cheeks. 'There is a town five miles further north,' he said. 'You'd be better going there.'

'It is a little far for us tonight.' Will continued to smile. 'It's already dark. We will head for the town in the morning, if that suits you.'

The man began to consult with the rest of the group and eventually they came to an agreement. 'One night only, Peter,' one of them said. 'We don't want any trouble.' He spoke very deliberately.

'One night is all we need,' Will kept his voice light.

'The squire and I can sleep with the horses, Father,' said Elric, delighted.

Peter gave Elric a not unfriendly cuff that the little boy evaded with ease. 'One night,' he said to Will. 'When your animals are settled, my wife will make you some supper. It will not be much, mind. We don't have much.'

'Whatever it is it will be very welcome,' said Will. 'Now, we need some oats, barley and hay. My squire will pay you well.'

Leaving Hal and Elric with Hosanna and Dargent, Will walked with Peter through the village. Most of the houses were invisible except for the dull glow of the fire in the hearth – small flickers of comfort in damp, wattle and daub mounds, some scarcely fit for badgers. Peter guided his guest to his own door and called for his wife.

The baby had stopped crying and Will could hear Elric's mother singing gently. She had a nice voice, the kind Will imagined his own mother had. He could scarcely remember her, since she had died when he was six, but the sound brought back vague memories of a time when, just like Elric, he had stared at knights passing through Hartslove and had yearned for a Great Horse.

The singing stopped. Elric's mother put the baby in a cradle and gestured to Will to sit on a rough wooden settle in front of the struggling flames. 'We have soup and bread,' she said, not grudgingly, but with a certain reserve. 'There are no spare eggs today.'

'Soup and bread will be fine,' said Will.

'Bring out the cheese too, Morwenna,' said Peter, sitting down opposite Will. 'Our guest should not go hungry, and take some supper down to the barn. We'll never get Elric away from those horses tonight.'

'He seems very keen on horses,' Will observed.

'Never stops talking about them,' Peter replied as his wife moved softly around, gathering things together. 'He runs pretty wild at the moment, but when he is older he will be taken into service at Hangem Tower so that he can learn more about them. Maybe one day he will be a squire. That's what we hope. It would be a better life for him than mine.'

67

A round cheese was fetched from a cupboard and Morwenna cut two fat slices before putting both loaf and cheese into a basket and filling a pitcher full of soup. Pulling a woollen plaid over her shoulders, she set off for the cow byre. Peter grunted as she went out of the door, then, chewing slowly on a bit of bread, scrutinized Will carefully.

'Going far?' he asked.

'Not so far,' Will said, softening his bread in his bowl. He tried to broaden the conversation. 'This looks like a busy village. Your son mentioned Constable de Scabious. He must be a powerful fellow.'

Peter's eyes never left Will's face. 'Constable de Scabious has aspirations,' he said. 'Do you know him?'

'No,' lied Will. 'But I hear he is a good friend of the king's brother, John. Does he keep a big household?'

Peter slurped his broth and shrugged. 'Depends what you mean by big,' he replied. 'He has soldiers. How many I couldn't say.'

'But you are sending Elric to him eventually, so he must be a good man.'

Peter spat into the fire. 'Good man, bad man,' he said. 'I just want my son to get on and the constable is moving up in the world. It seems we are to send up provisions for a marriage feast. His wife to be is a very grand lady.'

'When is this happy event to take place?' Will had to fight to keep his face expressionless.

'Very soon. The bride has arrived and a whole host of horses arrived with her. That is why people in the village are a bit unfriendly. Some say they saw a horse as red as fire against the sky.' He shook his head. 'We are supposed to be Christians here, but old superstitions die hard. The old women of the village never stop their mutterings about the devil and hell. Anyway, first there was that and then here you are looking for hospitality.'

Will was genuinely puzzled. 'But lots of people must pass through here,' he said.

'Pass through, yes,' said Peter, showing his gums in a mirthless smile. 'But did you not see the gibbets on your way in? De Scabious keeps them well filled. The sight does not encourage people to linger. Most people push on. You didn't.'

'We were tired,' said Will rather lamely.

'Aye,' Peter replied, getting up. 'Well, the rushes in the corner are clean and we've a spare blanket. You should sleep and then be off. I'll say goodnight.'

Will finished his bread, then he took the blanket Peter gave him, pulled off his boots and settled himself in front of the hearth. The fire cheered up a little and his eyes drooped. Morwenna returned and Will heard low voices but could tell nothing that was said.

After a few minutes, he saw Peter tiptoe out of the house muttering something about a sick cow in the byre. *I should get up and see if that's where he is really going*, Will thought, but after four nights on the road, his whole body rebelled against the idea of moving. *I'll go in a moment*, he said to himself. *I'll just lie here for a little while.* He slid further into the blanket. Oh, it was so comfortable. The fire flared, then sank. *I must get up right now*, he told himself firmly as he felt his breathing grow heavy. But before he could move even one leg, he was asleep.

In the dead, pre-dawn gloom, a rush of cold air and a thud to the back hit him at about the same time. With a terrible start, Will realized that the room was full of soldiers. He was ordered to get up. The baby began to wail.

'We have been sent,' said a man Will recognized as the constable's serjeant, 'to bring you to more comfortable quarters.'

'That is very kind,' said Will, trying to look unconcerned. 'But I shall be off very soon. There is no need.'

'Oh, but there is,' said the serjeant. 'It does not do to turn down hospitality.'

Will glared at Peter. This must be his doing.

The serjeant followed Will's eyes. 'This man's horse,' he demanded. 'Where is it?'

'In the barn,' Peter answered at once. 'It's in the barn. I can show you.'

The serjeant nodded. 'Let's go,' he said. Will pulled on his boots and watched as the serjeant took his sword for himself.

They walked in silence, Peter in front, the serjeant following, then Will, flanked by two soldiers with another behind him.

Suddenly Will began to talk very loudly. 'It is very kind of CONSTABLE DE SCABIOUS,' he almost shouted, 'to be so solicitous to travellers.'

'Keep your voice down,' the serjeant hissed over his shoulder and began to walk faster.

'What's that you say?' called Will. 'The mist is coming down? No, I don't think so. It is just the BREATH OF THE SOLDIERS making the air rather cloudy. SOLDIERS' breath always smells of onions, don't you find? Maybe one day they will invent something so that even these FOUR FINE FELLOWS HERE will smell only of mint or lavender.'

70

The serjeant strode on, swearing under his breath. The barn was in sight but Will's one-sided conversation never let up. In fact, his voice grew louder and louder until the serjeant, unable to bear it, stopped.

'SHUT UP!' he roared.

'Certainly,' said Will, for they had arrived at the barn. 'There is no need to shout.'

As the soldiers pushed open the door, Will held his breath. He could hear only the slow chewing of the cows in the darkness. He strained his ears but all else seemed quiet. Perhaps Hal had slept through his clumsy alarm call. But as the door opened wider, there was a sudden swish and thud of hooves. Already mounted on Dargent, Hal emerged full tilt from the shadows with Hosanna tossing his head and galloping by his side. Dashing round the soldiers, Hal let go of the rein and Hosanna made for Will, who caught the stirrup and leapt on.

The soldiers scattered, but as Will and Hal turned together to flee, a soldier emerged from the barn, triumphantly clutching Elric. The serjeant seized his chance. 'Stop! Stop or I shall cut the child's throat.'

Will spun Hosanna round. 'Leave him alone!' he cried. 'He has done nothing.'

'His life is in your hands!' shouted the serjeant, pulling out a dagger. 'It's up to you.' He twisted the little boy's arm behind his back. Peter sank to his knees.

Will hesitated for only a fraction of a second. 'Go, Hal,' he ordered under his breath. Hal began to remonstrate. 'Go!' ordered Will more loudly, wheeling Hosanna back to face the barn. 'Go at once!'

'I'll be back,' whispered Hal, and driving his spurs hard into Dargent's side, he sped away into the breaking dawn.

A cry went up as Hal disappeared, but the serjeant did not seem to care. 'Let him go!' he shouted. 'It's this one we want.'

Will rode back towards the circle of men. The serjeant was smiling. He was still clutching Elric, and the boy's chin trembled in an effort not to cry out. When Will dismounted, the serjeant let go and Elric immediately tried to run to Hosanna, but his father caught him and hurried him away.

Hosanna whinnied loudly as his bridle was seized and Will clenched his teeth. There was no more pretence about 'hospitality'. Instead, Will was marched roughly towards the soldiers' horses tethered behind the barn and manhandled on to a scruffy pack pony, his wrists tied tightly behind his back.

The serjeant gestured for Hosanna to be brought round for him to ride, but the horse would not stand still. Eventually, with two men to help him, the serjeant managed to mount. Will watched in silence. Then they set off for the tower. Keeping his eyes fixed on Hosanna's tail, Will was not completely despondent. Soon he would see Ellie, and Hal would surely be quick with reinforcements.

The serjeant was enjoying himself. Hosanna was much more comfortable than his usual mount, but just as he was congratulating himself on the morning's success, the gibbet's grisly human decoration rattled in the morning breeze. Hosanna shied and the serjeant fell heavily into the ditch. Swearing, the man scrambled out and drew his sword.

Will did not stop to think. He drove his heels hard into his own mount, shouting aloud as it wheeled round, drawn up short against the leading rein, 'Don't you dare touch my horse!' He twisted and struggled, desperate to see what was happening. 'Don't you touch that horse or you'll pay for it!' he yelled. 'By God, you'll pay for it!'

The serjeant hesitated, dropped his own sword and, with slow relish, slid Will's own sword out of its scabbard. Then he parted Hosanna's mane and raised his arm.

Will thought he would explode. 'No, no!' he cried. The sword came down, but at the last moment the serjeant twitched and severed a hank of hair which scattered and landed silently on the morning frost.

Will was shaking and leant forward, almost sick down his pony's neck. What a fool he had been. These people had no honour and no mercy. By the time Hal returned, they might all be dead.

The serjeant laughed.

The path to the tower was slippery and Will could hear the soldiers cursing behind him. Once inside the courtyard, he was pulled off the pack pony and shoved unceremoniously through a sturdy wooden door in a sunless corner well away from the gates.

He found himself in a damp cave, roughly twenty feet by twenty, with a sunken earth floor and slimy walls. Far from being able to see Ellie, he could see nothing at all, for the only daylight came through a small iron grille set high in the crumbling stone, designed deliberately so that while people could look in, no prisoner could look out. In the almost impenetrable black, Will could barely see his own hand in front of his face. As the key turned, he beat the door with his fists.

From a high window, Ellie watched, horrified, as both Will and Hosanna appeared then disappeared. For a few moments she thought it might be some kind of incomprehensible ruse concocted by Will and Gavin as part of a plan to rescue her and Old Nurse. But when she saw Hosanna hobbled and heard Will hammering, she was filled with dread and rushed down to the courtyard. She was halfway to the cellar when de Scabious caught her arm. She recoiled as from a snake.

'I have no desire to hurt you, Miss Eleanor,' the constable said in his most conciliatory voice, for, despite all evidence to the contrary, he really believed that she would come round to his charms eventually. 'But you must not go over there. If you do, I shall make sure our prisoner goes somewhere where nobody will ever find him.'

'Let Will and Hosanna go,' she said in a low voice, trying to still the terrible banging of her heart.

'Certainly. Once we are married.'

'We will never be married.'

'Oh, we will, when King John comes.' The constable rocked on his feet. 'I don't know why you are objecting, Eleanor. It's no good thinking about Master Gavin any more. It is quite plain: Master William has come alone because his sensible brother has given you up already. The Hartslove banner –' he enjoyed the flash of hope in Ellie's eyes – 'will never be seen here. The Count of Hartslove recognizes King John, even if his brother doesn't.'

'It's not true.' The light faded from Ellie's face but she would not allow her hopes to be dashed so easily.

'Then why is he not here, nor any of his knights? They have had plenty of time.'

To this Ellie had no answer. She pulled away and made once again for Will's cellar, but the constable

74

stood straight in front of her, this time with a far from conciliatory look on his face. 'A small warning, my dear,' he hissed. 'I mean what I say. If you go near the cellar or the stables, the prisoner will vanish and nobody will see him again. Is that clear?'

Ellie began to tremble. 'You are a wicked man, Constable de Scabious.'

'Oh no, my dear,' he said, smiling again and prinking a little. 'I am just a man who likes to make sure things go smoothly.' He gave a little hop. 'And now I have such a splendid new horse to ride, I am sure they will.' He threw this at her with his most triumphant grin.

Ellie sobbed with fury, but because she knew that the constable did not threaten in vain, all she could do was cry out both Will and Hosanna's names with as full a voice as she could, then flee back upstairs to Old Nurse.

Will heard Ellie's cry and answered it, crashing and shouting until the serjeant sent a man to threaten him into silence. Then he sat in the cellar cursing, icy drops of sweat beading his forehead as he thought of all that the constable might do.

In the late afternoon a pan of pottage and a pitcher of water were thrust in through the door but Will pushed them away. By evening, he was so cold he thought he might die. He could not survive this. At best it would take Hal three days to get back to Hartslove and, even then, what would Gavin do? Will was plunged into an almost deathly pessimism and lay down, his face in the dirt.

He did not move for hours. But as the day ended and the moon rose he was roused by a rumble, throbbing and persistent. It forced him to get up, and as he crouched, wiping the dirt from his eyes, he knew what it was. Hosanna's deep, familiar whinny was pulsing across the courtyard, filling the air with its music. Will remained absolutely still. The whinny grew louder and, in time, was answered by Sacramenta. Again and again Hosanna called out his great greeting.

Now Will could hear disconcerted soldiers rushing around the courtyard, nervously shouting for the horse to be quiet. But Hosanna took no notice. He would not stop until, one after another, all the other horses joined in and eventually the whole tower reverberated with their collective lamentation.

'I hear you, Hosanna, I hear you,' Will whispered as the waves of sound rolled round and through him. He could almost lean against them. By the time the throbbing grew less and the horses fell silent, he stood upright. Then he found the water and reached for the pottage. Mechanically he began to swallow. He did not lie in the dirt again.

At the top of the tower, Hosanna's song also drew Ellie to the window. She shut her eyes and when it began to die away, sank to the floor.

Old Nurse sighed, then looked sharply at her charge. 'Now, dear,' she said. 'Don't despair. Prince John, or King John, whichever it is, is Richard's brother and old Henry's son. We should at least have some faith in him.'

'Faith?' Ellie was scathing. 'And where exactly has faith got us so far, Old Nurse? We always say "keep faith", but what is the use of me keeping faith if Gavin won't?'

But Old Nurse refused to give in. 'We must keep faith because it is the only thing we've got, dearie,' she said simply. 'And it is a powerful thing, if you use it properly.'

Ellie reached for her necklace. At this moment, she wanted to rip the thing off. Gavin was failing her, and not only her, but Richard and Will also. She struggled, but the clasp would not easily be undone, and in the end she gave up. She ran her fingers over the stones. If she were to keep faith a little longer, it could not be out of desperation or duty to God. She needed something warmer to cling to.

As the last ripples of Hosanna's song rose into the night sky, it came to her. Of course. She did have something. She would cling to the memory of Gavin's face as he turned to make his vows, before de Scabious had ruined everything. Shutting her eyes, she concentrated until the image burnt bright in her heart. Then she leant back against the wall and let her hand fall to her side.

6

Having ridden as hard as he dared, Hal arrived back at Hartslove to find the place uncannily quiet. At first he was not too alarmed by the porter's reluctance to let him in. It was understandable, particularly since Hal's departure with Will had hardly been orthodox. Much more alarming was the silence. The workmen who should have been putting the castle to rights had vanished. Wooden scaffolding lay in piles, but where were the joiners?

Hal dismounted and, from the temporary stables, heard horses whinnying uneasily. He gave Dargent a drink at the water trough and found a space for him in a stall between two unfamiliar animals that had clearly been at Hartslove for several days at least. When he was confident that Dargent was comfortable, instead of going to the bakehouse, which was what he normally did, Hal made for the small door at the bottom of the keep, the same door from which Ellie had so blithely emerged on her wedding day, and made his way up the steps to the back entrance of the great hall. That door had been burnt, so it was easy for Hal to creep in.

Under the sagging beams, he saw Marissa and Marie together in a corner and two men sitting at opposite ends of a wooden trestle set up near the hearth. One of the men was Gavin, who looked hot and restless. The other was the man styling himself King John. A large fire spat, and the wolfhounds, lounging in front of it, raised their massive heads.

Hal drew back. He hesitated, then climbed further up the spiral stairs. By edging his way carefully through a hole in the wall, it was possible to crawl on to one of the blackened joists and shuffle into a position where, unseen, he could overhear the conversation below. His heart beat fast as his clothes snagged on the splinters and the wood creaked and shivered. He stopped several times, but nobody looked up as he pulled himself as far forward as he dared and then lay, every breath causing ashes to float around his head like a satanic halo.

Prince John – Hal refused to call him King – was leaning forward. He seemed very anxious that Gavin should understand exactly what he was saying. Gavin was sitting grinding his goblet of wine into the trestle in a manner, Hal thought, that would have earned him a stiff reprimand from his late father. John's voice was half pleading, half demanding.

'Your support would mean a great deal to me,' he coaxed. 'This county is an important one. If you declare for me, others will follow. You served my brother Richard well on crusade. Will you not do the same for me now that he is dead?'

'I always serve the king,' said Gavin. *Grind, grind, grind* went his goblet.

John tried again. 'Of course you do,' he said. 'And the de Granvilles have been well rewarded. But truly loyal service means serving the king at difficult times, at times when, perhaps, other people are not so loyal.'

There was a pregnant pause before John added in very deliberate tones, 'Such service commands even greater rewards.'

Gavin ground his goblet even harder. 'I do not want greater rewards,' he said. 'I am Count of Hartslove and happy to be so.'

'But you want to marry the heiress Eleanor de Barre,' John interrupted with a forced smile, wanting to slap the goblet out of Gavin's hand, 'in the full knowledge that she brings not only herself, but lands too. That's why your estimable father took her in, for goodness' sake, and loyalty to me at this point, Count, would make your union with Eleanor de Barre – how shall I put it – *possible* again. What is more, despite your commendable modesty, you know perfectly well that such a union would make you an even more powerful man than you are already. Come on, Gavin. With Richard dead you will have to be loyal to me sooner or later. A loyal man with a grateful king and an heiress for a wife – it's the wise man's dream.'

'I have it on good authority that you have promised Eleanor to Constable de Scabious,' said Gavin, ignoring all reference to Richard. 'He came to claim her himself. Look at the damage he has done to Hartslove in your name. You are sitting in the wreck of my wedding day, wreckage authorized by you yourself.'

John made a small disparaging noise.

Gavin stopped grinding his goblet. 'Are you saying that de Scabious acted with no authority?' he demanded.

John shifted, but continued to smile, if a little glassily. 'No,' he said. 'I am not.' He looked around and Hal stiffened as the prince glanced up at the gaping roof. 'He did go a little further than strictly necessary, though,' he said. 'I regret the damage. I shall have words when I visit him.'

'You are going to visit him?'

John nodded. 'I am,' he said. 'Directly I leave here and I am wondering exactly what to say to him. Or to Eleanor.' He tapped his fingers on the table almost dreamily. 'I could bring her back with me, of course. It would disappoint the constable, but would be quite easy. Just recognize that I am king, and get all your household and followers to do the same, and she is yours. It is as easy as that.'

'And if I won't swear loyalty to you, because you have brought me no proof of Richard's death?'

John pursed his lips and looked pointedly at the stump of Gavin's arm. 'Well,' he said, 'there might be some advantages for Eleanor in marrying de Scabious, worthless scum though he is.'

Gavin breathed heavily. John pretended not to notice. 'Perhaps they should marry,' he continued thoughtfully, as if debating the union of two dogs. 'A combination of Eleanor's spirit and de Scabious's cunning would produce children who would be useful additions to any kingdom.'

At that Gavin tried to spring up, but he needed the table to help him. 'You may or may not be the king, but you should watch your tongue.'

John got up too. 'Look, Count,' he said, deadly serious. 'Neither you nor I are fools. We both understand that the peace of this nation depends on the presence of a monarch who cares about what goes on here. England is my home. But what has Richard ever done for the place? He uses Englishmen as his bankers, milking them for money for a holy war he knows he can never win.

Where's the greatness in that? Have you not heard the joke doing the rounds, that Richard would have sold London if he had found a buyer? Nobody could write that about me. I may have my faults, but at least I know more about this country than how much silver you can extract from every last acre.'

'Richard will spend more time here when he gets back.' Gavin could think of no better defence.

John laughed out loud and it was not a nice sound. 'Even you don't believe that,' he said. 'Now, because of your gallant history, I am going to give you a little time to make up your mind as to your future course. Then I will return. Support me and you get the girl. Support my dead brother and you will be a traitor. Girls like Eleanor cannot marry traitors, so she will become Lady de Scabious. I know the constable is repulsive, but he is also ambitious and ruthless. I do not have to like him to recognize his usefulness.'

'Whatever I do, Ellie will never consent to marry de Scabious,' said Gavin.

'No?' asked John. 'I wonder about that. Your servants have told my men that your brother and that red horse everybody talks about have left here to find where de Scabious has his lair. Your brother is too impetuous for his own good. Alone, he stands no chance of rescuing Eleanor. Far more likely, don't you think, that his lonely –' John stressed the word to make Gavin wince – 'lonely raid will end in disaster. Maybe, even now, he and that horse find themselves – how shall we say it nicely? – detained.' He leant back. 'I shouldn't like to be detained by the constable,' he added, almost conversationally.

Marissa stood up and clenched her fists.

John glanced over at her and, pleased to find his

threats so effective, pressed his point home. 'All I am saying is that you do not know where your brother is, but if he and the horse do find themselves in the constable's custody, which, you must admit, is quite likely, Eleanor might find herself with little choice. She might prefer to marry de Scabious than witness anything unpleasant happening to either of them. You must see the risk.' He heard Marissa exclaim and watched Gavin's knuckles whiten. Then he gulped some wine. 'Look, Gavin, I am not a monster, even if it would be convenient for you to paint me as such. And my brother Richard is – was – not a saint. I may not be a Lionheart, but in many ways I will make the better king. Believe me, confirmation of Richard's death will come shortly. But if I wait for it before I take the crown we will be plunged into civil war. So, if you will not do as I wish and support me – and England – at this critical moment, I must find others who will. That is my duty as king. My father did not wear himself out on England's behalf to see everything he worked for disintegrate. And don't forget that when confirmation of Richard's death does come, I will remember those who put their faith in me and those who did not.'

Gavin stood in silence as John called for his horses and his men, but it was some time before the thump of the lowering drawbridge and the echo of hooves showed that Hartslove was at last free from his presence. Only then did Gavin sit down again and, as the hunting dogs pushed their great heads against him, Marie and Marissa crept away, holding hands.

Hal began to push himself back along the beam. He got almost to the end when he felt it begin to sway. It complained, then cracked, and finally, with a terrible tearing and splintering, broke off completely and crashed to the floor in a hail of powdery grit. Hal was pitched straight on to the trestle. He slid across, spilling all the wine before Gavin put out his arm and stopped his unexpected guest landing in his lap.

'What the –?' he exclaimed.

Hal tumbled into the rushes then picked himself up and began gingerly testing each arm and each leg. His normally freckled face was grey and his nose wrinkled as he coughed and sneezed.

'Hal?' said Gavin.

Hal wiped his nose. 'Yes, sir, it's me,' he croaked.

Gavin picked up a tankard from the floor. He could not stop his hand from shaking and his face was still blotchy with fever. Nevertheless, he banged the tankard on the table. 'I should have you sent before the justice for leaving this castle without permission,' he said. 'You stupid fool. What on earth made you risk a valuable warhorse by pushing it up the drawbridge? What Will does is his own affair. But you? You should have known better.'

Hal looked at the floor. Gavin's mouth was twitching badly and sweat soaked his hair. 'Alan sent two men out just after you had gone,' he said more quietly. 'They were brought back by John and he and his men have been here ever since. I have been a virtual prisoner in my own castle. You were lucky you didn't jump straight over the moat and into their hands.' He sat down. 'Goodness, though, I am relieved to see you back. Is Will outside? I must speak to him.'

'The earl has been taken by de Scabious's men.' Hal hated saying it and seeing how it made Gavin sag. 'I escaped because – but never mind that now. The important thing is that at least I know where the constable is, and Miss Ellie is there too.'

Gavin pulled himself up. 'Did you see her?'

'No,' said Hal. 'But she is there.' He watched Gavin rub his hands over his face as if he could rub the fever away.

It was a moment before Gavin spoke again. 'You heard all that the man who would be our king had to say?'

Hal blushed. 'I did, sir,' he said.

'Things are complicated, Hal. How many men would we need to take the place if it comes to that?'

'I don't know,' said Hal, feeling suddenly depressed. 'It's a tower, built to be impregnable.'

But Gavin wasn't listening. 'And even if we are successful, what then?' he muttered to himself.

'But Earl William is a prisoner,' said Hal, his voice growing louder in its urgency. 'We must go at once.'

'How can I go, Hal?' Gavin's voice ascended from a well of despair. 'I am so sick that I can hardly stand up, never mind ride. And I can't send my men out, in direct opposition to John, if I don't know that Richard still lives. Certainly I can't send them without me at their head to take the blame if it all goes wrong.'

He struggled to his feet and climbed on to the dais to sit in his father's old seat, one of the few things he had left. The wedding chairs he had had made for himself and Ellie had been burnt to cinders. He looked about him, feeling like a ghost in his own home. If he shut his eyes, he could still see Ellie in her wedding dress, wearing the green jasper necklace. His heart contracted. How could Will think that he, Gavin, did not love her? He loved Ellie as he had loved nobody else. But his love was not blind and he would not allow it to dictate his actions, even if Will thought this made him heartless. Surely Ellie would understand that?

Gavin sat for a long time, hunched into himself, and Hal had little choice but to wait.

Marie and Marissa reappeared carrying candles but Gavin was oblivious until Marie went to him, and with a gesture of utmost tenderness, put out her hand and touched his cheek. The effect was electric. Gavin's whole face lit with hope and longing. 'Ellie?' he breathed. 'Ellie?'

Marie shrank back. Whatever had possessed her? She never forgot the look of blank confusion Gavin gave her when he realized he had made a mistake. It was as if somebody had struck him. 'Marie,' he said, and sat up straight, trying to calm himself. 'Marie.'

Marie took a deep breath. She might be frightened of most animals, but the years after her sister's accident had cured her fear of sick people. 'Gavin, I can help you,' she said. 'But you have to rest.'

'There is no time. I must decide what to do. I cannot leave Ellie and Will in de Scabious's hands, but if Richard is not dead and I support John . . .'

His obvious anguish put unaccustomed steel into Marie's soul. 'You cannot decide in a fever,' she said, 'but I can make you better, and soon. Come.'

Gavin gave a wan smile. 'Even your potions can't give me back my wedding day or my arm,' he said.

'But I can give you back your health, and with that other things will follow. I know it.'

Marie would not give up now and, in response to her soft-spoken authority, he allowed her to help him up. Hal came to assist and Gavin found himself carried

86

into a small chamber that Marie had already made comfortable. Bowls and strips of cloth were stacked in neat piles in the corner. 'I'm going to dress his arm,' she said to Hal, rolling up her sleeves.

Hal was appalled. 'You can't,' he said. 'You're too young. Medicine is for old women or men from the university.'

Marie ushered him towards the door. 'How old-fashioned you are,' she said, and pushed him out so that she could begin her grisly work.

The squire returned to the great hall where Marissa was stroking the dogs. 'Your sister,' he said to her, 'is the bravest girl I have ever met.'

But Marissa was not listening. 'What can we do?' she agitated. 'We can't just sit and wait. We must do something now for Will and Hosanna.'

'And Ellie.'

Marissa made a dismissive noise. Now that Ellie was not here, she liked to pretend she did not exist.

'Well,' said Hal, thinking hard. 'I agree we must do something, but we can't muster an army on the count's behalf.' He weighed everything up carefully in the methodical manner of a good groom. 'To do anything at all, we need to know for certain whether King Richard is alive or dead.'

'You could go and find out.' Marissa was triumphant.

'I suppose I could try,' said Hal doubtfully. 'But I need to go back to Hangem, just in case there is an opportunity –' He broke off and stared into the fire. 'No,' he said finally. 'I should find out about Richard. That's what the earl would do.' He glanced outside. 'It's too dark to leave tonight and Dargent is too tired. I'll be off at first light.'

'Yes, at first light,' said Marissa, jumping up, impatient that there should be even a moment's delay. 'Do that.'

Nobody at Hartslove slept well, but when the abbey bell sounded through the dawn, and Hal, who had been through a dozen plans in his mind only to discard them, went to saddle Dargent, he found, to his intense frustration, that the horse had cast a shoe. Marissa hovered. Hal ran out, but returned, disconsolate, to saddle up the rangy black that Alan Shortspur usually rode.

'The farrier is drunk,' he said, yanking the girth strap. 'I'll have to leave Dargent here.'

Shouting to the porter to let him out, Hal settled himself, smiled apprehensively at Marissa, then urged the black horse over the drawbridge and was soon speeding his way to the coast.

Marissa watched him go, then turned away, dragging her leg. All that day, and the next, and the next, she was alone and never had time passed so heavily. Marie did not want her, for she knew the atmosphere in sickrooms gave Marissa nightmares, and the servants avoided her because of her temper.

She stood for hours just outside Dargent's box since, apart from the ruby brooch, he was the only thing of Will's she could find. Eventually she made herself go into the stable and stroke the horse's neck. Endlessly amiable, Dargent began to look forward to her visits.

More than a week later, the longest week of Marissa's life, she found him saddled up in the courtyard, and hesitated only slightly when asked to hold his rein while Alan, who was to ride him, went to give some last-minute instructions about the great hall roof. Climbing on to the mounting block, Marissa could see that the drawbridge was already lowered to let them out. She had no real intention of getting on at first. It was just a dream she had. But then there was a dispute and Alan called that Dargent would have to wait.

'I'll take him back to his stall,' Marissa heard herself saying, but she didn't take him back. Instead, she slipped her leg over his withers and before she knew it, with a heart beating fit to burst, she was trotting over the moat and out on to the open road.

7

John's journey to de Scabious's tower was a royal progress. When the sun shone, the knights in his retinue could feel its heat and they rejoiced doubly. Their lord's power was rising like spring sap. As he passed through villages, the prince heard himself addressed as king and did not contradict it. In the towns and monasteries from which he demanded hospitality, he made sure to sit a little above everybody else at supper. It was always a pleasure to be superior.

When he finally arrived at Hangem Tower, however, he was not very impressed. 'I can see why you want to marry the de Barre heiress,' he remarked to a toadying de Scabious as he dismounted. 'This is a dismal sort of place.'

The constable, who was in a panic about the quantities of food and drink he must offer his royal visitor, shuffled his legs and tried to smile. 'Oh, I quite like it up here,' said. 'But, as you say, it will not really do.'

indeed,' said John. 'A man like you deserves ~ else entirely.'

~s simpered. John looked round the court-
~he window. He saw a girl's face vanish
~. *Ah*, he thought. *Eleanor*. 'Well,

something to eat, man,' he said sharply to the constable. 'We have travelled a great distance.'

De Scabious led the way up the steps. 'The cooks have done their best,' he gushed, rubbing his hands together. As John made his way to the top table, de Scabious muttered to his own retinue to keep their appetites small.

'Why should we do that?' asked one. 'I thought this was a feast.'

'It may be a feast but there is not enough food, you numbskull,' whispered another as a cook dumped down four small legs of lamb. 'And that's because the constable is mean and the head cook is a dishonest knave. But, naturally, the king's men must not go hungry.'

Ellie was summoned. She persuaded Old Nurse to put on a clean apron and come down with her. As the old lady now reminded her daily, John was, after all, the son of old King Henry. He could not be all bad. If she found the right words, maybe he would make everything right again. When she found herself scrutinized, not unkindly, her spirits rose.

'Miss Eleanor de Barre?' he asked courteously enough. Ellie inclined her head. John looked her up and down. 'What it must feel like to be pursued by so many worthy men! I almost feel honour bound to join them.'

Panic washed over Ellie's face and she unconsciously put up her hand to touch her necklace. John laughed. 'Oh no, don't worry!' he said. 'I have my eye on bigger fish, although I must say,' and here he paused and let his eyes roam lazily over her once again, 'if you had more lands, I would certainly be tempted.'

Ellie's heart sank but she managed a stiff smile. 'Why is the constable allowed to keep William, Earl of

Ravensgarth, in captivity?' she asked, keeping her voice very civil. 'He should be released at once.'

'He will be released when he agrees to swear allegiance to me as his lord,' said John genially. 'Will he do that?' He took a whole chicken, pulled a piece off and, with de Scabious's famished knights watching his every move, threw it to the dogs.

'He is always loyal to the king.' Ellie made it a statement of fact.

John laughed. 'That's an old trick,' he said, 'but a neat one, particularly for a girl. Perhaps you could tell me which king, Miss Eleanor. Answer me that.'

It was impossible to smile now.

John grasped a lamb chop and bit into it contemplatively. 'Have some dinner,' he said, and when Ellie didn't move, made a dismissive gesture. 'You will be married by the end of two months, that's certain, whether you eat dinner or not.'

'Two months?' broke in de Scabious. 'I thought maybe, well, maybe this visit . . .?'

'Not this visit,' said John. De Scabious hid his disappointment under an obsequious bow.

Ellie tried to leave the table but she was not allowed, so she sat bolt upright and watched as John rejected most of the contents of de Scabious's kitchens and cellar and scowled at the makeshift musicians who twanged and plucked in the ridiculous minstrels' gallery.

Old Nurse, who had parked herself firmly next to Ellie, sniffed and settled her mouth in its most disapproving line. The food at this so-called feast would be only fit for the dogs at Hartslove. All her housekeeping instincts rose up in horror at the lumpy custards, stodgy tarts and half-cooked meat.

John smiled at Old Nurse's obvious disgust and, with conspiratorial secrecy, made a disparaging face. Old Nurse was quite unnerved and this amused the prince greatly. But he seldom took his eyes off Ellie, watching her as carefully as she watched him. As dinner progressed, her lips began to pucker slightly from the strain and John felt sorry for her. He hoped she would end up married to Gavin. Indeed, had he not decided on a very particular job for de Scabious, he would have ordered her release. It really was intolerable to think of such a pretty girl at the mercy of this portly puffball. But – and John gave a genuine sigh – until Gavin and Will declared their loyalty and the constable's job was done, life would be uncomfortable for all of them.

When dinner was over, he indicated that he wanted a private word with his host and was shown a small antechamber just off the hall. The room was a cheerless place, on which the few flames in the hearth made little impression. Two ancient wolfhounds were lying in the corner, scratching themselves. To try and create a more homely atmosphere, a huge and ancient tapestry had been hung from the top to the bottom of the wall, at right angles to the fire, but the prevailing smell was of rot. John sat on the edge of a chair and pressed on with his business, anxious to be gone. However, he had to be careful. He leant towards the constable, as if to draw him into his confidence. Oh, but de Scabious's breath was vile! If Gavin de Granville did not do the right thing, Ellie would have to be very brave.

'Constable,' he said, hiding his disgust in his most companionable voice. 'Your means are not large, but you have done your best to entertain me and my men. I appreciate it. Now. We have a small problem, which I am relying on you, relying on you, Constable,' he repeated pointedly, 'to fix. Once fixed, your life will be . . . I think transformed is not too grand a word to use.'

'You know you can rely on me, sire,' said de Scabious, licking his lips.

John looked at him long and hard. He needed to be sure of his man. 'I hear a rumour,' he said slowly and carefully, 'quite a reliable rumour, Constable, that my brother is still alive and that a ransom is to be demanded for his release.'

The colour fled from de Scabious's face. 'Alive?' he said stupidly. 'The king is alive? But I thought . . .'

John got up and stood behind him. 'He is not the king,' he hissed in his ear. 'Kings care for their kingdoms. Richard cares for nothing but foreign wars. After the Saladin tithe, what do you think a ransom will do? I'll tell you what. It will cripple the barony of England. We will all be made paupers. And for what? To redeem a king who will milk us again so that he can go back to Palestine and pursue an impossible goal. I tell you, de Scabious, those who are anxious for England's well-being cannot let this happen.' John walked round and sat down again. 'Do you see my point?'

The constable opened his mouth, then closed it again. He swallowed hard. He had gambled everything on Richard being dead. John had encouraged him. What was coming next?

John patted the constable on the arm. 'I see already that you and I understand each other very well, Piers,' he said. 'We are both men who think of England first and themselves afterwards.'

The constable smiled uncertainly. He understood

nothing, only that something was wrong when a king addressed a constable by his first name.

'You must act quickly,' John continued, holding out his hands towards the fire. 'And there must be no mistake.'

'No mistake?' said the constable, a horrible realization slowly beginning to dawn.

'No mistake,' said John impatiently. 'You know what to do?'

'Do?'

John was exasperated. 'Don't just repeat what I say, man.'

The constable could hardly speak. 'Are you saying that I should arrange to have Richard killed?' His voice was strangled.

John came close. 'Who should be king?' he asked softly, his words half a caress and half a menace. 'If Richard is king, where does that leave you?'

De Scabious's palms were sweaty. 'It will cost money.'

John shrugged. 'In the corner of the stable where you have put William of Ravensgarth's red horse you will find money,' he said. 'Use it wisely. There is a man – a foreign man called Abdul al-Baku – waiting by the sea. He has been sent, at my request, by the Old Man of the Mountains.'

At the mention of the Old Man, a small moan escaped from de Scabious's lips. The Old Man was a legendary assassin.

John watched, then leant forward again. The constable jumped as he felt a hand on his leg. 'That is all you need to know,' John said. 'Al-Baku is expecting you and is experienced in these matters. Now, sadly, I must be off

95

first thing in the morning. And doubtless you yourself will not want to waste time. The quicker you do your duty,' John threw a glance towards the hall, where Ellie and Old Nurse sat together, and made a lewd gesture with his hands, 'the quicker you collect your prize.'

De Scabious tried to laugh but it emerged as a bat squeak.

John was now halfway out of the room. As he reached the door, he turned. 'Remember, Piers,' he said, making his face deliberately stern. 'Remember how I rely on you. Oh . . . and also remember that I forget nothing.' He returned to the hall.

The constable sat in front of the fire for a few more minutes. His head was reeling. Richard alive! John had specifically told him this was impossible. The constable held on to his chair. Now his only choice was to do John's bidding, for if Richard ever returned, John would sell de Scabious straight down the river. Oh, what a fool he had been.

He got up, went to the door, shut it, returned to the fireside, swore long and loudly, using language he had learnt in the gutter, then threw his goblet of wine into the hearth and kicked one of the dogs as hard as he could. It howled, so de Scabious kicked it again and again. But then he began to think. Perhaps this was not really so bad. After all, if he did as *Prince* John asked, *King* John would be eternally in his debt. Richard would not come back. Richard *must* not come back. Then the constable would still get Ellie. He must fix his attention on that.

At sunrise, John left, and shortly afterwards de Scabious was standing in the courtyard rocking, as usual, on his toes. He was also ready to go, waiting only for Hosanna.

If he had to organize Richard's murder, it would be sweet to organize it from the back of William of Ravensgarth's horse. Gethin appeared. 'Hosanna is ready, sir. Shall I bring him out?'

'Take him over to the cellar,' de Scabious ordered. 'I'll mount over there.' Gethin walked Hosanna over and, really, the animal was a picture. The constable shook himself with delight when he thought of how he would look on the wonder horse of the crusade.

Will was sitting in the dark with his head in his hands when he heard de Scabious call out Hosanna's name. Instantly, he jumped up and grabbed the grille, trying to haul himself high enough to see, but it was impossible. Dropping down, he set up a ceaseless thumping on the door.

The grooms laughed and joked. 'Care for your horse more than girls? We know your sort.'

Will hardly heard them. De Scabious on Hosanna. It was an abomination. He ran round his cell crying out like a man possessed. Where was Ellie? If she was not being prevented, she would surely come to see him now. What had de Scabious done to her?

But Ellie did not dare to go near Will. She had heard John depart, and now she was watching the constable's preparations from above. When she saw Gethin bring Hosanna out and take off his hobbles, she came down to the courtyard, her heart sinking.

The horse himself, however, seemed unconcerned. Standing patiently in the sun, his coat shone like copper and his elegant ears were pricked and alert as the breeze rippled his mane. He took no notice of de Scabious, just nudged Gethin's arm occasionally with his nose. Gethin patted him. When polishing Hosanna's coat, he had noticed the horse's two healed crusading wounds and wondered about them. He didn't like the jokes at Will's expense and busied himself running his hands over the dents once again. Catching Ellie looking at him, he gave her a small nod.

De Scabious kept everybody waiting another twenty minutes before he eventually called for his knights to mount. He had needed some liquid courage to soothe his nerves. By the time he re-emerged, his nose was glowing and his step somewhat unsteady. He glared at Gethin and inspected Hosanna from all angles, making sure that Will could hear his disparaging comments. Rejecting the soft, supple bridle that Hal kept in such good order, he ordered it to be replaced with a stiff, highly ornate affair complete with barbed decorations, a spiked, ridged bit and an ill-fitting headpiece.

Gethin was unhappy. 'I don't think . . .' he said as Hosanna shifted and winced.

'You are not obliged to think,' de Scabious barked, before grabbing the reins. Hosanna fidgeted. 'This horse's manners will have to be seen to, Gethin. Fetch me a switch.'

The boy looked shocked, but did as he was told. It was immediately snatched from his hands by Ellie who ran over and broke it sharply over her knee. 'You leave that horse alone,' she could hardly get the words out. 'Do you hear me, Constable de Scabious. You lift a finger against that horse and I'll kill you.' Hosanna blew softly into her hair.

The constable gave a precious laugh. 'My dear,' he said, 'horses must have manners.' He gestured to the serjeant to take Ellie back into the tower and shouted to Will to be quiet.

But Will would not be silenced, calling his horse's name again and again. 'Hosanna! Hosanna!'

De Scabious, clicking irritably, sent Gethin for another switch. 'If the prisoner makes any more noise,' he said loudly, aiming his remarks through the cellar grille, 'there may be an accident. Horses do have accidents, you know.'

Will bit his fingers and ground his heels into the dirt, but he fell silent.

Hosanna braced his legs as the constable heaved himself on. 'Don't try anything, horse,' de Scabious muttered. To balance himself, Hosanna moved forward one pace. Immediately his reins were jerked while, at the same time, a pair of spurs dug into his side. Turning his head to avoid the bristling bit, the horse's flanks quivered, but he remained still. 'That's better,' de Scabious's voice was as high as his hands were heavy. 'Now keep doing as you are told.' He took the second switch from Gethin and gave it a little twirl. From the stalls, Sacramenta whinnied. Hosanna answered and got a crack across the withers. He swished his tail, but walked on without further protest.

As the gates swung open, Ellie's voice rang out. 'Constable de Scabious.'

The constable squinted.

'Constable de Scabious,' Ellie repeated, hoping her voice was carrying over to Will. 'Don't you forget. If you hurt that horse, I will kill you myself. I hope you understand that quite clearly.'

She was given, as a response, a proprietorial wave, before her husband-to-be flourished his heels, and Hosanna, bending his neck to a new and painful yoke, cantered out on to the track.

8

Hal reached the port of Whitby without mishap. But all along the way, in the taverns and even among groups of pilgrims, he heard, just as he had when travelling with Will, men muttering about Richard, some now openly mocking him as a crusader who failed to take Jerusalem and a king who couldn't even keep even his own lands intact while he was away.

'Haven't you heard? Richard died of despair in a German prison,' they told each other. 'Soon John will be crowned.'

But while their voices were loud, their eyes were furtive. Most knew that what they said was at best speculation, but the town was full of armed men who constantly referred to Prince John as king, and it seemed safer to show no reluctance to do the same.

As Hal made for the quayside and began to search for a galley, even the sailors were whispering tales they had picked up in the Levant: Richard had become a Muslim; Richard had drowned; Richard had been killed by a thief in the night. If anybody pressed too hard, they ran their fingers over their throats in theatrical mock executions and disappeared below deck.

Hal tried to take no notice, but it was difficult,

particularly as it took him two frustrating days to find a shipmaster who could offer him a passage. Then, to his misery and fury, the black horse, terrified by the choppy waters, refused to step on to the gangplank for loading.

A crowd gathered to watch the spectacle as Hal and six sailors first tried gentle persuasion, then a thorny cane, then brute force. But the horse plunged and reared, kicked and bucketed until eventually the captain stepped in. Even if they could get the horse inside, he would not take him. He could not risk a fracas in the hold. Hal, alternately crimson with humiliation and white with frustration, led the horse away.

If only I had Hosanna, he cried inwardly, for even Dargent often relied on the courage of the red horse to reinforce his own. *If only I had Hosanna.*

But there was no miracle. Hosanna did not appear. Instead, Hal took the black horse to the marketplace further down the waterfront to exchange for something braver. There were no takers, and the squire had to spend yet another night on dry land. After it grew dark, he found a cheap hostelry and sat brooding over a tankard of ale. So much depended on him and he was making such poor progress.

The fire drew other travellers and Hal found himself squashed in among men whose leathered faces, lewd manners and coarse conversation revealed them as mercenaries: swordsmen for hire. They tossed their money about carelessly, demanding more food and drink, much of which they vomited on to the floor. The innkeeper said nothing, just nervously scurried about doing their bidding. He wanted no trouble. Talk about Richard's fate was inevitable but it grew heated when the men could not agree whether Richard or John was most worthy of the throne. Hal's blood began to boil as they denigrated Richard's achievements and even called him a coward. He tried to slip out but he found his way blocked and soon he, like everybody else, sat silent as the mercenaries claimed the floor.

One member of the group, a small, wiry man with two fingers missing, seeing they had an audience, nudged his friends' ribs, telling them it would be great sport to take a straw poll. 'King Richard or King John!' he cried. 'Bolt the door, Innkeeper. We'll ask your customers who they prefer. After all, the people of England must have opinions.'

The atmosphere was tense as the mercenaries took lanterns and candles to shine in people's faces. 'King Richard or King John?' they demanded. The innkeeper was asked first. 'King J-J-Jo-John,' he stammered. The men cheered.

'I don't know,' ventured a beardless clerk, who had only come in to get some wine for his ailing wife. He tried to smile. 'I think we must wait and see.'

'Wrong answer!' roared his tormentors, and one, drawing a dagger, asked him to think again.

Spilling his wine, the clerk begged their pardon.

'Richard or John?'

He gazed wildly about, then he had a brainwave. 'We must wait until John is crowned. Then we can be sure.'

Missing Fingers pushed right up close. 'You are too lily-livered to be a true subject to any king.' He hawked and spat.

The clerk's smile froze on his face. It was not until the mercenary moved away that the young man put his wine jar carefully down on a table, looked a little puzzled, then fell backwards, quite dead, a neat red stain in the middle of his stomach.

After that, there was no more doubting. The inn echoed to cries of 'King John! King John!'

Hal wedged himself into a corner. He would rather die than renounce King Richard, but to die here, at the hands of these barbarians, when so much at Hartslove depended on him, seemed more stupid then heroic. Maybe he could remain unnoticed.

But the mercenaries were thorough and when they saw Hal half concealed, they pulled him forward. 'Now, my boy,' Missing Fingers said. 'Stand up here and tell us what you think. Richard or John?'

Hal was silent.

'Come now,' Missing Fingers rocked the table. 'Make your mind up. I believe you are the last.' He rocked the table again and sucked in his cheeks, the clerk's blood still wet on his knife.

'Not quite the last.' In a corner behind the table furthest from the fire, a dark figure swathed in a hooded cloak sat crumbling bread with long fingers. 'I have something to say on the matter.' The man's voice was muffled and the mercenaries swung their lanterns towards his face. Hal held himself tight. 'Come,' said the stranger. 'Come here and let me give you my opinion.'

The mercenaries lurched towards him. When only the trestle separated them, the stranger leant forward, as if to speak. Then he spat, hard and true, into Missing Fingers' eye, and at the same time heaved the table up and overturned it. The lanterns and candles flew into the air and steel flashed as the mercenaries bellowed and cursed.

Relief and jubilation gave Hal wings. He leapt lightly

103

over the mercenaries' heads and, drawing his sword, fought side by side with the stranger. Together they edged their way towards the door, which the innkeeper found the courage to throw open. The body of the clerk was trampled underfoot in the stampede to get out.

Hal and the stranger protected each other as best they could, fighting backwards side by side to give them the best chance against superior numbers. Eventually, spotting a narrow ginnel, they broke free and dashed away, losing their pursuers in the maze of dingy backstreets. When they judged it safe, they stopped to catch their breath.

Hal bent double, easing a stitch, then, when he could, stood up and leant against a wall. 'Who are you?' he asked. 'Because I owe you both my honour and my life.' He wiped his mouth and looked up, then stood in amazement, momentarily speechless again, as the stranger pulled back his hood and revealed his face in the moonlight.

'Do you not recognize me?' Kamil asked. 'Are you not the squire who looks after the red horse?'

Hal tried to find his tongue. 'Yes, I know you,' he said. 'How could I forget you? You are the man who helped to save Hosanna after the Battle of Jaffa. Of course I know you. You are Kamil. But I hardly expected to see you here. I don't understand.'

Kamil gave a short laugh. 'It is I who don't understand,' he said. 'What sort of a place is it when a brother tries to take the place of his living king?'

'Living?' Hal grabbed Kamil's cloak. 'What do you mean, living? Do you know for certain that Richard is still alive?'

'I have seen him,' said Kamil, unpeeling Hal's hands.

104

'I have a letter from him to give to the Count of Hartslove. Yes, he is alive, or he was, and in good health, when we talked a month or so ago.'

Hal almost sank to the ground. 'Oh, thank God,' he said. Then he was all business. 'There's no time to waste, Kamil,' he said. 'You must take the letter at once to the count, and I must go to the tower.' Kamil raised his eyebrows. 'My master is held prisoner,' explained Hal, his words tumbling over themselves, 'and Miss Ellie – well, it's too complicated to explain, but I must get word to them both that Richard is alive. So much depends on this. Have you a horse?'

'I do not,' said Kamil. Then he asked, almost casually, 'The red horse, Hosanna. Where is he?'

'Hosanna is with my master,' said Hal. 'I just pray Constable de Scabious – he's the man who is keeping them prisoner – has grooms who will look after him properly.'

'This constable must be a bad man if he does not treat the red horse as an honoured guest.'

Hal looked at Kamil. He had forgotten just how foreign he was. A horse, even a horse like Hosanna, an 'honoured guest'? He thought it sounded a little nonsensical. 'You will go to Hartslove with your letter, won't you?' He was suddenly doubtful. After all, Kamil was a Saracen and the Saracens were enemies.

'I will do my best, if you tell me the direction.' Kamil could sense Hal's mistrust and did not do anything to allay it. 'But I shall have to start tomorrow, after the horse market opens.'

Hal grinned and his face was suddenly open and friendly. 'I hope you choose better than me. I've got an unreliable black animal,' he said. 'Not like Hosanna at all. But now I think God was on my side when I chose him. He would not board the ship, you know, and if he had, I would have missed you. Hosanna would never have behaved in such a way.'

Kamil had little idea what Hal was talking about, but listened politely. They began to walk back the way they had come, keeping well into the shadows, for the black horse was stabled near the unfortunate inn. The animals were restive but nobody had interfered with them. Hal breathed a sigh of relief as Kamil helped him with the saddle.

'You'll go first thing in the morning? Keep south-west, and find the River Hart. Follow it upstream and eventually you'll see the castle. If you get to the abbey, you've gone too far, but one of the monks will help you. They are good people. Take care, Kamil. John's men are everywhere and the count may have unwelcome visitors. Ask for the river, don't ask for the castle.' Kamil nodded. Hal clicked at the black horse to wake him up. 'And thank you again,' he said. 'I'll not forget you saved my life.'

Kamil gave a half smile, but by the time the black horse's hoof beats were absorbed into the multiplicity of night noises, he was already making plans of his own. He hugged Richard's letter to him. If it were so vital, it must be worth something. *It must at least*, Kamil thought as he began to make his way back through the streets looking for somewhere safe to sleep, *be worth exchanging for a red horse*. He was so lost in his dreams that it was only after four mounted men had passed him, galloping fast in the direction Hal had taken, that he registered who they were. He was momentarily perturbed, but as there was nothing he could do, he continued on his way.

Hal heard the four horses too and at first tried to dismiss them. Horsemen could be riding fast for any number of reasons. It was not necessarily the mercenaries. He held his steady pace, trying to save the black's breath and legs, calculating how to get to Hangem in the shortest possible time. But as the hooves drummed closer his spine tingled and he urged the horse to go faster. Soon he was cantering, then galloping; an insane pace when he could not see the road in front of him. The black horse stumbled and slid, but Hal urged him on. Whoever was behind was gaining on them.

He crouched low as horses appeared at either side, and when Missing Fingers raised his weapon, he made the sign of the cross. But the sword was not for him. Instead it sliced clean through the black's jugular vein, and Hal was suddenly soaked in a spray of warm blood. The animal's legs begin to paddle as it sank to the ground, its throat rattling. Pitched off to the side, Hal was manhandled to his feet and, once hauled up behind Missing Fingers, his hands were tied to the saddle rings. The mercenaries were jubilant. They would take their prize to their camp and, when they had finished with him there, they would bring him before the new king and have him legally hanged for a traitor.

'No man gets the better of us.' Missing Fingers rolled his eyes at Hal. 'We may not find your friend, but you, at least, are going to pay.'

Hal said nothing. Silently, he prayed as his horse exhaled its last breath into the mud. But his prayer was not for the horse or for himself. 'Please God,' he pleaded, 'get Kamil safely to Hartslove and save my master and Hosanna.' Then he gritted his teeth and wondered just how much courage he was going to need.

9

Will was praying too, but he was praying for unconsciousness. After de Scabious left Hangem on Hosanna, all he wanted was to obliterate from his mind the loathsome picture of the constable on his horse. It scalded his thoughts. But when unconsciousness would not come, he padded round and round, scraping his shoulder against the sides of his green-slimed pen. He did this until his body was heavy with exhaustion. As he sank down he tried to console himself by recalling the sound of Hosanna's deep, confident voice as it had reverberated through the courtyard on the night of his capture. The horse would return safely. He must. Yet as soon as this faint hope took root, Will found himself assailed by other troubles.

For the first time, here in this hideous cell, he admitted to himself that Gavin was right. Ellie was not just his dearest friend: she meant far more to him than that. Gavin had accused him of being in love with her and Will must now acknowledge the truth. Whether Ellie loved him in return or not, he could not imagine a future without her. For a second, the admission filled him with a strange breathless exhilaration and the sensation that some niggling strain behind his eyes was dissolving away, allowing him to see straight for the first time since returning home from the Holy Land. He was a little dazed by the view. Yet the exhilaration vanished as quickly as it had arrived. What kind of a fool was he? Even if they escaped from their present troubles, Ellie was beyond his reach. He could never marry her. With King Richard's blessing, she had been betrothed by his father to his brother. Under King John she would be married to de Scabious.

Will felt his heart grow tight. It would be intolerable to see Ellie married, even to Gavin. He kicked out at the wall. As Earl of Ravensgarth, he was due a wife of substance himself. Why should he not demand that it be her? After all, he outranked his brother now. That must mean something. But even as he concocted wilder and wilder plans – some involving declaring loyalty to John, others involving fleeing the country – he knew they were doomed to failure. He could not betray his brother or his rightful king. If he did, Ellie would despise him – and he would despise himself – forever. Will momentarily envied de Scabious. A man with no honour might do as he liked. He buried his face in his knees. For most of his life, Ellie's marriage had not bothered him much. He had always known it was coming and had just accepted it, like war or the changing seasons. But now, even the memory of their childhood intimacy, their whispered dreams under the Hartslove chestnut tree, their teasing of the monks and the hours spent together in the stables, contained elements of torture. How had he taken her so much for granted? He prowled round his cell again.

When he could no longer bear to do this he sat, and within minutes the damp crept into his bones. Fingers of light struggled through the high grille, but were not enough to stop the cellar turning into an ice house. Will could feel his breath freezing almost before it left his lungs. He still had on his travelling cloak and his thick, quilted jerkin and chausses, but they might have been made of paper. He should walk round again, he knew that, but in his misery he just felt about for the corner with least water on the floor and curled up.

Gethin came in with his daily ration of pottage, but Will was too sick at heart to eat it and instead hurled it away. Nobody came near him again, not even to collect the pottage pan. The day dragged on and hours later, when it was nearly over and even the spluttering night torches that lit the tower had all but burnt out, he threw back his head and howled like a wolf.

The following morning, there was no food, only water. 'Punishment for keeping us awake!' shouted the serjeant through the door. 'I'll have you flogged if you make that noise again.'

By noon, Will's hunger was acute. The sun was up, but the cellar was colder than ever and he could hear himself beginning to wheeze. He shuffled about. He must eat or he would die. Dropping on to all fours, he found the pottage pan and began to search the ground for the bits of gristle that passed for meat in the slop, which he had splattered against the wall. He found one or two pieces and forced himself to swallow them. He even licked out the pan. But there was nothing else, no matter how carefully he felt around. He sank down against the wall and, because there was nothing else to do, began to scratch at the bottom of the cellar wall with the pan handle. The wall crumbled surprisingly easily, but Will had only made a small hole when the tin bent and buckled, too thin to be of any real use. He poked his finger through the hole but could feel solid rubble behind, and sat, almost beyond shivering. The hole seemed to mock him and he shut his eyes.

It was hard for him to tell when he first became aware of the scraping. Time had ceased to mean very much. His brain registered something, then discarded it, but when the noise persisted, Will suddenly found himself listening acutely. Surely it was too loud for mice and there was no squeaking.

He broke out in a cold sweat. *Oh Lord*, he thought. *Not rats. Please God, not rats.* He drew his legs closer to his chest. After a little longer, he fancied he heard shallow breathing. Fighting the impulse to shrink away, he strained his eyes and peered down. It was impossible to see anything, but he felt a small movement in the stone. Yes. There it was again. It was not his imagination. Something not very large was trying to push its way through, using the hole that he had made.

Ignoring the pools of water, Will lay down, steadying himself as tiny slivers of wall began to shave off. When a slightly larger chunk gave way, he grabbed what emerged. There was an indignant cry and, with disbelief and shock, Will realized that he was clutching a child's fist. He held on but, even in his surprise, he said nothing. The fist must belong to somebody. Let them speak first. From the other side of the wall, he heard sobbing.

'No harm, no harm,' the child was saying. 'I didn't mean no harm.'

Holding on firmly, Will whispered back. 'Who are you?'

There was a short pause. 'I'm nobody. Just a village boy. Who are you?'

'I'm nobody as well,' said Will. 'Just a visiting knight.'

'Funny place to be a visitor.'

'Funny way of doing no harm.'

There was another pause. The fist began to wriggle. 'You're freezing!' said the voice. Then, another question. 'Are you the Hosanna-man?'

'The Hosanna-man?'

'The man who stayed in our cowshed?'

'Are you Elric, son of Peter the cowherd?'

'Suppose I am?' The arm to which the fist belonged began to tug.

'Oh no you don't,' said Will. 'Not yet. Elric, how have you managed to crawl up here and get behind this wall?'

'Why should I tell you?'

'Why not? And anyway, I have your hand. I can wait.'

There was some more sniffing and tugging before Elric replied slowly and unwillingly. 'You don't know much about building, do you?' he said. 'How do you think they got the stone up here to build this place? They didn't drag it all up that hill. Some of it came from here. They quarried for stone, see, and left a passage behind, a big one, and this one branching off. They stopped this one up when they had finished and most of it has fallen in so nobody uses it now except us – me and my friends that is. We play here when we've finished our chores.' Elric stopped. 'You won't tell, will you? My ma says it's dangerous, but then she's always fussing.'

'Who on earth would I tell?' Will kept his voice very low. 'Did you say it just went to this cellar?'

Elric was coy. 'Why do you want to know? You are stuck where you are. And anyway, what's left of the tunnel is too small for you. I've had to push through the rubble to make this bit big enough for me.'

The arm pulled back, but Will would not release it. 'Elric,' he said, taking a gamble, 'I am the Hosanna-man. We are friends, aren't we? I would like to trust you with some of my secrets, just as you have trusted me with yours. Can I do that?'

'*You* trust *me*?' retorted Elric, his voice distorted by the wall. 'Why should *I* trust *you*, more like. In the village, they say you came to find out who was loyal to Richard and his men. Anybody loyal to John will be hung, they say, if the king returns. My da supports John. He says Richard has done nothing for us.'

Will tried a different tack. 'Did you like my horse, Elric?' he asked.

Elric sounded enthusiastic. 'Well, yes. He is a lovely horse, the nicest I ever saw.'

'I swear,' said Will, 'on my horse's life that my visit to your village was nothing to do with getting people hung.'

'Where'd you get him – Hosanna, I mean?'

Will smiled. 'It's a long story,' he said. 'One day I will tell you, and perhaps by then you will have a horse of your own.'

'A horse? Me?' Will could hear the boy snorting. 'Fat chance. People like me get an ass if we're lucky, or the loan of a mule if we become servants in a monastery.' But some of the hostility had gone out of his voice. Will relaxed his grip. Immediately the hand vanished and Will swore as he heard the scrabbling noises of full retreat.

Soon, even these scratchings died away and Will was left with just a child's fist-sized hole and the memory of small, warm fingers.

He'll not come back, he thought disconsolately. *Everything will be a game to him.*

Gethin came to collect yesterday's pottage pan, which

he had forgotten. When he saw the crumpled handle, he was disconcerted, shaking his head at Will. But he did not call the serjeant. Instead, he straightened the handle out before shutting the cellar door, and Will found himself resentfully grateful.

A little later, after he had scraped his fingers badly and been forced to give up trying to pull more bits out of his side of the wall, Will heard more noises and this time, when he sensed the fist emerge, he did not touch it. 'Hosanna-man?' came the whisper. 'Hosanna-man?'

Will lay down. 'I'm still here.'

'I have brought you something,' Elric said, 'because I liked your horse and I liked your squire and you did stop those men from killing me.'

Will was touched at Elric's order of priorities. 'What have you brought?' he asked.

Elric withdrew his hand and Will heard a careful tapping sound. The boy had brought a small hammer and he knocked down enough wall to allow Will to peer through. But it was no good. Will abandoned attempts to see and instead inserted his hand cautiously, using it as a feeling torch. There was something wet, then sharp teeth.

'Ouch!' he exclaimed.

'Don't put your fingers in my mouth!' Elric whispered. 'I wasn't expecting it. I have to lie flat on my stomach.'

'All right,' said Will. 'Take my hand and guide it.'

Elric took his hand and Will could feel the rough stone sides of a tiny passage, just big enough for a very skinny child. In front of Elric's arms was a bundle. 'We'll have to make the hole bigger to get it through,' he said.

Will thought for a minute. 'What if de Scabious's soldiers open the door wide enough to see it?'

'What's the matter with your brain?' asked Elric. 'We'll push all the stone out on your side, then, with some of the muck and slime, we can make a bit of paste, enough for you to cover the hole and make it look as if the wall is just crumbling a bit. Didn't you play hide-and-seek with your brothers before you became a knight?'

'I played mainly with a girl,' said Will.

'Phuh!' said Elric. 'That's shocking.'

Will couldn't help grinning. 'Yes, shocking,' he agreed. 'Right. Let's get started.'

Elric was small, but he was determined. The two of them worked without speaking, occasionally making contact with each other's disembodied hands. Will felt like a mole. Before long the hole was big enough for the bundle, which Will opened at once. Inside was a whole loaf of fresh bread, a small flagon of ale and a wizened apple. A feast.

'Thank you,' Will said, truly touched.

'But goodness, Hosanna-man, I don't know how you are going to eat them in there. The smell in your cellar is something awful,' said Elric cheerfully.

Will blushed in the dark. 'There is no drain,' he said. 'I am forced to live like an animal.'

'Not like a cow,' Elric said. 'They smell nice.'

'Yes,' agreed Will. 'We humans can write poetry and sing songs, but we are filthy creatures for all that. Now, Elric, do you think there is any way I could get out through your tunnel?'

Elric considered and his voice was doubtful. 'We could pull down the stones all the way back,' he said. 'But the roof might cave in. Even with the tunnel this small, odd bits fall on top of me – more every time I come through.'

Will considered. 'How far is it to the big tunnel you told me about?'

'About half as far as from my house to the cow byre. Where this tunnel joins the main tunnel, there is a kind of cave.'

'And you can easily walk from there down into the village?'

'Well,' said Elric, 'you can stand in the main tunnel, but it's very steep. It comes out behind our house. But if you go the other way, you come out into that small chamber with the tapestry. Do you know where I mean?'

'No.'

'Well, it's a room off the main hall. There's a big tapestry on the wall.'

'How far is it from the cave to this tapestry room?'

'Oh, I don't know. The tunnel winds round quite a bit. If you say sixty paternosters you are there.'

'Sixty paternosters?'

'Yes,' said Elric, suddenly sneezing from the chill and the dirt. 'Sometimes my friends and me have bets to see who can get to the castle and back quickest. Some of us sit in the cave and count our paternosters. Sixty is the quickest so far. Sixty there and sixty back, that is.'

'Can you really count to sixty?' Will was impressed.

'Well, something like sixty,' said Elric cautiously. 'You use all your fingers and thumbs six times. Any dunce can count to six.'

Will made no comment about that. 'Your friends might be cheating,' he said instead.

'I can tell you only had a girl to play with,' said Elric pityingly. 'Boys would never think of cheating. And anyway, we always have to bring back some of the tapestry threads. I had to be careful the other night. The dust is something awful and we have taken so many threads now that there is a bit of a hole – we don't want to get caught.'

'You were playing there the other night?' Will wished very much that he could see Elric's face.

Elric ignored the question because he was full of one of his own. 'Hosanna-man, is King Richard really dead?'

'Actually, nice as Hosanna-man is, my name is really William – Will.' Will felt it best to avoid questions about Richard. 'And although I am at present a half-frozen prisoner lying in a pool of human dung, I am the Earl of Ravensgarth.' But he couldn't resist. 'No. I do not believe King Richard is dead.'

'Well, he soon might be,' said Elric. 'When I was behind the tapestry I heard Prince John tell Constable de Scabious to see to it.'

Will almost choked. The king was alive! He knew it! His blood began to stir and then, at once, he was filled with dread. De Scabious might be a coward, but he was cunning and would be desperate. His whole future depended on Richard being dead, just as Will's depended on him being alive. In prison, Richard would be easy prey for a professional assassin looking for gold. Will's heart raced.

'Elric,' he said, trying to conceal his agitation in case he frightened the boy off, 'does anybody else know what you heard?'

'No,' said Elric. 'I told you. My da and ma would kill me if they thought I came up here.'

'Oh yes,' said Will. 'But, Elric, do you ever see the girl in the castle, you know, the young one with auburn hair, who walks about with a fat old nurse?'

'Sometimes,' said Elric. 'If I help my ma carry the laundry back.'

'Do you ever speak to her?'

'Do you think I'm stupid? The serjeant would hang me.' Elric's voice was full of fear.

'Of course,' said Will. 'Sorry.' His frustration grew.

But Elric was nothing if not inventive. 'If I brought you a quill and parchment, you could write. Ouch!' He banged his head on the stones above him in his excitement. 'I could come to the tower with my ma and see if I could pass your girl a letter in among the clothes. I could do that.' His voice echoed around the cellar. 'I could steal the quill and parchment from the priest.'

'Sssssh!' said Will. 'They would roast you AND hang you if they found you now.' There was a pause. 'Ellie's not my girl. And anyway, I can't write.'

'You can't write?' Elric was incredulous. 'I thought knights were supposed to be clever. Even I can write my name. An old man in the village taught me. I think he was a monk once. We used to throw stones at him because of his strange accent and one day he ran and caught me. I thought he would beat me, but he just asked my name and taught me to write it. He's dead now but I've not forgotten.'

Will was hardly listening. 'Look,' he said. 'I know it might collapse, but could we try to make this tunnel bigger? I can't escape, since if de Scabious finds me missing, who knows what he might do to Ellie and Old Nurse – she's the fat old lady – and Hosanna and Sacramenta. But just being able to get out of this cellar for a bit –'

'Sacramenta?'

'Sacramenta is Ellie's horse. De Scabious's men caught her and she is being kept in the stables here. She's

118

Hosanna's mother. But never mind that. If I could get out into the tower itself, first of all I might not freeze to death, which I certainly will soon, and maybe I could speak to Ellie myself.'

'We could make the tunnel bigger,' said Elric without much enthusiasm. 'But if the roof does fall in . . .' His alarm was evident. 'I don't want to be buried alive!'

'Sssssh, Elric! We will be very careful,' Will said as gently as he could, sensing that the boy was about to take off. 'I would never, ever, leave you buried alive in the tunnel. I promise you, on my own life.'

There was silence, then Will heard the scraping sound again. 'Are you going now?' he asked quickly.

'No, Hosanna-man, I'm digging,' said Elric, 'although I will have to go soon. I told my da I was going to gather kindling. We really need tools but I am just seeing how well the stones come away.'

Will smiled. Elric dug for two paternosters, after which the stones began to fall in.

'Stop! Stop, Elric!' Will waited for the cascade to dwindle to a trickle of pebbles and mud. 'We can't be safe unless we have some light. Next time you come, can you bring a flint and taper? I think the light would be too dim and too low down for anybody to notice from the tower courtyard.'

Elric's voice was muffled. 'I'll come back tomorrow –' Will just caught the words – 'if I can.'

After Will had consumed the food Elric had brought, he leant back and shut his eyes. He tried to plan, to work out what use he could make of the tunnels, since he could not leave alone. Just thinking about the reprisals if he was discovered to be missing made him dizzy.

119

Eventually he fell into a kind of doze. When he woke he tried to ease some feeling back into his legs, then waited and waited for Elric to reappear. He heard the horses released into the courtyard for some exercise, but still the boy did not come.

Will grew quite desperate. He dared not dig and risk a rockfall. That would mean the end of everything. He began to recite his prayers. *Six times your fingers to get to the castle and back*, he thought to himself. *Perhaps if I practise now, by the time I have finished, Elric will be here.* He began. '*Pater noster, qui es in caelis, sanctificetur Nomen tuum . . .*' He said the whole thing over and over, but eventually gave up in disgust.

When Elric finally appeared, two days later, Will almost cried with relief. 'I'm sorry,' Elric panted apologetically. His father had made him stay and muck out the cowsheds as punishment for not bringing back the kindling he had promised. But Elric had used his time well and, between stints with the spade, had squirrelled away flints, tapers, a small pickaxe and meat saved from the village dogs.

Now that they could see, the digging was easier. Elric lay on his stomach and pulled the stones down while Will pitched them carefully into the cellar. Soon they had to buttress up the roof, for large boulders became dislodged causing them both agonies of terror. They worked in silence, with Will keeping his ears open in case de Scabious's soldiers suddenly and uncharacteristically opened the cellar door wide in the middle of the day, and also for rumblings within the rock that would intimate that the tunnel was about to collapse. Elric stayed for an hour or two, then grew tired and needed fresh air, but Will did not stop, resting only when his back ached and all his nails were broken. He tried to eat the food Elric brought but his throat was lousy with dust.

For the next six days, sometimes with Elric and sometimes without, Will worked like a madman. Every second, new terrors assailed him. Maybe, right now, de Scabious was on his way back and Richard's fate – and therefore Ellie's, Gavin's and his own – was sealed. Then, what was happening to Hosanna? Will could not bear to think. Taking endless risks, he pushed his way further and further through the tunnel, crouching under the vast weight of shifting granite that at every moment threatened to descend.

He left his cell in the morning, directly after his pottage tin had been collected, and spent the rest of his time hacking, shoving, scraping and pulling, wedging the taper where he could and calculating the passage of time by its burning. Late in the night, he would crawl back into the cellar and lie with his eyes open, too worn out for sleep. But it was worth it, for when Elric climbed up after breakfast on the seventh day, he found Will had made it through into the cave.

'I've done it,' Will said rather unnecessarily, 'and I have pulled enough rubble up into the hole in the cellar to hide it from somebody not looking very hard, and anyway, nobody ever seems to come right in. But it's taken us so long, I'm frightened de Scabious is just about to return. He mustn't find the cellar empty or who knows what he might do. When is he expected?' He was gabbling, at once exhilarated to be out and appalled by the possible consequences.

Elric shook his head in answer to the question about de Scabious. He felt suddenly shy. Will did not notice as he held what remained of his taper aloft. The tunnel

121

before him was blackly expectant as he tried to decide what to do. In the end, temptation proved too hard to resist. 'I'm going to risk it,' he said. 'Come on. Let's have a quick look before I get back to the cellar. Then you must go home and try as hard as you can to find out about de Scabious's movements.'

Elric needed no further encouragement to begin his paternosters and, with the little flame casting huge shadows in front of them, he followed Will into the bowels of the tower.

10

Constable de Scabious did not have a happy trip on Hosanna. The ridged bit and attached chain meant that pressure on the red stallion's tongue was intolerable, making him constantly toss his head. The delicate edges of his lips were soon a mess of pink spittle as the roof of his mouth was rubbed raw and his gums cut to pieces. Sweat poured from his two crusading scars as the constable pushed him on at speed but kept an iron grip on the reins, preventing him from stretching his neck. Up hills the strain was intense. Very quickly, the muscles in the horse's back knotted and his normally fluid movements became jerky and stiff. But there was no let-up in the pace. De Scabious sensed the horse's discomfort and became liberal in his use of the switch, secure in the knowledge that Hosanna no longer had the strength to buck him off, even if he wanted to. And that was not the worst of it. Sitting smugly in a saddle built for a much larger horse, the constable's lumpen weight was unevenly distributed, rubbing tender withers to ribbons within minutes. They had not made more than half a day's journey before Hosanna's shoulders were strained, his legs swollen and his flanks criss-crossed with small angry-looking red lines. His coat began to stare and his heart to beat unevenly.

By the time the sea shimmered on the horizon, every step was agony. As the constable spurred him on down the uneven road leading to Whitby's noisy quayside, Hosanna kept his footing with difficulty and shrank further and further into himself. De Scabious ignored his distress. The town was busy and the constable's eyes darted about as he puffed out his chest. Whoever was coming to find him on the king's business should be in no doubt about his importance.

'Go and arrange suitable lodgings for me,' he ordered his men. 'I have things to do and I prefer to do them on my own.'

The men were only too glad to leave the constable alone. 'Let's go and get a drink,' one muttered. 'As far away from de Scabious as possible. I don't want anybody to think I am responsible for Hosanna. He looks like something a tinker would be ashamed of.'

'What's that you say?' De Scabious's nose for disloyalty was sharp.

'I said, we'd go and find an inn since, after our journey, we look like tinkers and don't want to shame you,' the man said hastily.

Moored to the wooden jetties, a small commercial fleet from Genoa was busy unloading spices and cloth from the East. As de Scabious watched, a barrel of dates cracked and broke open. Immediately a group of raggedy urchins descended on it, pursued by a Jewish merchant waving furious arms. The urchins were much too quick and the merchant eventually kicked the barrel away in disgust. The constable smirked as he watched the drama unfold. No urchins would get the better of him!

He dug his spurs once more into Hosanna's sides.

The wind blew in chilly from the sea but had lost its winter bite. Enjoying the first real intimations of spring, old men stood gossiping while small boys ran hither and thither, almost as busy as the rats scurrying down every gangplank. Gruff shipmasters shouted unloading instructions, and great bales of coloured silks and velvets swung away from the decks of larger vessels nodding peacefully on the waves out in the deeper water. The bales hovered over small rowing boats waiting to take the precious cargo ashore. The little craft rocked madly when the cloth thumped into them. Occasionally the operation went wrong and a bale would spill great coloured sheets on top of the boatman. Emerald-green velvet or blood-red silk would float like giant stains on the water, and haberdashers, seeing their profits vanish beneath the waves, would noisily berate the sailors for their clumsiness. The mishaps sometimes ended in tragedy, for the cloth was heavy, but nothing stopped the great flow of the day's business.

Standing near one of the Genoese ships was a group of tall, dark men inspecting a line of horses of different shapes and sizes. They carried curved weapons and their faces were haughty. De Scabious narrowed his eyes. Maybe, among this group, was the man he was searching for.

Kamil was looking with distaste at the horses and listening with even more distaste to the whining of the sellers.

'Only six years old, sir. Yours for fifty shillings, or take him and this palfrey, both for seventy shillings. A bargain, sir, a bargain.'

Both horses were fit only for the knacker. He ran his hands down the legs of another, offered for sale by a fat man, whose bulk had caused the horse to fall and break its knees. 'Just ten shillings,' the man wheedled.

Kamil turned on his heel. None of these would suit him. Last in the line was a grey held by a girl whose clothes had once been rich. Overcoming his natural reluctance to approach a Christian woman, Kamil looked at the animal's mouth and legs.

'This horse belonged to my husband,' the girl told him. 'He died on crusade. I have nothing left to sell.'

Kamil had no interest in her story, nor much in the horse. It was too common for his taste and its coat was coarse. Nevertheless, it might have to do. 'How much?' he asked.

'How much will you give?'

Kamil considered. 'Six shillings. That's all.'

The girl looked disappointed and even shed a tear, but she accepted and, after kissing the horse's nose in a fond farewell, handed it over. Kamil vaulted on, secured his pack of belongings and began to ride away. But halfway out of the town, his conscience smote him. The horse might not be to his liking, but it was worth much more than six shillings. It was a mean, dishonourable thing he had done. He was set against going back, but then twitched the reins. If the girl was where he left her, he would make things right.

The roads were clogged and, almost stationary behind bulging carts and straggling groups of beggars, Kamil soon regretted his decision. Standing up in the stirrups, he could see the quayside and it soon became clear that the girl was no longer there. Kamil sighed at his own stupidity. Of course she wasn't there. Why would

126

she hang about? He would not be able to make things right and this would always be a mark against him.

He set off again, angry with himself, but as he turned away from the main thoroughfare, his eye was arrested by something in the milling throng. It was nothing, he told himself, nothing except a glimpse of colour. Nevertheless, he hesitated before setting off up the road out of the town again; stopped, started, then quite suddenly pulled the grey round.

The horse, fed up, baulked, refusing to move at all, and it was as Kamil was trying to coax it to go forward that he saw, mostly hidden by people and surrounded by carters and pack ponies, another horse moving slowly and uncomfortably towards the group of horse sellers. He lost all interest in the grey as his heart began to race. That's what had caught his eye before. That colour. That red colour. He surely could not mistake it. He tried to reason with himself. Hal said that Hosanna was stuck in a tower somewhere and there must be many blood-red horses. But still. Kamil slipped off the grey and let it go.

Constable de Scabious rode Hosanna past the jetties, searching out foreign faces. There were many and he gave each man every encouragement to approach him, raising his eyebrows and showing the gaps in his teeth. John had said the man would find him. Well, the constable was ready. One foreigner, winked at by the constable, made a remark which elicited laughter of a not altogether friendly kind from his companions. At once de Scabious's eyes stopped smiling, although his teeth remained bared.

Kamil pushed through the crowd until he was so close he could almost touch Hosanna's tail. His hand crept under his cloak to the neat red plait hanging from his belt. Now he was at the horse's girth, now at his shoulder. Now he could plainly see the two scars and at last he put his hand on Hosanna's neck. Under the sweat and grime, the two dents were piercingly familiar. Kamil felt light-headed and looked up to find Constable de Scabious staring down at him. He withdrew his hand and pulled his hood over his face.

The constable nodded with satisfaction. *Ah! Just as John said. This must be the person.* Feeling de Scabious shift, Hosanna eased the weight off one sore leg and was immediately chucked in the mouth. He gasped a little and a teardrop of blood landed on Kamil's shoulder. It was almost more than the young Saracen could stand. He wanted to pull de Scabious off and kill him there and then, but there were more certain and subtle ways to regain possession of Hosanna. The man who stole was unworthy of the prize. Despite the unjust bargain he had concluded with the girl over the grey horse, Allah was still offering blessings. Hosanna was a present from heaven and Kamil only had to find the right way to take him.

The constable cleared his throat. 'I'm busy taming this horse,' he said, appearing to want to take Kamil into his confidence, something Kamil found a little surprising. 'Abdul al-Baku?'

Kamil frowned, then gave an almost imperceptible nod. 'You are looking for him?' he asked casually.

The constable leant down further. 'I believe I am,' he said conspiratorially. 'Can we have a word?'

Kamil inclined his head.

'Come,' said the constable. He kicked Hosanna in the ribs and the horse grunted before limping forward. Kamil walked by his side in silence.

In a narrow lane the constable heaved himself off. Released from de Scabious's iron grip, Hosanna's head sank to the floor. Immediately the constable jerked it back up. Kamil winced, but nevertheless remained in the shadows. He remembered the mercenaries and was ready for any tricks. But there were none.

'Abdul,' de Scabious said, his eyes popping with nerves, 'you are an acquaintance, are you not, of –' and the constable whispered here – 'Rashid, the Old Man of the Mountain?'

Kamil's mouth twitched as he tried not to shiver. This was unexpected indeed. Nobody ever mentioned the Old Man lightly. He waited, wondering what was to come.

The constable grew braver. 'There is a certain prisoner – an important prisoner – an enemy of your people and mine. Do you understand?'

Kamil was disgusted by the rancid smell of de Scabious's breath and his sly calculating eyes, but he gave an enigmatic smile.

'Ah, I see we understand each other well.' De Scabious's confidence was increasing. 'We would all be better off if this prisoner – the enemy of your people and mine – if he could be, well, be *persuaded*, using –' the constable licked his teeth – 'the ultimate in persuasion, you understand, the *ultimate*, not to return here. Neither, I am sure, do you want him returning to your country. Nor can he be left where he is. So, he can be nowhere. Do I make myself clear?'

Kamil inclined his head again.

'We must make sure this prisoner is nowhere as soon as possible,' the constable added, 'as soon as possible.' He did not wish to live in this limbo of uncertainty for a moment longer than necessary. 'Do you think you can do this?'

Kamil still said nothing and de Scabious, perplexed, felt his confidence evaporating. 'Now look –' he began, yanking Hosanna's head up once again. Then he found Kamil's face suddenly very close to his own.

'Assassins,' Kamil said quietly. 'You need the help of the assassins to get rid of King Richard.' He hoped his disgust was not too evident.

De Scabious nearly jumped out of his skin. 'Sssssh!' he exclaimed, looking over his shoulder. However, he was relieved. If the man could talk of assassins, he must be the real thing. Who else would be so bold? He fumbled in his purse and brought out a small pouch full of coins. 'This now,' he said. 'And another when we have proof that you have done your work.'

Kamil looked coolly at the money as de Scabious shook the pigskin purse as if Kamil were a performing lion waiting for a treat. There was a long pause. 'No,' Kamil said. 'No money.'

'No money?' exclaimed de Scabious. 'What, then?'

Kamil pretended to think. Then he put his hand on Hosanna's neck. 'I have no horse,' he said. 'I will take yours.'

The constable was completely taken aback. 'But you will be going over the sea tonight,' he expostulated. 'Get a horse in Flanders.'

Kamil shrugged. 'Your horse, or I don't do it.'

De Scabious persisted. 'You can't have this horse,' he said. 'I will buy you a much better horse. Come, we will find one back in the marketplace.'

But Kamil wouldn't move. 'This horse, or you must find somebody else,' he repeated.

'This horse is no good.' De Scabious, most reluctant to part with such an effective bargaining tool over Will and Ellie, grew querulous. 'I can't give him to you. I'm too fond of him.'

Kamil shrugged, and took the biggest gamble of all. 'Then I go,' he said, and started to walk off.

The constable stared after him. These slippery foreigners. Why couldn't he just take the money? Kamil had almost disappeared by the time de Scabious made up his mind. 'Oh, have him!' he shouted.

Kamil forced himself to turn the corner as if he had not heard, before reappearing. He would not allow himself to hurry, but underneath the cloak his hands were damp and shaking. The constable wondered whether to try again with the money, but one look at Kamil's face was enough to have him hauling off the saddle.

'You keep your side of this bargain, or I'll have you hunted down and hung,' he grumbled, angry at being thwarted, but cheering up rapidly at the thought of the gold he could now keep for himself. He would give himself a few treats, a week or so's holiday by the sea even, before going back to Hangem. The tower was secure and it would help pass the time until his wedding.

The saddle fell with a clank to the ground and Hosanna shuddered as the skin on his back was flayed away. When the constable pulled off the bridle, revealing a bit stained crimson, Kamil half raised his hand. De Scabious was immediately defensive. 'The horse gives a good deal of trouble,' he whined.

Kamil made no remark. He simply drew out, from his bag, a thin, silken rope. Deftly turning it into a halter, he slipped it over Hosanna's head.

De Scabious smiled his oiliest smile. 'I think our

transaction is sealed,' he said. 'I will learn if you have fulfilled your part of the bargain through a message you will send to King John. If no message comes, I am told that the Old Man of the Mountains can be relied upon to remind you himself.'

'I need reminding of nothing,' said Kamil, fixing de Scabious with an ominously inscrutable expression.

'No, indeed,' said the constable nervously. 'Let's hope not at any rate.' He turned away and kicked aside the underblankets, which were blotted with blood and hair.

Eventually he grabbed a passing boy. 'You,' he ordered. 'Carry this saddlery to my lodgings. There's a groat in it.' He loaded the boy up and, without another word to Kamil, disappeared with the boy dawdling behind him.

As soon as the constable was out of sight, Kamil threw back his hood. 'Red Horse!' he exclaimed. 'Hosanna! Do you still know me?' Hosanna fixed Kamil with his clouded eyes and rested his torn mouth on his arm. Kamil was overwhelmed. He took Hosanna's face between his hands and pressed his forehead against the white star still shining fair against the chestnut. Kamil's black hair and Hosanna's russet forelock ruffled together in the breeze and neither moved for some time.

When he felt calmer, Kamil encouraged Hosanna to walk on. 'We'll find a ship straight away,' he said, 'and leave this benighted country before war breaks out. Hal knows that Richard is alive. The de Granvilles don't need my letter. I can leave with a clear conscience.' He began to guide the horse through the narrow streets.

Now that he could see them clearly, Hosanna's wounds made him burn with indignation. 'We Arabs at least know how to treat our horses,' he muttered. People stared at them and, while Kamil was not surprised, he was alarmed by the attention. 'Try to hurry,' he urged. 'One of those Genoese ships will take us.'

They reached the quayside and Kamil began to negotiate a passage. Terrible comments, which Kamil tried to ignore, were passed about the state of the red horse and as he concluded his bargain with the shipmaster, he felt sharp fists on his back. Turning round, he found himself accosted by the grey horse's weeping mistress. 'Where's my horse?' she sobbed. 'What have you done with him? Is this what happened to your last one?'

Kamil did not try to explain. 'Your horse is here somewhere,' he said easily. 'But I no longer want him. Here –' he fumbled in his pouch – 'take this.' He handed over 100 shillings, not even bothering to count it out. The girl fell back in amazement, then grabbed the money, hid it under her skirt and fled.

The shipmaster looked on with both concern and amusement. 'Lovers' tiff?' he asked. 'The horse looks like he has borne the brunt.'

Kamil thrust more money at him. 'I want to board now,' he said.

The master looked into the wind. 'Good timing,' he said. 'We'll be out of here in less than an hour.'

Taking hold of the silken rope, Kamil began to lead Hosanna forward. He was smiling as he remembered how Hal's plans had come to nothing because his black horse was a coward. Not so Hosanna, who, Kamil knew very well, would load on to any ship in any circumstances. 'Come,' he said. 'Let's go home.'

Hosanna moved obediently, but when they reached the gangplank, he stopped.

'Come,' Kamil repeated, tenderly rubbing Hosanna's blood-caked velvet nose. But Hosanna remained stead-fast. Kamil leant down and picked up a hoof, to place it on the ramp. Maybe the horse's wounds had rattled his nerves. But while Hosanna raised his foot willingly enough, he would only put it down on dry land.

The shipmaster watched the procedure with interest. 'I saw one of these cowards just yesterday,' he said. 'A boy with a black animal. It wouldn't load either. Horse training isn't what it used to be. Now, shall we use a whip, or shall I get the sailors to bump him on? He looks such a miserable animal we could probably carry him if you insist on taking him, although it doesn't seem worth the trouble to me.'

Kamil tried to remain calm. He dropped the rope, unsure what to do, particularly as Hosanna was droop-ing, finding it difficult to stand. The horse leant against Kamil's breast, causing Richard's letter, inside his tunic, to crackle. Kamil stroked the horse's ears and Hosanna sighed, closing his tired eyes.

'What's it to be, then?' demanded the ship's captain. 'We must get going. Shall we manhandle him on, even though he looks only good for the slaughterhouse?'

Kamil shook his head. Most reluctantly, hardly be-lieving what was happening, he turned away from the sea. Immediately, Hosanna hobbled after him.

'You, foreigner,' the shipmaster shouted, throwing back Kamil's money, 'treat your next horse better.' The sailors laughed as the young man's cheeks flamed.

Hosanna walked quietly now.

'I'm not going without you,' Kamil murmured. 'So I shall just have to wait.'

They walked out of the town and up a sandy track for

about half a mile. It was steep and they took their time. Where the sand gave way to grass, Kamil, not knowing what else to do, turned inland until the gurgling of a stream was louder than the drag of the waves. Here, he found several good-sized sheep bothies amid the yellow gorse, all of which appeared to be abandoned. One of these would do for tonight. Hosanna was beginning to stiffen up.

Once inside the bothy, Kamil extracted a bowl from his bag and went outside to fill it with water. Then he stripped off his silk tunic, tore it up and used it to wash Hosanna's wounds, first his mouth, then his back, then the criss-crossed stripes sliced into his skin by the thin switch. The water was changed many times as it went from clear to pink to red, but finally Kamil was satisfied and laid out ointments he had brought from the Orient. Choosing carefully, he spread some over the horse's body.

Hosanna stood all the while, his eyes following Kamil's every move. As his old friend worked, he sighed and several times Kamil had to push down a lump in his throat. *I am growing sentimental*, he thought as he covered Hosanna in his cloak and busied himself finding twigs for a fire. He blew on the flames and watched Hosanna as he rested.

We'll go to Hartslove, Kamil decided. *It seems I must.* But even cleaned up, the horse was in a poor way. They would have to move slowly. No matter. Now he had what he wanted, Kamil began to lose any sense of urgency. The red horse was his, bargained for, not stolen.

At dusk he checked the horse's wounds again. There would be scars, but they would heal. As the sun vanished, they stood together at the bothy opening, looking up as the night sky rolled itself out. When darkness fell, Kamil sat cross-legged and Hosanna, in a gesture of supreme trust, lay down, put his head in Kamil's lap and went to sleep.

The horse spent all next day in or near the stream, allowing the cold water to massage his legs and cool his bruises. Kamil sat on the bank or stood in the water too, gently separating each hair of matted forelock, mane and tail and washing off the last remaining sweat and filth. Hosanna drank deeply, curling his lips as the water stung the raw patches on his gums and flooded the bloody indentations on the roof of his mouth.

At about midday, both he and Kamil heard the bell of Whitby Abbey calling the monks to sing the office. Hosanna raised his head. Kamil knew he should pray too, but somehow, in this strange country, it did not feel right. Instead, with some misgivings, he set off back to the town to get provisions and equipment for the journey, leaving Hosanna dozing among the sheep.

But all was well. A whinny greeted his return. Already the cloudiness was lifting from the horse's eyes and Kamil, sharing the bread he had bought, felt hopeful and glad.

As the sun rose the following morning, he twisted a thin length of hide to make a bitless bridle and fashioned a saddle from an old sheepskin and a leather strip. 'I can't use my coloured cord and ride with no saddle at all,' he said to Hosanna. 'From what I can see, it is not a very English way to go about things.' He was anxious to move on, for he did not want to bump into de Scabious or the mercenaries. Packing away anything that marked him out as a Saracen, he made sure that when he and Hosanna set off nothing, except perhaps the colour of his own skin and the very distinctive red of the horse's coat, looked out of the ordinary.

They walked in companionable silence, covering only a few miles to begin with. However, after a day or two, his wounds markedly improving and the spring sun warm on his back, Hosanna began to lose the terrible shrunken look that pain brings with it. Only then did Kamil vault lightly on and begin the long climb to the top of the moors.

It was a glorious journey. Up in the clear air, Hosanna recovered his strength almost by the hour and his spirits rose. With no audience except the curlews and the hawks, Kamil pretended that they were back in the desert, he a powerful emir and Hosanna his crusading charger. *And surely this is not a pipe dream*, Kamil thought. He would deliver the letter, and after that, the de Granvilles would feel obliged to help him get home. He would make a new life for himself in Palestine. He watched a buzzard circle on broad, motionless wings, its plaintive cry and heavy flight reminding him of Richard. Yes. Hosanna had been right to refuse the ship's gangplank. Now he could claim Hosanna not just by bargaining right, but with honour.

As they covered the miles, for the first time Kamil was able to think of his dead adoptive father without bitterness. That evening, at sunset, he asked Hosanna to perform an old trick he had taught him just before the last battle of the crusade. At the appropriate command, Hosanna reared, striking out as if at an enemy. As he plunged back to earth, Kamil was filled with gratitude and that night, as he heard once again the distant toll of an abbey bell, he bowed his head and lifted his own heart and mind to Allah.

11

Ellie often heard abbey bells, but they brought her no comfort for they could not answer the question that nagged her all the time as the days dragged on: where was Gavin? Was he really not even going to come for her? Old Nurse, watching Ellie's youthful freshness wither and her brow crease, grew mournful. 'I really am a ball and chain,' she said one evening as the girl stared out at the sun setting over the woods miles below. The snow was gone and the trees were showing their buds. 'I know you. If it was not for me, you would find a way out of here.'

Ellie stopped staring. 'You are a comfort and support,' she said wearily. 'Please, Old Nurse. Don't torture yourself. How could I leave, anyway, with Will locked in the cellar and Sacramenta locked in the stables. And how could we leave Hosanna with Constable de Scabious? It's not you who is preventing me from trying to escape. It is everybody else too.'

Old Nurse sighed. The old Ellie was slowly diminishing. This new Ellie did not run up the tower steps or walk with springs in her feet. She looked beaten, almost submissive.

'Come,' Old Nurse said. 'Come and try to sleep.'

Ellie obeyed, but long after the old woman was snoring her eyes were still wide open, so she got up and drew a thick cloak round her. The night was clear and from the window's height she felt close to the stars. *Will must be freezing*, she thought, and hated herself for being warm. She could hear raucous laughter below her and the sound of barrels being rolled over cobbles. The serjeant was having a party celebrating the constable's continued absence.

Early next morning, she dressed and went out to the courtyard. The soldiers lay in heaps. The party had clearly been a good one. Ellie wandered about. She was forbidden to visit Sacramenta, but when she saw Gethin alone in the armoury, she ventured inside and sat down near the fire. The youth was concentrating hard as he stitched a bridle. He did not speak, but every now and again stole a glance. Ellie looked so like his dead sister. She was certainly as pale. The only colour about her was the green jasper necklace. He cut his thread thoughtfully and hung the bridle on a hook. It didn't feel right to him, somebody looking so sad. He sat down again. Then, with purely animal instincts, he got up, rummaged in a corner and found a large brown blanket. Tossing it over Ellie's head, he swiftly wrapped her in it and picked her up.

At first she resisted, but Gethin was strong. He waited until she stopped thrashing about, then seized a lantern and swung her over his shoulders. Without saying a word, he carried her straight across the courtyard and glanced quickly round before opening the door of the stables and slipping inside. Sacramenta whickered and Gethin clicked his tongue at her. Finding herself on the floor, Ellie emerged, blinking, stared up at Gethin, then got to her feet, poised for flight. But, suddenly realizing where she was, her face lit up. In a trice, she had found Sacramenta and buried herself in the mare's mane.

Gethin said nothing, but after he had taken the animals, two by two, to drink at the trough and finished his work, he brought the blanket over and waited. Reluctantly giving Sacramenta a last kiss, Ellie lay down and allowed herself to be rolled up again, and once she was safely back in the armoury, Gethin was pleased to see that she had more colour in her cheeks. He shook out the blanket, put it back in the corner and began to repair a broken saddle tree.

But Ellie did not leave. A far more daring idea was forming in her head. The soldiers were still snoring. Frightened of alarming the boy so that he would never allow her into the armoury again, Ellie was nevertheless determined. Wrapping the blanket round herself once more, she stood by the door and whispered, 'Cellar!'

Gethin's ruddy cheeks became even ruddier and his broad face evinced a mixture of fear and apology as he shook his head. He pointed to the floor. The pottage pan that had contained Will's breakfast had already been collected. There was no reason to go to the cellar again.

'Please,' breathed Ellie, and she smiled at him, a smile of such heartfelt pleading that it would have melted the resolve of somebody much less susceptible than Gethin.

He wrenched his eyes away from hers, but, although every cell in his body told him 'NO', he could not bear to refuse. He peered out of the armoury. Deep shadow still covered the wall behind which Will was imprisoned. It might be possible. Taking a shaky breath, he tried to steady his heart. Never in his life had he contemplated such disobedience to orders. Never. Then, suddenly, blowing out his cheeks, he seized Ellie and again set off across the courtyard, this time almost at a run.

Just outside the cellar door, he had misgivings, wondering if she would be prepared for the conditions in which men shut up other men. But Ellie, nervous that he would change his mind, was already slipping down. She agonized as he fumbled with the key, then nearly retched as he opened the door and the smell wafted out. But she did not stop. Silent as a ghost, she vanished inside. Gethin shut the door and locked it. By the time he got back to the armoury, he was green.

Ellie had to put her hands over her mouth to stop herself from gagging. The air was suffocatingly thick and without light she was completely disorientated. When she felt able, she took her hands away from her face and gingerly put her arms out in front of her.

'Will, it's me,' she whispered, trying not to breathe. 'Gethin let me in. Will? Will? Where are you?'

She felt for the wall, and recoiled at the water running down it. Slowly, she made her way round the cell, sliding through the gunge, her heart crashing in her ears. She made her way round twice. Then she began to shiver uncontrollably. Will was not here. He definitely was not here. Oh God, what had they done with him? Beside herself and not caring what the soldiers might do to her, Ellie slithered back to the door and raised her fists to beat on it. She must know where Will was. Surely they could not keep that from her. But she only hit the door once before pure animal fear made her whip round. Draughts like icicles were fingering her ankles and creeping up her legs. She thrust out her hands to ward away some unseen, unspeakable evil.

'Help me, Mother of God,' she cried silently into the darkness. 'Oh help me, Mother of God.'

As her panic rose, she dropped the blanket and began to fumble madly round again, not looking for Will this time, not looking for anything except escape from something she felt was about to envelop and smother her. The draught caught the bottom of her dress and made it flap. Faster and faster, Ellie scrabbled round the cellar, crouching lower and lower, until her frantic fingers suddenly found themselves scratching not against stone, but against thin air. She was brought up short. Trying to control the tremors in her legs, she made her fingers scratch again. And again and yet again.

What she could feel was a broad crack, where the stones were haphazardly pulled together. If she pushed her finger through ... yes, oh YES! That was where the draught was coming from, not from some demonic creature's jaws, but from a hole.

Weak with relief, Ellie leant her head against the wall, oblivious of the slime that oozed on to her hair. She almost laughed out loud. There was no evil beast, just a gap, through which fresh air was pouring. Gingerly, she pushed her hand inside and immediately a small cascade of rock landed near her feet. She moved her arm up and down. This was not even a hole, it was a tunnel, and if Will was not in the cell, this was the reason why.

At that moment, she heard the door opening again. In an instant, she pulled her arm back. Making no sound, she stumbled towards the light, snatching up the blanket from the floor as she went. The door must not open any further for she had no idea how far she could trust Gethin. She reached him just in time. His face was red and strained. He was not regretting his kindness, but he would not rest until Ellie was back in her chamber, and when she presented herself with such alacrity, his relief was palpable. In silence the girl wrapped herself in the now vile and stinking blanket and Gethin, after relocking the door, quickly slung her over his shoulder and hurried away.

They were inside the armoury before they realized they were not alone. Elric's mother had drawn up a stool in front of the fire. 'I've brought laundry,' she said to Gethin. 'There are clean blankets here.' She smiled at him, but her smile faded when Ellie dropped to the floor. Gethin stood quite still, frightened out of his wits. However, Ellie knew at once what she should do. Walking straight up to Morwenna she held out the blanket.

'I apologize about the mess,' she said. 'I was not feeling very well and came down to use the sewer, but I slipped and fell in. I'm so sorry to cause you extra work.' She gave a tentative gesture of pleading.

Morwenna got up. The lie was so blatant. She felt sorry for Ellie, but her fear of de Scabious was greater. She could hear the serjeant coming across, the keys at his belt clanking. If she was caught in here now with Ellie, it would be assumed that she was part of whatever had been going on. Pictures of Elric being taken from her and finding himself at the serjeant's mercy hit her like a series of punches, and before Ellie could even put out her arm, the woman was at the door, calling for the soldiers.

The serjeant came across, nursing a thunderous hangover. 'You're late with the laundry, you lazy hag,' he growled. 'Let's hope your son is a better timekeeper than you when he eventually comes into the constable's service. If not, we'll soon make him hop, skip and jump.' Morwenna tried to say something, but he roared, daring her, a lowly laundress, to address him directly. 'You should beg my pardon for your impudence,' he barked, before making an aside that had the soldiers grinning and laughing.

Morwenna blushed then came back into the armoury, her lips a thin line. She did not speak but looked at Ellie and handed her a servant's dress and hood from her basket. Gethin turned puce and looked into the fire as Ellie changed and rolled her own stained clothes into a bundle. When she walked with Morwenna across the courtyard, the groggy soldiers took no notice of them. They parted at the bottom of the tower steps and Ellie ran back to Old Nurse. The old lady was beside herself.

'Ellie, oh, Ellie,' she cried. 'I woke up and you were gone. Dearie, never do that again. Where on earth have you been?'

'Never mind, Old Nurse,' laughed Ellie, stripping off the servant's clothes. 'Get a fire going. We'll have to burn all these dirty things. Is there any hot water?'

'But –'

'Not now. A fire and hot water first.' Frowning, Old Nurse built a bigger blaze and Ellie pushed all the damning evidence into the hearth, where they took a while to catch alight.

'Take care,' said Old Nurse. 'They are wet. We don't want too much smoke.'

She clucked about. Ellie was chilled to the bone with what appeared to be weeds in her hair and a very peculiar expression on her face. But at least the stricken pallor of the past weeks had been replaced by a look that was more familiar. Old Nurse filled a basin and rolled up her sleeves. 'Now, where on earth have you been?' she asked, bustling, scrubbing, rinsing, rubbing and finally washing Ellie's hank of hair and whirling it about like a horse's tail. Ellie was wiping between her toes, but she looked up and it was not only the scrubbing that made her face shine.

'Oh, Old Nurse,' she said, keeping her voice down despite her excitement. 'I couldn't sleep so I got up early and went outside into the armoury. That dim-looking boy, the one they call Gethin, well, he took me into the stable and I saw Sacramenta. Then, oh! Old Nurse, you can't imagine. I went into Will's cell.'

Old Nurse let go of everything and sat down heavily on the bed. The danger! She could have done with some fortifying wine, but she had none. 'You saw Master Will?' she repeated.

'Hush!' warned Ellie. 'No, not exactly. The thing is, Old Nurse, he wasn't there.'

Old Nurse clutched the fur rug. 'What do you mean, he wasn't there?'

Ellie seized Old Nurse's hands. 'I was frantic,' she said. 'It was so dark, and the filth –' She pulled the old lady closer to the fire. 'Anyway, there was a draught and,' her voice was almost inaudible, 'I found a tunnel, Old Nurse. Will must have escaped.'

Old Nurse took a moment to understand fully what Ellie was saying. Then she stood up. 'And what will happen when de Scabious comes back and discovers this?' she asked, her face now as red as it had been white. 'What then? My sweet, the constable is not going to like that. No. He won't like that one little bit.'

'But by that time Gavin may have come and we may be rescued!' said Ellie, willing to believe anything in

146

her new state of hopefulness. 'Will must have gone to get him.'

Old Nurse sat down again. 'Ellie, my dear, dear child. Have you not been listening? What's the use of that if King Richard is dead? Your best hopes lie in getting John on your side, and that's not going to happen if Gavin attacks de Scabious.'

'Richard's not dead,' said Ellie obstinately.

'I'm afraid,' said Old Nurse, frowning, for she did not want to send Ellie back into a decline, 'that Gavin thinks he is. This is why he is not here already.'

Ellie sprang up and droplets flew from her hair. 'Never say that in my presence again,' she cried. Then she dropped her voice so that it was both low and menacing. 'Old Nurse, I love you very much. But until we have proof, until we have proof, you hear, that things are otherwise, our king is Richard. And whatever happens to us here in this tower, at least Will is out of it so I can sleep and,' Ellie hesitated only momentarily, 'even die, with an easier heart.'

The fire roared a little, and as Ellie threw back her head, the sparks caught the green jasper, making it glitter.

Old Nurse looked at the girl she had known from a baby, whose childish tears she had dried and whose bruised knees she had bathed, and then she did something she had never done before. She curtsied. She did this as best she could, for she was hardly the shape for it and many years out of practice. 'My Ellie,' she said, once she was safely back on both legs. 'How proud Sir Thomas would be, if he could see you now.'

Ellie knelt down in front of the fire again. Suddenly, her elation and bravado vanished and she felt drained

147

and exhausted. But it had been worth the risk to know that at least Will was away. Old Nurse drew up a chair and picked up a hairbrush. As she worked, she sang an old song that her own mother, another Old Nurse, had taught her when she was even younger than Ellie. Her throaty tenor was soothing to both of them and, when she insisted that Ellie should rest in bed for an hour or two after her ordeal, the girl slept and got up refreshed.

But the fat old lady did not sleep. She sat staring at Ellie's necklace, weeping silently for what had been and for what she feared was to come.

12

It had taken less than an hour for Marissa to regret riding Dargent out of the Hartslove gates, but she had been too proud to go back, assuming she could have found the way, which was doubtful. The horse was willing enough, but, used to the clear instructions of Will or Hal, he grew nervous at Marissa's uncertainties. Every so often he stopped and neighed loudly. The girl could feel his whole body quaking and although she tried to soothe him, the tone of her voice was unconvincing.

'Come on, Dargent,' she said, hating the wheedling sound she made.

When they reached yet another crossroad, the horse tossed his head. 'Straight on,' said Marissa. 'I'm sure Will's prison must be straight on.' He reluctantly obeyed.

After a little while, they took a right fork in the road, then another one, then a left until after less than half a day, Marissa realized she was hopelessly lost, not even knowing which direction she was facing. Dargent could feel his rider's confusion and, wrenching the reins from her hands, he began to nibble at the spring leaves within his reach. Both were relieved when other travellers came by, led by a group of monks. Marissa settled Dargent next to them, hoping they were going north, for that is where she felt she should be heading, but really just glad enough of the company.

A few journeymen of slender means had also latched on to the monks. They eyed up their new travelling companion, wondering what she was worth. But something in her expression made them pass her by. Some women just looked like trouble.

At nightfall, Marissa shivered, regretting very much that she had not brought a cloak. However, the monks were kind and took pity on her. In the morning, she got back on to Dargent, feeling quite proud of herself.

'I am travelling to rescue somebody,' she told one of the brothers grandly. 'I'll do it or perish in the attempt.'

He lowered his eyes before Marissa could take offence at his look of amused disbelief.

From the top of a ridge above the road, Kamil could also see the monks. Unwillingly forced to descend from the high ground to cross the river, he took his place behind them as they all headed for the bridge, for the river was too deep to ford. Kamil hated the crush, but he was not unduly worried about people's curious stares. Despite some suspicion when he bartered for food, he had encountered no hostility and was enjoying the rising spring, with its torrential showers and sudden, dazzling sunshine. He thought King Richard was wrong to dismiss England, for it seemed a fruitful place and even though the snow stubbornly clung to the high ground, Hosanna was already finding plenty of tender new grass. He and the red horse settled themselves at the back of the procession.

But out of his sight, beside the bridge, the mercenaries were hanging about once more. Having had their fun

150

with Hal, they had despatched him to John for hanging and were travelling along the trade routes looking for further diversions. Monks were always good sport and Missing Fingers and his friends soon blocked the road, demanding to know for whom the monks were praying as they walked and chanted.

'For the king,' came the stock answer.

'But which king?' Missing Fingers grinned. It was almost too easy.

There was silence. Then a young monk unwisely piped up. 'For Christ our King,' he said brightly.

Missing Fingers drew his sword and poked the young monk on the chin. 'But we have an earthly king as well.' He raised his eyebrows. 'Now, who would that be?'

The young monk shivered. 'Well, now,' he stuttered. 'Th-th-that will be your master and ours.'

'The king needs a name,' Missing Fingers persisted.

'We just call him the king,' the monk whispered.

The mercenaries laughed. 'Shall we force our holy brother to choose?' they asked each other with mock seriousness.

'Yes, yes,' came the response. The crowd was growing all the time.

'Name him,' said Missing Fingers to the monk. 'Name him right now. Which is it, Richard or John?'

The monk just shook his head. Missing Fingers got off his horse and, as he did so, spied Marissa.

'Well, what have we here?' he brayed. 'A fair maid in need of protection! What a piece of luck! Protection is just what we can offer.' His friends whistled.

'Keep away from me!' Marissa stared straight in front of her.

But Missing Fingers sidled up to Dargent. 'That would

be failing in my duty,' he declared. 'I'm supposed to help people in distress.'

'I'm not in distress.'

'Well you soon will be.' And with that, Missing Fingers pulled out a dagger and pricked Dargent's hind quarters. It had just the effect he desired, for the horse, first surprised, then maddened, leapt forward and bolted. Marissa was at once thrown backwards, losing her reins. She recovered enough to grab the saddle, but then could only cling round Dargent's neck as he thundered over the bridge, scattering the crowd, some of whom had little option but to leap into the river.

'Lady riders!' bellowed Missing Fingers, thrilled with himself. 'Now I'll go and rescue her!'

But before he could clamber on to his horse he found himself flat on his back, bleeding heavily from his head.

Kamil had not intended to get involved. It was none of his business, he reasoned with himself. But Hosanna thought differently. When the procession had stopped he refused to stand still, and when Missing Fingers drew his dagger he reared and plunged through the gawping spectators until he knocked the mercenary over and, leaving the imprint of a shoe on his forehead, galloped away in pursuit of his friend. Kamil was powerless to stop him.

Dargent headed straight up a path leading through some fields, then up through trees and eventually out into open country. He might as well have been riderless, for Marissa, terrified by the speed, could do nothing to slow his headlong flight. The ground grew rough, and several times the big bay almost fell. From behind, Kamil could sense the rider's fear and now he urged Hosanna on. Not that Hosanna needed urging. Flattening himself out, he quickly began to catch up. At first, hearing the pounding of hooves almost on top of him, Dargent panicked and galloped faster, but something in the rhythm of the vibrations resonated in his mind and soon the horses were galloping side by side. Marissa could not look, but Dargent could and his ears slowly crept from flat back to pricked forward. Too breathless to whinny, he checked and then, automatically, tried to tuck himself in behind the familiar red tail.

When he was able, Kamil leant down and grabbed Dargent's rein. He did not recognize the horse although, like Hosanna, he had been on crusade, but he could feel that capture was not unwelcome. The reckless gallop soon became a canter, then a trot and finally, as the horses slowed to walk, Marissa fainted. She came round to find herself stared at by a dark-eyed stranger and her first reaction was to be defensively angry.

'What do you want?' she demanded, sitting up, feeling fragile as a leaf but determined not to show it. Kamil said nothing and moved away. Marissa put her hands on the ground to steady herself, and as she did so, saw Hosanna. The shock was very great. At first she thought she must be mistaken. She stood up and straightened her dress, acutely conscious that she and this stranger were quite alone. 'Who are you? Where did you get that horse?' It was all she could think about.

'I am just a traveller,' replied Kamil curtly.

'Not from here,' said Marissa, and her voice, despite her fright, was tart. 'Nor from anywhere in England.'

Trying to disguise her limp, she hurried over to where Hosanna was standing, blowing. When he turned to her and she found herself reflected once again in his wise

153

eyes, she knew she had not made a mistake. 'Hosanna,' she said, without thinking. Kamil listened intently. Suddenly panicking, Marissa felt for the ruby brooch. She almost cried with relief when it was still there and put her hand up to touch the horse's white star. Then she turned on Kamil.

'This horse is not yours. He belongs to William Ravensgarth. How did you come by him?' She was imperious in her questions. 'Are you a friend of Constable de Scabious?'

'I have no friends here,' said Kamil carefully. He had no idea who this girl was and the fact that she knew Hosanna troubled him deeply. He wanted to get away from her. 'Can you ride again? If so, I shall leave you.'

'Leave me? Not on Hosanna. He's not yours.' She fixed him with a glare.

'So you say.' He took Hosanna's rein. She could not stop him.

'Please,' said Marissa, suddenly desperate. 'Where are you keeping Will? I only want to see him.'

'I am not keeping him anywhere.' Kamil vaulted on.

'How did you get his horse, then?'

'I bargained for him.' Kamil wheeled Hosanna round. 'Now, if you don't mind, I will be on my way.'

But Marissa was determined. She found a pile of stones and struggled into the saddle. Kamil ignored her and rode off, but Dargent was soon stuck to Hosanna's tail and would not be shaken off. Eventually, Kamil had to accept the unwelcome company and he and Marissa rode on together, their hostile silence in noticeable contrast to the easy familiarity of the horses.

Hours later, as the sun began to set, Kamil, as was his habit, searched for the bothies he had come to rely on and eventually found one filled with sheep fleeces. He made a fire and, with surly courtesy, shared his food, then spread some of the woolly hides out for Marissa to lie on. The girl said nothing. She knew with certainty that Hosanna would not leave her behind.

Kamil looked down on her as she slept. *Why*, he thought to himself, *she's barely more than a child.* He noticed the scars on her arm and her twisted leg as he covered her with Dargent's blanket and went outside to sleep himself.

In the morning, after he had got the horses ready, he tapped her with a stick until she woke. She came out of the bothy to find Hosanna at Kamil's shoulder, licking his hand for the salt. 'He likes you,' she said, with surprised resentment.

'We're old friends,' Kamil replied.

Marissa was jealous on Will's behalf. 'I don't know who you are,' she said. 'Constable de Scabious may have imprisoned Will and given you Hosanna, but that makes no difference.'

Kamil watched as the horse moved over and sniffed Marissa's hair. 'But I think you are one of those Saracens,' the girl said, almost spitting the word 'Saracen'. 'In any case, I feel sure you are our enemy.'

Kamil did not respond.

Marissa grew peevish and when Hosanna moved back to Kamil, she got up and went to stand beside him. Kamil stood up too, and he and Marissa glared at each other over the horse's withers, Hosanna's great red mane spread over their fingers. Almost without thinking, Marissa stroked and divided the long hairs, wondering about the shorter hairs where the serjeant had let Will's

155

sword fall, then began to braid. Hosanna lowered his head so that she could reach and although it was such a small, polite gesture, Kamil's heart sank a little.

Gradually, as she plaited, Marissa wove her yarn, telling Kamil how she had come to Hartslove, how she admired Will and Hosanna, and how she had been sent to find them both. 'Will loves Hosanna,' she said, 'but he also loves me.' To add weight to her words she let go of the braid to show off her ruby brooch. But as she held it up, Hosanna tossed his head, unravelling all Marissa's work and knocking the brooch from her hand. The girl quickly retrieved it from the ground, attached it to her undershift and, undaunted, began her braiding all over again.

Finally, Kamil spoke. 'We must hurry to the castle,' was all he said, and although he betrayed nothing, he felt that every moment Hosanna was somehow slipping away from him. It had been too good to be true when the red horse was delivered into his hands. Now something else was at work. He said nothing to Marissa about his letter from Richard, only fingered it over and over as he repeated to himself, 'You are mine, Hosanna. You are mine.' He needed to believe it.

They pressed on, but not as fast as Kamil would have liked, for Marissa was not up to it. There was no question of asking the way, for it was clear that Hosanna's compass was set, and the following afternoon Kamil found himself gazing into a pretty valley below him.

He called to Marissa but she shook her head. 'I don't recognize this place,' she said. 'Not that that means anything. Marie – that's my sister – and I never went over the Hartslove drawbridge again after we arrived.'

Hosanna, however, was insistent. He stepped eagerly

down a goat track leading round a fold in the hill, aiming for the glistening river below. Kamil allowed the horse a free rein. Finally, from a spit of rock, a small fortress was visible just under the skyline. Squinting against the sun, Kamil could make out the jousting field and the road down which, three years before, the crusaders had left with so many, then limped home with so few.

Marissa brought Dargent up beside him. She shaded her eyes with her hand. 'Yes, that's Hartslove,' she said.

They rode on and could soon make out the scaffolding up which men were climbing like ants, pitching a roof back on the keep. The drawbridge was firmly closed. Suddenly, Hosanna stopped and his flanks fluttered as he whinnied long and hard. In a moment the orange-streaked sky was filled with answering greetings as the Hartslove horses welcomed him home.

It was not until they were almost at the ford in the river that Kamil was aware that a number of mounted men were approaching fast out of the woods to the left. Those mercenaries again. Angry at being made fools of, they had been searching for Kamil and Marissa and now they had found them. With drawn swords they were spreading out, intent on separating the two horses.

Kamil's jaw tensed and Marissa's eyes were wide and startled. Sticking closely together, Hosanna and Dargent increased their pace, speeding through the ford, then galloping up into the water meadows, their wet tails slapping their legs.

The mercenaries followed. Kamil glanced to right and left but there was no escape except into the castle. He tried to think quickly as Hosanna's mane lashed his face and Marissa's hair flew loose. Berating himself for not being more careful, he nevertheless revelled in Hosanna's floating gallop, but as the ground rose Dargent began to labour.

Marissa had none of Kamil's confidence. She sat, almost paralysed as the horse struggled, his ears flattened against his skull. All she could see was the water in the moat glinting black. Kamil crouched down. 'Gather yourself up and ride that horse,' he shouted as Dargent's breath came in great gasps. 'Don't just sit there. He can go faster. He must go faster or we are lost.' Marissa could barely hear his words but she knew what he was saying.

An arrow whistled past her head. 'Help me, Hosanna,' she wailed, keeping her eyes glued to the red tail in front of her. Then she gathered the reins, braced her body and rode for her life.

From his chamber in the keep, Gavin was conscious of Hosanna's great whinny as it echoed across the valley, and of the answering ripple. At first he wondered if he were still delirious and hearing sounds from years gone by, but he knew this was unlikely, since under Marie's firm ministrations, his body was recovering. Already that day he had held a council of war, and although he was still riven with uncertainty about Richard and almost prostrate with grief, guilt and worry about Ellie and Will, he could stand and hold his sword again. Before Hosanna's whinny had died away, he was halfway across the courtyard.

Somebody hollered from the top of the battlements. 'Sir, your brother's two horses are fleeing towards us, but although it's definitely that de Neville girl on Dargent, the man on Hosanna is not the Earl of Ravensgarth.'

Gavin ran to the gatehouse. The porter huffed and puffed beside him. 'Alan Shortspur thinks this is a trap. The man on Hosanna clearly wants us to lower the drawbridge, but if we do that we'll be overrun because the ruffians pursuing them are too close. We have not even got our armour on, so we are hardly equipped for battle. We must keep the drawbridge up, sir.'

Gavin climbed up inside the wall and peered out. He exclaimed loudly when he saw the horses almost finished and their pursuers almost on them. Hosanna was stretched right out, his white star pulsing.

'Christ help us,' muttered Gavin. 'But I can't let him down, whoever his rider is.' He ran down the steps. 'When I say "now",' he bellowed to both the porter and the soldiers rushing about in a frenzy, 'let down the drawbridge, but not all the way. Keep it about four feet from the ground and hold it steady. Get every man you can to help with the winch. Do you understand?'

The porter began to remonstrate. 'The enemy will overrun us.'

Gavin silenced him. 'Not if we are quick enough. Now, do as I say, right now. There is no time for argument. The horses jumped out. They must jump back in. They can do it, so let's just hope that the others cannot.'

Marie had been grinding herbs in the kitchen when she heard the commotion. She liked it in the kitchen for the servants respected and even admired her, recognizing that she and she alone had been responsible for saving Gavin's life. Now she ran to him and all her new-found self-assurance vanished. 'Marissa can't jump,' she grasped his sleeve. 'She can't do that.'

'She will have to try,' said Gavin, taking her hand. 'It's the only way we can let them in, Marie. We cannot risk

159

an invasion of enemy knights when we are not in a fit state to defend ourselves. Have faith.'

Then there was nothing to do but watch and pray.

In the end, it was only Hosanna's unflinching nerve that kept Kamil heading for the drawbridge. The horse was almost flat on the ground and Kamil had never ridden at such a speed. It was difficult to see or hear, for there was roaring in his ears and his eyes were wind-whipped. Squinting sideways, he could just make out Dargent's bared teeth and the sweat staining his neck. But it was not over yet. Only twenty strides from the moat, Missing Fingers barely six sword lengths away and the drawbridge still firmly shut, Kamil's heart was hammering. There was no hope now. He closed his eyes, waiting for the sting of enemy steel. But when he opened them again, a miracle had happened. The draw-bridge was being cranked down and as Hosanna and Dargent summoned their last ounces of strength, it hung, suspended in the air.

It was clear at once what was required. Kamil slowed a fraction so that he and Marissa were knee to knee. 'When I say go,' he shouted, 'kick Dargent as hard as you can.'

Marissa did not blink. Kamil could not know if she had understood so he pulled Hosanna back, and, leaning over, he hit Dargent as hard as he could. The horse took off. Marissa, every sinew dissolving into liquid fear, urged him forward with her voice, her heels and her hands. But while Dargent made it on to the drawbridge, he had leapt too far to the left to leave space for Hosanna alongside. As the great ramp swung up, causing him and Marissa to tumble into the courtyard, Kamil and Hosanna saw daylight for one brief second before they jumped straight into the moat and darkness closed over their heads.

Marissa pushed Marie aside as she got up and staggered as best she could to where Dargent lay, completely winded, on the cobbles. She flung herself down beside him, calling his name and looking round for Hosanna. It was only then that she realized she had made the leap alone.

On the edge of the moat, the mercenaries spread out and emptied their quivers into the water, furious at once again being denied their prey. Occasionally they got a glimpse of a red head and redoubled their efforts. Gavin frantically ordered his archers to return arrow for arrow, but it was only when Missing Fingers and five of his cronies were lying dead on the ground that the rest wheeled away, gesticulating and shouting abuse, but beaten – for the moment, at any rate.

When they were clearly retreating, the drawbridge was lowered and Marissa was the first on it, limping inelegantly as fast as she could, peering down for signs of life. There was nothing. The girl stood, hunched above the water. Then, before anybody could stop her, she stripped to her shift, revealing her damaged leg and scarred arm to the world. Marie tried to hold her back, but Marissa gave an odd smile, shook her off, filled her lungs and dived.

The soldiers gaped, open-mouthed. In the air Marissa was transformed into an arc of grace. Her lame leg no longer dragged, but rested neatly against its counterpart. The scars on her arms looked not like teeth marks, but like small stones of red jasper. She created barely a ripple as she broke through the discouraging surface, then propelled herself down, down into the cold and began systematically to feel for bodies. She found nothing for what seemed like a lifetime. She heard the soldiers groan as she came up for air, then down she went again. It was impossible to see much in the murk. Silken tendrils of watery plants caressed her legs. Occasionally she felt the bones of long-dead animals bump against her skin. The water was heaving with the detritus of a hundred years of castle history, and Marissa had to fight through it all.

Then, just as she thought her lungs would explode, she felt something that was neither plant nor bone. Her hands were entangled in a skein of something spread out like a feathered fan. A horse's tail. She kicked forward.

Kamil was underneath Hosanna, his fingers pulling hopelessly at the horse's saddle. A thick snake of weed had curled itself through the stirrups. Kamil had managed to pull some of the leaves away, but thin, branch-like stems, strong as twisted steel, meant that Hosanna was still trapped. The red horse could no longer even struggle, but was entirely at the mercy of the water and, although Kamil's hands were still twitching, he too had resigned himself to a watery grave.

Marissa felt for the ruby brooch. She pulled it off her shift and used the pointed end to stab and stab at the fronds until they were perforated enough for her to break. As they snapped and sank away, a dozen more tried to take their place but Hosanna, freed at last, began to rise to the surface, dragging Kamil with him. Desperate for breath, Marissa prayed. 'Please God, help us,' she begged.

Her strength was almost gone when a rope dangled above her. She grabbed it, then saw a shadow and a dipped oar. Somebody had found a makeshift raft.

Willing hands reached out, pulling Kamil on to it and securing Hosanna so that he would float to the draw-bridge where two dozen men were waiting to winch him out. Marissa, her shift weighing her down, swam slowly alongside, pummelling the horse's chest. Water poured from his nose and mouth but nobody could tell if he were alive or dead. Marissa's own breath came in great gasps.

When Hosanna was laid out in the courtyard and Kamil carried in on a hurdle, Gavin was completely taken aback. 'Kamil,' he kept repeating. 'Kamil.'

Kamil opened his eyes and was as sick as a dog. He pushed Gavin away, only wanting to drag himself over to the horse's body. When the Hartslove knights saw he was a Saracen, however, they began to mutter and some tried to seize him.

Gavin drew his sword. 'Keep back,' he ordered. 'This is not the time.' The soldiers obeyed.

Kamil's teeth were chattering as he watched the water flowing from Hosanna's nose. 'We were going to get out,' he choked. 'That weed . . . It just caught . . .' He spread his hands helplessly.

Marissa concentrated all her efforts on her pummel-ling, pausing only to attach the ruby brooch back to her shift. She would not allow herself to think what would have happened had she not been wearing it.

Alan Shortspur ordered great wedges of straw to be set up so that Hosanna's body would be higher than his head to help the draining process. Blankets were brought. Everybody tried their best, but it seemed hopeless.

Eventually, Marissa turned to Kamil. 'Pray with me,' she ordered. 'We must save Hosanna for Will. I don't know what else we can do.'

'Pray to save Hosanna for Will?' Kamil was too shattered to do anything but repeat her words.

'Yes, for Will,' Marissa said. 'Now. Lord, with Thy Grace anything is possible. Do not take from us this horse, Hosanna. Keep him safe so that he and Will may be reunited forever. In Thy Mercy. Amen.' Silence. 'Say Amen, Kamil.'

'I can't.'

'Say Amen. Do you want Hosanna to die?'

'Of course not.'

'Then say Amen now. What does it matter if the word is wrong for your god? He will understand and if he doesn't, he's not God.'

But it was not this that was bothering Kamil. He could pray for Hosanna. He had done it before. But he could not pray for him to be reunited with Will.

Marissa stared at him, incredulous, and her voice rose. 'Say Amen, Kamil. If you don't and Hosanna does not survive, it will be your fault. Say Amen. Say it.' She began to moan, convinced that Hosanna's life depended on this one small thing. 'I'm begging you.'

Kamil looked down. The horse seemed lifeless. 'Amen,' he said dully. It did not seem to matter now.

Marissa resumed her pummelling and Kamil turned away. He did not turn back until the girl's sobs finally came. They poured out and she welcomed them. Kamil slid to his knees beside her. 'You tried your best,' he said.

Marissa could not speak, but she shook her head and pushed her hair from her streaming eyes. Through her tears, a quivering smile was trying to break through. 'He's breathing,' she said, and collapsed.

Relief threatened to overcome Kamil too, but even as

his heart swelled, his 'Amen' also rang in his ears. It rang all the harder when he realized that Richard's letter, his most powerful bargaining instrument, was in soggy tatters. It would be useless because unreadable. And now he had been trapped by a prayer. Hosanna coughed, then began to struggle slowly to his feet, leaving puddles of weeds and water. His breathing was sticky and gulping, but Kamil held him and stroked him until his panting became more even and the horse could support his head himself.

'The worst is over, I think,' said Marissa, but, though her tone was unusually kind, Kamil could barely look at her. For him, the worst was just beginning. It now seemed years since he had parted from Saladin; an age since his meeting with Richard. He had been lulled into a false sense of security by little more than a piece of luck and some good English weather. Only now did the truth really strike him, that here he was, in a foreign, hostile country on the brink of civil war, able to see, but apparently never to own, the only living thing he cared for. He briefly touched Hosanna's two crusading scars and looked into his eyes. An injury, probably from the detritus in the moat, had caused a mark like a feather to appear in the left one. The pain of that, coupled with the agony of emptying his sodden lungs, caused the horse to groan, and Kamil groaned with him. Then they were parted.

Kamil was immediately and not very politely seized by two overzealous soldiers and manhandled into the great hall. With naked swords, they pushed him behind a screen where Marie had ordered hot water and fresh clothes to be laid out. Standing guard as he changed, the tone of the soldiers' remarks was predicated on their belief that Kamil could understand nothing they said. As he stripped, and the insults about foreigners in general and him in particular degenerated from the unpleasant to the scandalous, an anger black as the moat water possessed him. What did he care for their wars or for Richard? Stuffing the disintegrating and now illegible remnants of the letter into his belt, he hated them all.

When he appeared from behind the screen, Alan Shortspur addressed him. He had only one question: 'Where is the Earl of Ravensgarth?'

'Alan, be quiet and get out of the way.' Gavin could still hardly believe it was Kamil in front of him. Surely he should be in the Holy Land with Saladin? Marie hovered anxiously. Gavin was not yet fully recovered and she did not want all her good work undone. He smiled at her and nodded, then turned back to Kamil. 'You must understand,' he said, 'that life for us is already full of danger. Now you arrive riding Will's horse, and with my ward. My brother and my bride are prisoners and even Will's squire, Hal, who left for the continent to find King Richard, is rumoured to have fallen into the hands of mercenaries. In God's name, where do you fit into all this?'

Kamil stood stonyfaced. He would not be interrogated like a criminal, although the news about Hal disconcerted him.

'Perhaps he doesn't speak our language,' said Alan.

'He speaks our language perfectly well,' Gavin retorted. The two joking soldiers blushed a little. 'I know this man. He is one of Saladin's emirs.' Alan drew his sword. 'Oh, put it away,' Gavin ordered. 'He is completely unarmed.'

Kamil remained silent. *Let the Christians destroy*

166

themselves fighting each other, he thought. They were nothing but infidel dogs.

Gavin watched, then ordered everybody to leave.

Alan remonstrated. 'If he was to attack you, sir —'

'He will not,' said Gavin curtly. 'But even if he does, I expect I can still wield a dagger.'

Alan flinched and withdrew.

Pulling two chairs to the hearth, Gavin motioned to Kamil to take one. 'I think we have been through too much, you and I, to play games,' he said. 'Now tell me, how did you come by Hosanna?'

'I bargained for him from a fat man at a port. The man wanted something from me. I took the horse from him.'

'Constable de Scabious!' exclaimed Gavin. 'Oh God, poor Will.' Now even he looked at Kamil with suspicion. *Perhaps*, he thought, *Saladin has sent him, at John's request, to cause even more confusion.* Everybody knew that Muslims were devious. He shifted in his chair and fingered the hilt of his sword. But Kamil hardly noticed. He fiddled with the hank of Hosanna's hair and something fell from his belt on to the floor.

Gavin leant forward. He looked once, then again, and his face lost the healthy hue that Marie had so carefully restored and became pale as death. 'My God,' he whispered. 'My God.' He leant down. 'I can't be mistaken. That is Richard's seal.' He stared at it as if it were gold. 'Where did you get it, Kamil? Where did you get it?' He made to pick it up but, quick as a flash, Kamil got to it first. Gavin stretched out his hand, but Kamil held back, hardly daring to hope. 'The seal,' Gavin said hoarsely. 'Who gave it to you?'

Kamil looked at him straight. 'King Richard, not so much more than a month ago,' he said.

167

'You saw him?'

Kamil nodded. 'He sent me here from his prison in Austria, to give you this, as proof that he lives.'

Gavin held out his hand again. 'Richard is alive,' he said. 'Richard is alive.' He seemed almost incredulous. Kamil watched him and kept the seal just out of reach. 'Give it to me now,' Gavin said. 'God be praised! I could never have hoped for this.'

But Kamil still held back. Oh, Allah was still looking after him! The fulfilment of Richard's request could surely negate the prayer.

'This seal for the red horse,' he said quietly. Gavin did not seem to hear him, so Kamil repeated his demand a little more strongly. He must do this right. He must not lose the red horse again.

'This seal for the red horse,' he repeated once more. He could tell that Gavin was not listening, so he said it again even more loudly. Everybody must hear this. There must be no misunderstanding. Gavin's arm was still outstretched and Kamil allowed him to touch the seal now. 'For the red horse,' Kamil said one last time. He waited for a second, then let go.

Gavin took the seal and held it up. The engraved wax dangled luminous in the firelight and Gavin's eyes were bright with tears. Kamil leant back and the braid of Hosanna's hair swung gently. He watched as relief flooded Gavin's ravaged face like waves smoothing sand. Only then did he himself relax. 'We have a bargain,' he said, and his heart began to sing.

It had grown dark and neither man had noticed Marissa, dressed in rich yellow velvet and with her fair hair spinning down her back, walking up from the end of the hall in a pool of candlelight. She looked very different from the scruffy girl Hosanna had rescued on the bridge. Marie walked slightly behind, her eyes always assessing Gavin's state of health. But as they approached, he leapt up and strode down the hall towards them, his voice stronger than Marie had ever known it.

'Come,' he called to her. 'King Richard needs us. We must go and fetch Will and Ellie. All will yet be well but I need you to help me to organize the provisions we will need for a journey.' Marie ran after him and Marissa was left to face Kamil alone.

'A seal for Hosanna?' Her fury shook the rafters. 'I heard you, Kamil.'

He barely looked at her. 'A king's seal,' he said. 'King Richard's. The Count of Hartslove exchanged it for the red horse. We made a good bargain. The horse for a king. It absolves me from your Amen.'

'The horse is Will's.' Marissa's eyes were daggers. 'Or even mine. After all, I saved both you and Hosanna from the moat. Without me you would both be dead. How could you demand such a price?'

'It seemed a fitting price.' Kamil could not quite look Marissa in the eye. 'Gavin is Will's brother. He has the right. Hosanna is mine.'

Marissa took a step closer. 'How can you take such a horse in this way? You demean yourself.'

Her voice jabbed like a needle and Kamil wanted to thrust her away, to ignore her, to pretend he had never met her. After all, what was she? Only a Christian girl. She knew nothing. He would leave now. His job was done. Pushing over his chair, he made his way swiftly to the stables, hating Marissa for following him as he walked along the row to Hosanna.

The horse was restless despite his exhaustion. The

grooms had changed his blankets so he was comfortable, but he could not settle and when Kamil approached, he pushed against his stable door. Kamil began to soothe him but Marissa frowned. 'I'm sure he knows that Will is in real danger,' she said. 'He can sense it. The seal you brought will frighten John. Anything could happen now.' Her voice accused him.

Kamil slid the bolt, went inside Hosanna's box and locked it behind him. 'You are very concerned about Will,' he said. 'When are you to be married?'

Marissa flushed. 'When he comes home,' she said, but added bitterly, 'He will never be happy without Hosanna.'

'He will have you.' Kamil clenched his fists. This girl was intolerable. He leant against Hosanna's shoulder. 'He can surely spare the red horse.'

'You know he can't,' said Marissa. 'And Hosanna will not be happy without him. Look how he frets. It is as if he knows you are going to take him away from where he belongs. I bet,' she said slowly, suddenly inspired, 'that if you try to take him away he won't go.' Kamil's hands ceased to stroke. 'Yes,' said Marissa, sensing a crack in Kamil's stony reserve. 'I bet he won't go. Take him out and see.' She unlocked the stable door. 'Go on.'

Kamil stood back. Hosanna seemed keen enough to get out, but what would happen if the girl were right? What would he do if the red horse refused to cross the drawbridge or stood in the middle of the road, clearly reluctant to accompany him back to the coast? Kamil could see it all: the cruel disappointment; the laughter of the soldiers; Marissa's triumphant smile. Damn her. He could feel the ground shifting under his feet.

'I know he won't go, and I'll be there to watch,'

Marissa pressed on, waiting for the final hesitation that would tell her she had won.

Kamil's face grew black as night, but he was not finished yet. 'I have a different proposition,' he said, touching Hosanna's scars. He thought quickly. 'If I stay and fight with the Count of Hartslove to rescue the Earl of Ravensgarth, but in the process the Earl of Ravensgarth dies, will the red horse be mine then?'

Marissa's face lost all colour. 'Will will not die,' she whispered. 'That is impossible.'

'But if he does, will my bargain with the count stand?'

The girl faltered. 'If Will dies because you do not fight as if he is your own brother, even to sacrificing your own life for his,' she said, 'I do not believe Will's horse will live happily with you.'

Kamil resumed his stroking. 'It's a bargain, then,' he said. 'Now, get out.'

The following morning, when the Hartslove soldiers prepared to leave for Hangem, Kamil, mounted on an eager Hosanna, was the first over the drawbridge.

13

As Ellie rested after her visit to the cellar, hopeful that Will had escaped and was now at the head of a rescue party, deep within the tower Will waited for something – he was not sure what. His first sight of the tapestry room had been delayed because a fresh rockfall had prevented even somebody as small as Elric getting through. Will was forced to wait as the little boy went back to the village to steal more tools, for the ones they had were too small for this new hurdle. They had soon set to work and cleared it but it all took precious hours. What was more, Will could see that it would not be long before the whole tunnel collapsed. He made Elric promise that once he had rescued Ellie and got away – he would not admit that there could be any other outcome – the little boy and his friends would never use it again. Elric promised faithfully as he unpacked quantities of stolen food.

'You are a one-boy forage party,' Will told him as he tore into bread and cheese. 'We could have done with you on crusade. Richard might even have knighted you.'

'What's Richard like?' asked Elric, thrilled by the picture Will conjured up. 'My da says that we hear of him, and we pay for him, but we never see him. He hates him, but he would have died for old King Henry, at least that's what I heard him tell the priest. King Henry passed through here often enough and once, when my da was young, he actually sat and listened to the villagers' complaints. Why has your Richard never done that?'

'He has other concerns,' said Will. 'Bigger ones, like Jerusalem.'

'But what bigger concerns can you have if you are king, than your people?' asked Elric, puzzled.

'I know it is difficult to understand,' said Will, 'but I promise you, Richard is a good man and a great king. Maybe his father was here more often because he didn't go off to fight the Saracens, who are, don't forget, Elric, God's enemies. Most of them anyway. And we had to get Jerusalem back.'

'But you never did, did you?'

'Well, no,' said Will, feeling pressured. 'But we did our best.'

'So, if Richard comes home, will we have to pay more money for another crusade?'

'I don't know.' Will was exasperated by his own confusion. 'Look, Elric. All I know is that Richard is our lawful king. When he comes back, maybe you can talk to him yourself.' He picked up one of the candles. 'Go home now,' he said. 'You've been here long enough today. But thank you. I could have done nothing without you. I'm going to see if I can get all the way to the tapestry room now. It may be my only chance. Once de Scabious is back, who knows what will happen to me and Ellie.'

'Why don't you come to the village with me?' asked Elric. 'You might be able to get away to Hartslove and bring a whole army here.' His face glowed at the thought.

'It would all take too long,' said Will, who had been

173

over that possibility a dozen times in his head while he was digging. 'I simply can't leave Ellie here with just Old Nurse. Now, it really is time for you to go home.'

'I suppose,' Elric agreed reluctantly. 'I hope more rocks don't cave in, though. Oh, and when you get to the room, you'd better watch for the old dogs. They lie in front of the fire.' He had just one more thing to say. 'I know my da doesn't feel any loyalty to Richard . . .' He hesitated. 'But I think lots of people hate the constable although they daren't say so. Maybe, if they thought he really was finished, some of the villagers might help you.'

'Elric, if they would, it would be tremendous,' said Will, shining the candle backwards for a moment. 'That would terrify him because, you know, for all his blustering and his gibbets, he's just a coward.'

At the mention of gibbets, Elric's enthusiasm died. 'I only said "might",' he said. 'People would be frightened in case the attack failed and, anyway, even if we beat de Scabious, what happens if Richard doesn't return and John is king? We would all be strung up.' He shuddered. 'I couldn't see my mother hang, even for you.'

'Of course you couldn't,' said Will with a mixture of understanding and exasperation at the boy's nervy courage. 'You have done enough already.' He squeezed Elric's hand. 'Get yourself home and wish me luck.' Then he vanished amid the echo of his first paternoster.

Beyond the rockfall, the tunnel dived steeply down at first, curling and weaving through the foundation rock of the tower. It was very damp and occasionally, where the water flowed rather than dripped down the walls, Will paddled through mud. Although he could stand up perfectly straight, he had some difficulty keeping his feet and, above him, the rock occasionally juddered, making the hairs creep up the back of his neck. The tiny bones of mice and bats crunched under his boots and he had to grit his teeth when the crunch turned to a squelch as rotting corpses of rats heaped the path. Soon the candle went out and Will, shivering with cold and dread, threw it away. He lost track of his prayers but it hardly mattered for he could do nothing but struggle blindly on, trying not to cry out when he touched something he did not even want to imagine.

Eventually the tunnel flattened out, then began to rise again as it neared its end. So glad was he to see it that Will had to stop himself from rushing towards the small faint haze that could only be the back of the tapestry. He stilled his breathing and sternly reminded himself that the horrors of the tunnel would be nothing compared to the horrors that would await him if he were caught. He crept closer. It was soon clear why the tapestry was there. The wall had crumbled away and the tower's occupants, too lazy to repair it, had covered it over instead. From the bristling web of sticky cobwebs spread thick and unbroken, Will could tell that de Scabious had never looked behind it. The only fingers that had disturbed it recently were those of small boys pulling out threads.

He approached cautiously and touched the tapestry gently. Immediately, an army of spiders swung crazily, spinning more and more silver tracery into the mass behind them. A cloud of grey dust billowed out and for a moment Will thought he was going to sneeze. Bending double and clamping his hand over his nose and mouth, he held his breath. The sneeze passed and, sweating slightly, he took care not to touch the tapestry again.

Instead, he looked for the place where the weave was thinnest and peered through. Just as Elric had warned, in front of the fire he could see two indistinct lumps of dog. There was a high-backed oak armchair facing the hearth in which, so Will rightly assumed, de Scabious did most of his plotting. Otherwise, apart from a small table laid with a jug and a tankard, the room seemed to be empty. A tiny window, high up in the outside wall, showed a charcoal sky. Opposite the tapestry was the door, which was open.

Will let his eyes travel slowly up and down, taking in every detail, but when they reached the fire again, he became rigid. One of the dogs had raised his grizzled head and was gazing directly at him. The dog's nose was twitching and its throat ticked with the beginnings of a growl. Its companion also opened a suspicious eye, but, finding the effort too much, licked its chops a few times and settled back to sleep. The first dog, however, was more tenacious. With a huge effort, it got up, padded over and sniffed about. Cursing his luck as the dog opened its mouth, Will shut his eyes, ready for the bark that would bring the soldiers running. But nothing happened. When he opened his eyes again, he found himself staring straight past some yellow fangs and down a pink speckled throat. The dog was yawning. Then it padded back to the fire, leaving a small streak of dribble on the floor.

Will began to breathe again, then got the fright of his life when the chair was suddenly scraped back and a figure, which he recognized as the serjeant's, rose to its feet. The man had been asleep. He stretched, belched, then, warming his bottom against the fire, bellowed for Gethin. It took a while for the youth to appear, and, in the meantime, the serjeant amused himself by turning the dogs' ears inside out. When Gethin arrived, the serjeant slopped back into the armchair, laughing unpleasantly as the dogs regarded him with mournful eyes.

'The constable returns tomorrow,' he said, 'and you must get the stables ready for visitors. He has sent word that his wedding is to be very soon now. He has decided he can wait no longer. Have we enough stores?' Gethin muttered something. 'Well, send down to the village,' said the serjeant, leaning back. 'The peasants must provide what is due. Now. Send one of the maidservants for that girl. I'll break the good news that before the week is out, she'll be a married woman.'

Very slowly, Will leant down and felt for a sharp stone. He had no idea what he would do with it, for he knew that even if he managed to kill the serjeant and spirit Ellie away down the tunnel, they could not leave, just the two of them alone, without Old Nurse, Sacramenta and Hosanna. Nevertheless, he felt better with something in his hand. When Ellie appeared, and was pushed over to the tapestry side of the room, Will stared so hard he was sure she must feel the force of his eyes in the back of her neck. He was shocked by how thin she was but, when the serjeant began to tease her, was glad to see that her spirit was undiminished. Indeed, she seemed almost unnaturally calm. If the serjeant hoped for hysterics he was disappointed, for she greeted the news of her imminent wedding with complete silence. Irritated, the man got up and raised his hand to her. Will gasped but Ellie never flinched.

'I hardly think,' she said, 'that even Constable de Scabious –' she made his name sound like a disease – 'will want a wife with a black eye.'

The serjeant dropped his hand and glared at Gethin. 'Send her back to her chamber,' he said.

Ellie left the room, keeping as far away from the serjeant as possible. If Will had put his hand out as she passed, he could have caught her arm. The desperate urge to whisper her name almost overcame him, but he held his tongue. There was too much to lose. He waited until she had vanished, hoping that the serjeant would leave the room, but he did not, and more soldiers came to join him. They would not be drunk tonight. There was too much to do before the constable's return.

Will returned to the cellar, concentrating only on what his next move should be. Hosanna would be back tomorrow. Thank God. He scrambled through the hole, neatly blocked up the tunnel entrance and crouched in his usual corner. Sleep was impossible. A multitude of plans hatched in his head, all of which had to be discarded. How he needed Gavin now! If he could only know the Hartslove men were coming. But Will imagined that his brother had long since transferred his allegiance and that of his soldiers to John and this was why de Scabious had confidently set a date for his farcical marriage. *If my freedom comes at the expense of Ellie*, Will thought in despair, *it will not be worth having*. When dawn broke, his plans were no further forward, except that he knew he would have to remain in the cellar now in case the constable demanded to see him as soon as he arrived back, and that it was time to ask Elric to steal something even more difficult than a crowbar. Will needed a sword.

The sun was halfway up a pale but breezy sky when the cellar door opened and the usual pan of pottage was dumped inside. A blackbird alighted briefly near the grating, twitched its tail cheerfully and was gone. Will began to flex his muscles, first his arms, then his legs. The digging had kept him fit. As he loosened himself up he could hear more soldiers than usual in the courtyard.

'Scrub those cobbles, you lazy rats,' the serjeant was bellowing with exaggerated impatience. 'What have you all been doing, hanging around in the guardroom? I'll have the fireplace in there stopped up.'

Soldiers shuffled past, complaining under their breath. On impulse and reckoning that Gethin would be too busy to collect it, Will broke the pottage pan to form two odd-shaped daggers. They were not strong but would be better than nothing. When he had finished, he hid them carefully behind some loose stones.

By noon, activity in the courtyard was increased by the chatter of women heading for the kitchens. Pacing up and down, Will knew that whatever his plan was, it would have to be accomplished that night, when the constable would be tired and many of the soldiers would be drunk. Maybe he could use fire to cause a diversion and force the gates open. Maybe he could capture de Scabious and frighten him until he crumbled. Maybe then he and Ellie could seize a cart for Old Nurse and, with Hosanna and Sacramenta, gallop away. The plan sounded improbable, even to Will, but he could think of no other.

Ellie too was planning, and equally frustrated. She had been so happy yesterday, when she discovered Will's cellar was empty. It never occurred to her that his absence might be temporary. But after her evening encounter with the serjeant, her nerves were fraying again. De Scabious

179

was returning. This dreadful wedding loomed so close. But if Will had escaped where was he now and how long would it take him to get back? Maybe – and Ellie's legs felt weak at the thought – maybe he had escaped just after de Scabious left, but something had happened to him. Or maybe he had got back to Hartslove but Gavin had refused to help him.

'Or maybe I imagined it,' she said to Old Nurse as she stared gloomily out of the window.

'Imagined what, dearie?'

'Imagined that Will was not in the cellar,' replied Ellie impatiently. 'I mean, it was dark.'

'But you felt the tunnel entrance,' said Old Nurse, dropping her voice and tapping Ellie on the shoulder to remind her not to speak too loudly.

'Yes, I did. I really did. I really did, didn't I, Old Nurse?'

'That's what you told me.' Old Nurse remained placid. 'And you're not given to fancies.'

'Then why does nobody come to help?' Ellie despaired. 'Soon it will all be too late.'

Old Nurse made no comment. She let Ellie's frustrations run their course, before suggesting that they stitch some of her most precious possessions inside her cloak, so that if rescue did come she could be sure of leaving nothing behind. Ellie agreed at once. At least it was something to do. She was still wearing the green jasper necklace, but, out of her pocket, brought Gavin's battered wooden dog, which was now missing an ear. Old Nurse fetched needles and thread and began to sew.

The sun was still high in the sky when there was shouting from the battlements. Ellie rushed to the window, hoping against hope to see the Hartslove standard. But all that greeted her was the constable's high voice calling for the serjeant and the sight of her tormentor not astride a graceful chestnut stallion, but sitting in an ungainly heap on an ugly roan palfrey. Ellie gasped, then, her hand over her mouth, she flew down the tower steps and into the courtyard, searching frantically among the returning horses for the familiar red colour and white star. None of the soldiers would meet her eye. Careless of her dignity, Ellie eventually ran to the constable and shook his leg.

'Where is Hosanna?' she demanded. 'Where is Hosanna?'

De Scabious's tongue flicked over his lips and he rolled uneasily in his saddle. 'Have you no welcome for your bridegroom?' he wheedled.

Ellie shook his leg harder. 'Where's Hosanna?' she repeated.

'Hosanna?' The constable was deliberately vague. 'Oh, Hosanna! That dratted horse of William Ravensgarth's?' He tried to sound as if he had never heard the name before. 'Hosanna,' he said, 'is, quite simply, dead. He slipped and fell. The roads really are shocking. Anyway, there was nothing to be done. A butcher dealt with him, my dear. Never mind. He was really quite unsuitable as a warhorse for a knight in the late twelfth century. We have to progress, you know. We need bigger, stronger animals these days.'

There was a moment's complete silence as Ellie tried to take in what the constable had said.

'You have killed Hosanna?' It started as a disbelieving question, but as Ellie said it again, and saw the nervous tick in the constable's eyes, it began to turn from a question into an unearthly wail. 'You have killed Hosanna,' she repeated, softly, then louder as her voice crept up. 'You have killed Hosanna.' Again and again she forced out the words – impossible words, but the only ones she found she could utter – until she was shouting them so loudly that they filled her head, pushing out everything else.

Unable to make out anything very clearly amid the hubbub, Will nevertheless heard Ellie's cry and, breathless with foreboding, jumped to clutch on to the grating. But it was no good. He could see nothing and threw himself against the wall, hammering it with frustration. It was only when the soldiers fell silent, terrified and appalled by Ellie's ceaseless lamentation, that everything became apparent and Will felt as if the blood were draining from his body. It was at first impossible to move, then he too began to shout and to bang his fists against the door. He must have misheard. Surely he must have misheard. Ellie could not be saying what he thought she was saying. He roared and howled until his fists were bloody and his throat raw, begging to be let out. From high up in the tower, Old Nurse dropped everything and began to lumber down the stairs.

A stinging slap brought Ellie to her senses. Deafened by the noise, de Scabious dismounted and hit her smartly across one cheek. She choked, but could still hear hammering and moaning. It was a second or two before she realized that the noise was not coming from her, but from Will's cellar. Her whole body shook as the living nightmare grew darker and deeper. Surely Will was not in the cellar? But it sounded like him.

De Scabious's head was splitting. Ellie's animal laments had turned into sobs, but now Will's had taken their place. Finally his temper snapped. 'Get Master William out of the cellar,' he shrieked. 'I'll teach him to make such a din.'

At that moment, Old Nurse appeared. She thundered across the courtyard and made to take Ellie in her arms. But the girl seized her shoulders and shook them. 'Old Nurse, Old Nurse,' she wept. 'He's killed Hosanna. He's killed Hosanna.'

Old Nurse held Ellie as tightly as she could and added her own horrified chorus. 'If this is true, you are a filthy, wicked man. A filthy, wicked man. May God damn you and yours to hell for eternity.'

De Scabious span round. 'You fat hellcat,' he snarled. 'I'll deal with you later.'

The serjeant was busy with his keys. As the prison door was unlocked, Old Nurse could hear Will's cries clear as day. Whatever Ellie thought, he was certainly in the cellar now. It nearly broke her heart to see him dragged out, blinking, into the daylight. He was almost unrecognizable, with his ragged clothes and stricken face. But there was nothing wrong with his lungs.

'What have you done with my horse, de Scabious? What have you done with my horse?' he yelled, kicking and twisting in the serjeant's grasp. 'If you have hurt him, you will die for it. I swear it, you'll die. And when you're dead, God will punish you and your punishment will never end.'

De Scabious, keeping carefully out of reach of Will's flailing feet, nodded to the serjeant, who threw Will to the ground and slashed the cellar key across his face. This achieved nothing. The pain and blood did not stop the shouting for even one second, so the serjeant punched Will's stomach and back until his shouting became weaker and eventually there were just groans. De Scabious rubbed his hands together.

'Hosanna is dead,' he said, recovering himself as his head stopped ringing. 'You had better get used to it. The butcher who slaughtered him was very efficient. I don't believe the horse suffered – at least –' he couldn't resist it – 'not very much. That is the end of the matter.' He turned his back and began to walk away.

'The end of the matter?' Will hauled himself to his feet. 'No, de Scabious. Do not think, even for a second, that this is the end. I will pursue you to the ends of the earth. I'll find you and rip out your guts and serve them to the hounds. I'll never forgive you. Never, do you hear me?'

He bent down, picked up a stone and threw it. It hit the constable hard behind his knee. He yelped and swore, his little eyes like red gimlets and his hand on his sword. But Will would not be cowed and his curses and Ellie's now made a fearful duet.

'Keep Eleanor quiet, Old Nurse!' screamed the constable, who could take no more.

But Old Nurse joined in herself. 'You are filth, de Scabious!' Her roar echoed round the walls. 'Utter filth. You disgrace your name. If any of the soldiers here had any gumption, they'd leave you now, before the devil comes to claim you, because he will, you ugly piece of excrement, he will, and when he does, everybody with you will be damned.'

Her imprecations grew louder and louder and more and more earthy until the constable was reduced to putting his fingers in his ears. 'Chuck them all in the cellar!' He had to make his voice high as a banshee's to be heard. 'Chuck them in and throw away the key. Here,

184

I'll do that bit myself. Let them all rot. Even the girl. Just get them out of my sight. Go on, go on, get on with it. Don't stand there like cabbages. Get them out of my sight. GET THEM OUT OF MY SIGHT!'

The soldiers surged forward as de Scabious grabbed the iron keyring from the serjeant. All three prisoners were bundled through the cellar door and the constable, fumbling and blustering, ground the key into the lock before running jerkily to the well and throwing it into the bottomless depths. 'There,' he skipped with demonic triumph. 'That's what happens to people who make me angry.' He bounced up and down on his tiptoes, then up the steps to the hall.

The serjeant hurried after him. He had never seen de Scabious quite like this before. 'That will teach them a lesson, sir,' he said nervously, for he was not sure of his master in this mood.

De Scabious ignored him. He was trying to pick up a flagon of wine but had to use two hands. Not bothering with a goblet, he tossed half the contents straight down his throat, giving himself the hiccups. Only then did he feel able to speak. 'It was – *hic* – clever – *hic* – about the key, wasn't it? I know we have – *hic* – another one,' he spluttered. 'I will marry that – *hic*, oh damn-*hic*nation – that girl, whether she likes it or not. She can throw herself off the battlements – *hic*, *hic*, aah! – after our wedding night. But I will have her, do you hear, I will have her.' The constable was clutching his chest.

The serjeant felt it safe to wink with leery complicity. 'The spare key is in the stables,' he said.

The constable grunted as sweat ran down his chins. 'I knew it. Have a drink yourself, Serjeant.' He passed over the flagon which the serjeant, who had smelt the constable's breath on more than one occasion, caught up with false enthusiasm. 'Drink, drink,' the constable urged. 'Stick with me and by next week, who knows? You may be a constable yourself.' The serjeant drank.

In the cellar, Will, Ellie and Old Nurse clung to each other, their relief at being together utterly destroyed by grief impossible to bear. They pitched and swayed as wave after wave engulfed them.

'My beautiful horse, my beautiful Hosanna. And I thought de Scabious could not hurt you. How could I have been so stupid?' Will tore his clothes in his agony.

'It's not your fault,' sobbed Ellie. 'Oh, Will. Oh please don't let it be true.'

Old Nurse rocked back and forth, her arms ready to support, just as they always were. She too mourned Hosanna, but her grief for the horse was intermingled with frantic concern for the two people she loved as her own. Gradually she brought them gently but urgently back to their own predicament.

'Master Will,' she whispered, for she was not sure if people outside were listening, 'we thought you were not in here.'

Will took no notice of Old Nurse's words at first. He was crouching down, his hands covering his face, scratching his cheeks in an effort to steady himself, hardly noticing the physical pain the serjeant had inflicted, so great was the pain in his head and in his heart. 'Hosanna butchered. I see these terrible pictures in my head. I want to be sick, Old Nurse. The last voice he heard will have been de Scabious's. Oh God! Some brute butcher with a blunt knife.' Will's voice rose. 'I shall go mad.'

'Master Will, you will not,' said Old Nurse sharply.

'For Ellie's sake. Hosanna may be gone, and that is damnable, but I know the constable. For all his threats and tossing away of keys, he will not have finished with us yet.'

'I don't care about anything any more.' Ellie slumped in Old Nurse's arms.

'You will care if the constable decides to come for you,' said Old Nurse grimly. 'My sweets, this is a terrible crime but we must keep our wits.'

'Yes,' said Will, making himself stand up. He shook his head and when he spoke again, his voice was hard as nails. 'You're right, Old Nurse. Killing Hosanna finishes nothing. Rather it begins something else. Vengeance. Vengeance for Hosanna. What do you say, Ellie?' He found her hand in the dark.

The girl's voice was muffled but her sentiments were clear enough. 'Vengeance,' she said. 'Yes, Will. I'm with you all the way.'

Will kept her hand, took Old Nurse's and led them the few steps to the far wall, then bent down and began to pull at the stones. 'There is a tunnel,' he said. 'A boy called Elric, son of Morwenna the laundress, showed me. He crawled up from the village. This tunnel leads to a bigger tunnel, which itself leads from the village in the valley to the tapestry room in the tower. That's the room where the serjeant had you brought yesterday, Ellie.'

She started. 'How do you know?'

'I was there,' said Will. 'I was behind the tapestry.'

Ellie could hardly take it in. 'I knew there was some way out of here,' she said, trying to get her thoughts in some kind of order through the fog of Hosanna. 'Gethin let me in, Will, and I couldn't find you. It was horrible. But I found the beginning of the tunnel. It seemed too good to be true. I thought you had escaped back to Hartslove and I was glad. But now . . .' Her voice broke.

'This tunnel is our escape and the beginning of our revenge,' said Will, not allowing himself to take Ellie in his arms, which is what he badly wanted to do. In a world without Hosanna, she was even more precious. He blotted out any thought of Gavin. 'Help me open it up properly. Old Nurse, you can listen at the door and tell us if you hear anything from outside.' He spoke mechanically. The only way he could make his brain or body work was to concentrate on his hatred.

It did not take long to clear the stones, and Ellie at once felt her way round the hole. It only took her a second to point out the obvious.

'We can get through here, Will,' she said, 'but not Old Nurse.'

'You must leave me, then.' Old Nurse's answer rumbled out without hesitation. 'I can look after myself. Don't you fret.'

'I will never leave you, Old Nurse,' Ellie said flatly.

'My sweet, my life has been the best anybody could have.' Old Nurse fumbled over and patted Ellie's arm. 'Don't spoil it for me now. If you remain here with me because I am too fat to escape, I will die the unhappiest death imaginable. You couldn't be that cruel. And who knows, my angel, if you and Master Will get out, you may rescue me yet. Now, be off with you. I have plenty of thoughts for company, particularly as I haven't yet devised a good enough punishment for de Scabious. That will keep me warm for a long time.'

'Old Nurse is right,' said Will. He found the old woman's hand again and pressed something into it. 'I made this knife out of a pottage pan. It is small, but it is very sharp. Old Nurse, you have been like a mother to us.' He tried to make his voice sound normal, but felt he might never sound normal again. 'Better than a mother. You have never failed us. We will try not to fail you now, but we may, and if we do I hope this makeshift knife is of some use. Let's pray for each other, and may God have mercy on us and none whatsoever on Piers de Scabious.'

He slipped the other home-made dagger into his own tunic and rejoiced when it pricked his skin.

In the dark, Old Nurse's tears flowed freely, spilling into and over the deep crevices that lined her face. But she never allowed her voice to waver. 'No time to waste, dearies,' she muttered. 'Away with you.'

Before they could move, however, through the tiny grille came the sound of terrible rowing and the sudden violent scream of a man in pain. The scream was followed by the scrape of feet and the crack of whip against skin.

'There, and there, and there!' The prisoners could hear the serjeant's voice as he worked himself up into a towering rage. 'You traitorous dog! A whipping is too good for you.'

Outside the cellar, there was a scrabbling noise. Will, Ellie and Old Nurse flattened themselves against the far wall as a key was turned and the door flew open. In an instant, Old Nurse was standing in front of the tunnel entrance, her bulk easily hiding it and her skirts covering the disturbed stones.

A moment later, Gethin landed face down in the dirt at her feet. He bunched himself into a ball, tensing for another whip sting. It never arrived, for the serjeant had finished with him and was looking for someone else. Ah!

189

There she was. Knocking Will to one side, he grabbed Ellie. She struggled wildly as she was swept towards the door, and the serjeant swore and clutched her hair. He missed and instead caught the green jasper necklace, breaking the clasp. The circlet of stones tumbled to the ground and, in a moment, Ellie found herself once again in the daylight, with the cellar door banged behind her.

The serjeant's mouth was so close to her ear that the grease on his breath crackled. 'I found Gethin stealing the spare key,' he said, the malice in his voice matched only by the malice in his eyes. 'Luckily, I caught him just in time! Gethin!' he shouted. 'Your punishment is that you can starve in there with a powerless earl and a fat old woman. Mind you, she's so padded with lard, I'll bet she is the last to die. But that doesn't matter since nobody is ever going to open that door again.'

Ellie clawed and scratched at the serjeant's face. Her fury gave her such strength that she managed to rake his forehead with her nails before he wrenched her arms behind her and secured them with a rope. Then, seething and smarting, he marched her over to the well, dangled the key in her face for a few moments and dropped it in.

From the top of the steps, the constable was watching. All this was the fault of that wretched horse! If only he had not been obliged to get rid of it, he flattered himself, he might have won Ellie round as soon as it was obvious that the de Granvilles were finished. No girl, at least no girl in the constable's acquaintance, had ever given up social advancement for something as ephemeral as love. But that horse. That damnable horse. De Scabious wished he *had* had Hosanna butchered, for all the trouble he was causing. He made no move to prevent his bride's arms being bound for she would have to learn who was master now. Nevertheless, when the soldiers began to taunt her, he hid behind the hall door.

'Tell the serjeant to lock her upstairs in a room with no windows,' he said to one of the serving girls who was watching, agog, all that was going on. 'She'll soon come to her senses.'

Will listened in helpless agony to Ellie's struggles as she was dragged away, but when he could hear nothing more, he fell on to his knees and scoured the ground until he found her necklace. He crushed it so hard against his hand that the stones bit into his palm then, with one stride, he reached Gethin, yanked him to his feet and shook him. His anger made him vicious. 'What were you doing that made them come and take Ellie away?' he menaced through gritted teeth.

Gethin tried to answer, but Will threw him backwards and he landed on Old Nurse. 'Master Will,' she begged, 'it will help nobody if you turn into a monster.' Her reproof hit home. When Will spoke to Gethin again, his tone, although curt, was more civil. 'You know what that man did to my horse?' he asked. 'What is he going to do with Ellie?'

Gethin stayed near Old Nurse. 'Earl William,' he said, searching for the right words, and hoping against hope to find them, 'I am not a brave man, but that horse, well, he deserved better. And as for your Miss Eleanor . . .' Gethin hesitated. How could he explain, without causing offence, why the thought of her skeleton lying in a stinking cellar was too much for him? 'The second key was in the stable,' he said finally. 'I thought maybe the constable had forgotten. He has never used it. But he hadn't forgotten and the serjeant came in when I had it in my hand. I don't even know what I was going to do with it.' With that, his flow came to an end and a dull, repetitive thud told him that Will was beating his knuckles against the wall.

Old Nurse felt her way over. 'Now, Master Will,' she said. 'Come on, dearie. Don't rage. Think. The time for rage will be later. Don't let that man get his hands on my Ellie. Off with you. Get up that tunnel and get her out of here.'

Will heard her, but his mind leapt from one dreadful image involving Ellie to another involving Old Nurse. 'Do you know what they might do to you if I manage to spirit Ellie away, Old Nurse? Do you?' he demanded.

'Ssssssh! Quiet!' Old Nurse exclaimed, shivering only slightly. 'Now, get away with you, Master William. We've been through all this. I'll survive. You see if I don't.' She hugged him, then urged him on. Will turned to Gethin. 'Are you with me? Because if you are not, I'll have to kill you.'

It took Gethin no time to choose. 'With you,' he said, and an excitement entirely new to him coursed through his veins. 'I'm with you. But I've never heard of any tunnel.'

'No need to hear any more,' Will replied. 'Just bend down and follow me.' A minute later, both men had disappeared.

Old Nurse sat heavily and allowed the dark to close in on her. It would take her some time to die, but she was a patient woman, used to waiting. She fingered the knife that Will had given her. If her suffering became intolerable, she knew what to do with it.

14

Gavin travelled to the tower with twenty men and five carts of siege machinery. Marie's prayers and Marissa's exhortations to hurry rang in his ears long after Hartslove was lost to sight. Alan was left behind to finish the work on the castle's defences. Gavin had chosen to ride Dargent, who was a little bruised after his tumble down the drawbridge, but willing nevertheless.

Hosanna strode out strongly for Kamil, occasionally tossing his head to shake the last of the water from his ears. Despite Marissa's best attempts, a few bedraggled weeds still clung to his mane and Kamil pulled them out as they went along. Some of the time, the young Saracen daydreamed that he was not in England but somewhere far away with just Hosanna and a hawk for company. It might be possible. Will could die. But even as Kamil hoped, his conscience was uneasy. It was wrong to wish a man dead so that you could have his horse. If Hosanna was his at the end of this venture, he must be won honourably. Will could not die for lack of any action on Kamil's part, for that could never be forgiven. He glanced over at Gavin. With Richard's seal at his belt, it was clear that the Count of Hartslove did not need to dream. In his mind's eye, de Scabious was already finished and, what was more, he seemed certain that when confronted with proof that Richard lived, John would not want to jeopardize his own future for a fat constable and a girl he barely knew.

With each day of the journey, Kamil's face grew more gaunt while Gavin's lost its haggard sheen and filled out. His eyes were bright – almost too bright. There was no tremor in his left hand and when challenges were issued by those intent on blocking their way, he drew his sword cleanly and held it steadily. 'I feel as if I've been living in hell,' he told Kamil, 'and can only now see my way out.'

They pressed on fast. In every settlement they passed through, Gavin made sure to show Richard's seal and announce that the king was alive and would return. There was not universal rejoicing. Some who had suffered from Richard's obsession with holy war jeered, but for the most part, although nobody volunteered to join Gavin's meagre forces, the villagers felt happier after hearing the news.

However, as the cavalcade got further north, people began to stare at Kamil and one morning, small boys threw stones at him, calling out, 'Saracen-man, Saracen-man,' and other words that their mothers forbade them to use at home. Kamil did not respond, except when a pebble hit Hosanna's rump. The horse grunted and Kamil's sword was out in a second. It was enough. The boys vanished.

When, five days later, the evening of de Scabious's return home, they reached the final split in the road to Hangem, Gavin stopped. 'The tower must be at the end of the track leading up to the left,' he said. 'This right-hand one looks as though it leads to the village. We'll go there first. If we show Richard's seal, the villagers may be willing to help us.'

The horses picked their way down to the valley floor. As they passed the gibbet, Gavin's heart lurched. The corpses, now stinking, were unrecognizable, but they had clearly hung too long to be Will. Gavin ordered them cut down. 'The constable has made his point – whatever it was,' he said. 'It is enough.'

As he rode among the houses, anxious faces peered out and doors were barred. He halted at the foundations of the church and Kamil dismounted to stand by his side. 'Go round and tell them we come in peace,' Gavin ordered one of his knights. 'Tell them that when he returns, Richard will hear their grievances.' He dismounted himself. Although nobody appeared, he sensed a tinderbox atmosphere. It would take more than a seal and the cutting down of some corpses to gain the villagers' trust.

When ten minutes had passed, Kamil grew impatient. Spying a woman trudging down the path, half buried under a huge bundle, he leapt back on to Hosanna and was after her. The woman dropped the bundle and began to run away, but Kamil was too quick and used the horse to push her towards Gavin. She looked both terrified and mutinous, but before Gavin could reassure her, a small tornado shot out from behind a sheep hurdle and began to hammer at his ribs. 'Get off my mother!' the boy shouted.

'Elric! Oh, please don't hurt him!' Morwenna pleaded, trying to grab her son, but Elric pushed her away, utterly humiliated by her intervention. He wriggled round and the first thing he saw was Hosanna. His jaw dropped.

'It's the –' he began, but Morwenna stopped his mouth. It was not safe to say anything.

'You have seen this horse before, I think,' Gavin said, following Elric's eyes.

'Never,' Elric replied at once, but his face betrayed him.

'What is your name?'

'What does it matter to you?' Morwenna interrupted quickly.

A group of villagers now cautiously began to gather. Gavin waited until a good number stood in front of him, then addressed them. 'We come with good news,' he said. 'King Richard is alive and will return. Constable de Scabious is a traitor. But we are not come to shed blood. We are come to free his prisoners, one of whom is my brother and the other my betrothed wife. We have no quarrel with you. We have simply come to take them home.'

The villagers muttered among themselves. Morwenna looked round and Elric took advantage of the moment to make his escape. 'Elric!' Morwenna cried. But he took no notice. Instead, he shyly approached Hosanna, who leant down and his forelock tickled Elric's nose. The boy laughed and the villagers inched forward. They stared and pointed at Kamil, who glared at them and then drew his sword as Peter rushed forward brandishing a hoe. He had seen Gavin arrive and had run in from the fields, fearful for his wife and son.

'No, Peter!' cried Morwenna, conscious that Kamil could kill Elric in seconds. 'That weapon is no use. Please.'

Peter frowned at her.

'Is this your boy?' asked Gavin.

Peter spat. 'He is my son,' he said. 'And if you hurt him, Constable de Scabious and King John will have something to say. Come here, Elric.'

Elric did not move.

'Constable de Scabious will have nothing to say in future,' said Gavin, remaining determinedly polite. 'You have not heard. King Richard is not dead and John's writ does not run here, so we have come to take the tower and release its prisoners. Will you help us?'

'Help you?' scoffed Peter. He moved to stand beside Morwenna and turned to the villagers, raising his voice. 'We should do nothing to help these people,' he declared.

'But he has shown us King Richard's seal,' a man at the back shouted. 'He's telling the truth about that at least.'

'A seal can be forged,' Peter replied. He looked round. 'Where did he get it, do you think?'

'It was brought from Richard himself by this man.' Gavin pointed to Kamil.

'A foreigner.' Peter spat again.

Morwenna took his arm. 'Don't make them angry,' she begged. 'One of those prisoners gave himself up to save Elric's life. Have you forgotten?'

Peter shook her off. 'Elric's life would never have been in danger if those men had not come here in the first place.' He stood four-square in front of Gavin. 'We will not help you. Just leave us alone.'

'Give us food and firewood, then,' said Gavin, 'and we won't trouble you further. Now, we must waste no more time. We go in the name of God and the king.'

'God and the king,' the Hartslove men echoed.

Kamil felt small hands tugging at his boot. 'Can I go with you?' begged Elric.

197

His father's heavy arm crashed on to his shoulder. 'You're going nowhere,' Peter said. 'Now get away from us.' He shook his hoe at Kamil, who shrugged and cantered off.

The Hartslove knights met the baggage train as they climbed the approach to the tower. Gavin ordered the animal lines to be drawn up out of sight of de Scabious's archers and the grooms to stay with them at all times. It would not do to lose the warhorses, for there seemed little possibility of finding replacements locally. Then he ordered camp to be pitched, cleverly using the slant of the hill to disguise how few men he had.

That night, as he and his knights settled down to plan, Kamil slipped off and sat with Hosanna. He watched the red horse for a long time, mulling over his bargain before finally finding some blankets and snatching a few hours' sleep.

Oblivious of all this activity, Will and Gethin were climbing to the tapestry room. Will felt utterly finished. He had lost Hosanna. He had left Old Nurse to face her death alone and there was no guarantee that he would rescue Ellie. As he felt his way along the slimy walls, almost gagging on the rotten air, he felt a dreadful sense of responsibility for their predicament, as if some wrong turning had been taken early on, and this, rather than anything de Scabious had done, had precipitated the collapse of his world. His thoughts were very bleak. Maybe he was being asked to pay for the sins of previous de Granvilles. Or maybe, and here Will faltered in his stride, maybe it was his own jealousy over Gavin and Ellie that had turned God's thoughts to punishment. He climbed faster. 'I'll hate You forever if You punish Ellie for my sins,' he said aloud, then jumped at the echo of his voice. How petty he sounded. He was glad when he could see the filter of light through the tapestry and stopped to whisper to Gethin to take care of the dust.

'No more talking, now, not even whispering unless what you have to say can't wait.' They crouched down, trying to make out whether the tapestry room was empty. It was not. De Scabious appeared occasionally, but soldiers milled about all the time and even settled themselves down to sleep in shifts. There was no opportunity for Will and Gethin to try to get to the door. Frustrated, they watched and waited. As the hours wore on, grief spread its deadening blanket over Will and he found it harder to concentrate. The night slouched past and, long after it had become day, Will was startled by Gethin tapping his shoulder.

'Somebody behind us,' he mouthed. His breathing was shallow with fear for he had heard many stories about demons. But this demon turned out to be tiny and, as Gethin seized it, it squeaked.

Will was exasperated. 'Elric! Go back. It's too dangerous for you here.'

'But –'

'Ssssssh!'

Will pulled the boy a short way down the tunnel, almost tripping over a sack. Elric was not pleased to find Gethin with Will, for he did not want to share him. For a moment he wanted to sulk, but his news was so momentous that he couldn't.

'Yesterday afternoon,' he whispered, the words tumbling out, 'men came to our village. I would have come before, but after they left, my da locked me in the house. He doesn't trust me any more. Anyway, when the men came to the village, one said he was your brother and said that King Richard was alive. Oh! And I don't know how, but another is riding your horse.'

'My horse?' Will said sharply, trying to take in all that Elric was saying. 'And the Hartslove knights? Oh, thank God for them, at least. Now, maybe, there is hope. But, Elric, you are mistaken about Hosanna. He is dead. De Scabious had him . . .' His voice, to his shame, trembled a little. 'The constable had him butchered.'

'He can't have,' said Elric cheerful now that he had Will's undivided attention. 'I saw him.'

'Did you hear somebody call his name?'

'Well, no,' Elric admitted. 'But it was him. Do you think I'm stupid?'

He suddenly found his head almost ground into the dirt. Will's fist was unforgiving. 'Don't say it was Hosanna. It can't have been.'

But Elric was unrepentant. 'It was,' he insisted, rubbing his face. 'Don't you want him to be alive?'

'Look,' said Will, 'if it really was Hosanna, my brother Gavin would be riding him. Or my squire, Hal, who you met. Was it either of them?'

'No,' said Elric, frightened now, but determined not to give in, 'it was somebody else. I don't know who. He looked funny. Then your brother brought all his men up here. They've got siege machines and everything and they're going to rescue you. I followed them and I saw your horse again, only he was grazing at the back. He let me touch his star.'

Will dropped Elric and put both hands on the wall to steady himself. It could be true, what the boy said. The constable could have been lying. Will shut his eyes. He wanted, above everything, to believe that Hosanna was alive, but he would not allow himself to forget that Elric had only seen Hosanna once before.

The boy waited impatiently. Will's doubts seemed ridiculous. And anyway, he had something else important to say. 'I didn't come just to tell you about your horse and the knights. Here.' He felt for the sack.

Gethin felt inside the coarse cloth. 'Swords,' he said to Will with delight. 'Two sharp swords.'

'I stole them,' said Elric, thoroughly pleased with himself.

'Where from?' asked Gethin.

'From the knights outside the tower.'

Will rocked backwards, nonplussed. 'You stole these swords from the Hartslove knights?'

'They seemed to have plenty, but I knew they wouldn't give me any if I asked,' said Elric defensively. 'And your horse helped me. He was eating near one of the wagons. I slid underneath his stomach. Then he walked to the end of his tethering rope and I hid right behind him until I could get away without anybody seeing me.'

Will felt a weight lift from his heart. He would not yet allow himself to rejoice, but he could see it all, the horse grazing, seeming to do nothing but doing so much. Maybe the boy was telling the truth.

'I know two swords are not going to be much good against all the constable's soldiers,' Elric held one up for Will, deeply resenting the fact that Gethin was holding the sword he had thought to wield himself. 'But it was the best I could do.'

'They are more than we could have hoped for,' said Will. 'And anyway, with Gavin outside the tower, there will be plenty more swords on our side.' He ran his finger over the flat blade and his confidence began to return.

'If only my da would tell everybody in the village to help,' sighed Elric. 'He's not a bad man. It's just that he is frightened of being on the wrong side.'

'I know,' said Will. 'But never mind about the village, Elric. Will you do something else for me? Go to my brother and tell him about the tunnel. He could send men up to meet me and Gethin. Attacking from two sides would give us double the chance of success. You could show them the way. Would you do that?'

'Why would they believe me? They would think it a trap.' Elric sounded uncertain.

'Not if you give my brother this,' Will answered, and feeling about in his tunic, he brought out the necklace of green jasper and pressed it into Elric's hand.

The boy peered down. 'It's just a girl's trinket,' he said disdainfully.

'Take it,' said Will.

Elric slipped it into his pouch. 'I'll be as quick as I can.' He hesitated only for a second. 'My da will kill me if he finds out.'

Will caught his arm. 'I know,' he said, 'but Gethin and I must stay here in case de Scabious brings Ellie down. I'm sorry.'

Elric shook off Will's hand and was gone.

De Scabious had seen Gavin and his knights arrive outside the tower at sunset but, still recovering from the turmoil of his welcome, had chosen to ignore them. Hangem was well defended and could hold out for a long siege. Nevertheless he had gone to bed feeling uncomfortable. All this uncertainty was a strain. Sitting in the great hall the following morning, moodily pulling bits off a haunch of venison for his breakfast, he picked his teeth and suddenly decided to wait not a day longer. It was quite unnecessary, really, for John to witness his wedding and, after the event, what could anybody do? No, he would be married within the hour, using whatever means required to make Ellie say the words of consent, and then nobody, ever, would be able to deprive him of his new prestige. He was thankful he had had Ellie locked up in a room with no windows. She would have no idea that Gavin was outside the tower's walls.

He belched and wiped his mouth on his sleeve before practising his husbandly smile in the reflection of his tankard. The distortion was such that he even gave himself a fright. He slammed the tankard down as his serjeant hurried in to announce that Gavin had sent a message demanding Ellie's release.

The constable poured another drink. 'Come to reclaim the girl, has he? Well, he has taken his time, I must say.'

The serjeant sniggered.

De Scabious thought for a few minutes. 'Actually, we should invite the count in.' He showed his filthy teeth. 'That's it. We'll invite him in. After all, he can hardly refuse an invitation to see his lady-love without branding himself a coward, can he? And I'll have a little surprise for him. *He* can witness our wedding.'

'Shall I send for a priest?'

'Don't bother,' said the constable, and his cheeks went slightly pink. 'John's permission is all I need and I have that. He may turn up in time himself. But it doesn't matter. Eleanor will give her consent. I guarantee it.' The constable winked. 'Women, Serjeant,' he said, 'just need managing properly.'

'Shall I go and give Eleanor a little preliminary "management"?' asked the serjeant, flexing an arm muscle.

'Don't overstep the mark.' De Scabious's voice cranked up an octave. The serjeant turned off his smile and the constable lowered his voice again. 'Go and prepare the tapestry room,' he ordered. 'Make sure the fire is blazing and that sort of thing. It's just right for an intimate wedding. Then send two guards up to Eleanor's chamber and bring her down. No – on second thoughts, send four guards. And tell them that they are entirely responsible for her. If she harms herself, I'll have every soldier here hung and left for the ravens.'

The serjeant hurried off. Goodness, but the constable could be touchy.

De Scabious made his way out of the great hall and into the courtyard. The sound of a horse neighing and stamping irritated him. A young stable boy who was passing saw the constable heading for the stalls. 'It's that chestnut mare we caught instead of that stallion. She's really restless today. Gethin used to take her out, but he'll not be doing that any more,' the boy said, thinking to ingratiate himself. Instead, he found himself the object of uncomfortable scrutiny.

De Scabious rocked on his toes. 'Now then,' he said, 'do you want to be helpful to me?'

The boy looked sly, and nodded.

'Good,' said de Scabious. 'Go and get the horse and tie her in the corner near the cellar. Then bring out bundles of hay and pile them up against the cellar door – lots of them, until the door is covered, do you hear me?' He paused. 'It may be,' he continued, clasping and unclasping his hands, 'that later today I will give the order to set the hay on fire, so keep a lighted torch next to it. Do you understand?'

The boy's face lost its slyness. 'But that means –'

'But that means what?' asked the constable blandly. 'Come on. What?'

'Nothing,' said the boy, looking at the ground. 'I'll get a pitchfork.'

The constable watched until the hay pile began take shape. He would make sure Ellie saw it too. Then he sauntered over to the gates. They were quite thick enough. A few knights from Hartslove could never hope to breach them, even with a full-frontal attack. Nevertheless, he could not control a small nervous throbbing in his eyelid. 'That assassin will be well on his way by now,' he repeated to himself again and again. 'Gavin de Granville may have turned up here, but he has already lost.' Not wanting to expose his own head, he asked an archer to peer over the wall and recount what he could see.

'The enemy are heavily armed,' the archer called down, 'but they've only two very basic siege engines and not much cover. But I can't see how many of them there are, because some are out of sight below the hill. Will King John be coming to help us?'

'Very likely, but we may not need him,' said the constable, deliberately offhand. 'Now, I want you to go out and offer the one-armed Gavin de Granville an invitation to come inside. Don't be alarmed. He won't hurt you. We have too many hostages for that. I want you to tell him that I will allow him to come in and see Eleanor. You can also tell him that if he doesn't accept my invitation, I will make sure Eleanor knows it.'

The man came down from his perch and wrapped a piece of white cloth round a pole to wave as a sign of parley. 'Very good,' said de Scabious, and pushed him out.

*

Gavin was discussing where best to place the siege engines when they were warned of the man's approach.

'Which one of you is the count?' The archer was edgily cocky. 'It must be you.' He let his eyes rest provocatively on Gavin's empty sleeve. 'Constable de Scabious sends you an invitation to come in and see Miss Eleanor de Barre.'

Gavin heard the man out without changing his expression, but when he turned away, his eyes were shining. 'Of course I will go in,' he said to Kamil. 'When all the constable's supporters see Richard's seal and hear that John is no more king than I am, they will surely melt away or come to join us. That's the way of these people. Cowards attract cowards.'

'It's dangerous, though, sir,' said one of his knights, doubtfully. 'I mean, the constable may be a coward, but once he has got you in the tower, who knows what tricks he might play?'

'But I have the seal,' Gavin insisted.

'Well, yes,' said another, who thought that Gavin set rather too much store by a piece of wax. 'But de Scabious will declare it a forgery. You may have the seal, but you can't absolutely prove it is genuine.'

'No, but it will sow doubt, and maybe that is all that's needed,' said Gavin, unwilling to have any obstacles put in his way. 'After all, we just want to leave with Ellie, Will, Old Nurse and Sacramenta. Once we get them away, we can finish off the constable in our own time. But I think the seal should at least secure the release of the prisoners. Somebody might even be able to give us news of Hal. Alan heard that John now has him.'

Kamil stepped forward. 'If you go in, I'm coming in with you,' he said.

'No,' said Gavin. 'I think I should go on my own.'

'That would be foolish.'

'Somebody should go with you,' said the first knight. 'After all . . .' He did not dare mention Gavin's arm.

Kamil had no such compunction. 'You can only fight on one side,' he said. 'I'm coming.'

Gavin did not argue further, but went at once to fetch Dargent. In the horse-lines he found a commotion going on.

Elric, red in the face, was trying to dodge through mock defences that the knights had set up. Each time he was caught, he was made giddy, then let loose to try again. It was an amusing game. Gavin frowned, but as he went forward to remonstrate, something flew out of the boy's tunic, momentarily sparkled green in the sun, then disappeared into the grass. Gavin jumped. Running forward, he searched the ground until he found what he was looking for. There was no need of an examination. Filled with trepidation, he shouted at the knights to let the boy pass. Elric was panting and felt slightly sick.

'You must tell me where you got this.' Gavin threatened the boy with his hand.

'Your brother – Earl – William – Will – gave it to me.' Elric's world had not yet stopped turning.

'Why does he have it?'

'How should I know? He said it would make you trust me.' Elric's balance began to return.

'We saw you yesterday. Elric, isn't it?'

'It doesn't matter,' Elric said, uncomfortable at being the centre of attention. 'But I have a message for you from your brother. Do you want it or not?' He sounded more defiant than he felt.

'Tell me –'

But at that moment, Kamil appeared with Dargent. 'We must go,' he said.

Gavin mounted. 'Quickly,' he said to Elric, 'we have no more time. You say Will had a message?'

'I can get men into the tower without being seen,' said Elric a little sullenly, for he felt he was being treated like a child. 'If they follow me, your brother is waiting.'

Gavin hesitated. He looked at the necklace again, then slipped it down the front of his shirt. At the feel of it, his confidence grew. 'Do whatever this boy tells you.' He touched the bump the green jasper made. 'It's time to have faith again,' he said, allowing himself a slight smile. Behind his back, the knights shook their heads doubtfully, but Gavin had already gone.

He and Kamil cantered to the tower gate and silently endured a short but insulting speech from the gatekeeper. They were to go inside on foot. Gavin's lips were set as he dismounted and, despite the green jasper, a sudden nausea overcame him. Kamil fell into step behind him.

'Only the count,' the gatekeeper said.

Gavin recovered himself. 'Tell me,' he said, 'do you have a right arm?'

The man laughed scornfully. 'Of course.'

'Well,' said Gavin, 'you would never leave it behind, would you? This man is my right arm and I never leave *him* behind.' He pushed his way through and Kamil slipped in after him.

The courtyard was full of soldiers, and Gavin noticed the hayrick being secured in one corner, although it was too high for him to see Sacramenta, now tied behind it. The sun had vanished and a leaden pall descended as a few flakes of snow began to drift down, a final wintry flurry. It reminded Gavin of the weather on his wedding day. He was jostled up the steps into the hall and was very glad to feel Kamil at his side. Constable de Scabious was not there. And nor was Ellie. He began to feel some tightness in his chest and started violently when the serjeant approached from behind. He was grinning. 'The constable has told me to bid you welcome,' he said. 'I am to offer you a drink.'

Gavin dashed the proffered wine to the floor. 'Enough of this,' he said.

The serjeant clicked his tongue as if reproving a naughty child. 'Clumsy,' he murmured, and the soldiers began to laugh. Gavin ignored them. The serjeant was sorry not to get a rise. 'You don't seem quite dressed for a wedding,' he remarked. Surely this would do it. 'But then it isn't your wedding, so I suppose it doesn't matter. Have you bought the happy couple a gift?'

Gavin did not allow himself even to blink. He made himself think only of Richard's seal and Ellie. The constable and his odious sidekick would soon have their smugness punctured. At the door leading into the tapestry room, the serjeant halted, as if he had just remembered something. 'Oh yes. Your weapons,' he said. 'We will leave them at the door. That's customary at weddings, I think. I'll help you. Really, buckles are impossible with one hand, don't you find?' His grin was nearly splitting his face but Kamil pushed him out of the way and undid Gavin's sword belt himself, reluctantly handing over his own also. The serjeant placed them both with mock deference on the floor.

The soldiers had had no difficulty bringing Ellie down the steps into the tapestry room. She had neither fought nor screamed. It was as if she had retreated into herself. Her eyes were dead and she asked no questions. Occasionally she fingered the bare place on her neck where the green jasper should have been, but apart from that her movements were minimal.

De Scabious was waiting for her, bouncing on his heels. This was quite a moment in his life. Everything was ready. When Ellie appeared, he was wise enough not to approach her, but indicated only that she should stand on the side of the fireplace furthest from the door. Ellie did not acknowledge him and when he tried to address her, looked steadfastly into the flames. Even if Will was behind the tapestry, she did not see how he could rescue her now.

But Will was not behind the tapestry. Before Ellie had been brought before her bridegroom, a low grumble had echoed up from the bottom of the tunnel, and he and Gethin had rushed down to try to quell the noise. If he were to realize it was there, de Scabious could block the tunnel mouth in seconds. To Will's frantic frustration, in the cave where the tunnels met, they had found Peter and a dozen angry men armed with farm implements, determined to get into the castle, offer their services and claim a reward from a king they still determinedly believed to be John.

As Ellie faced de Scabious, Will and Gethin had their backs to the wall and were fighting fiercely and silently, trying to disarm the villagers rather than kill them, all the while knowing that their one opportunity to get to Ellie might be passing them by. The battle was very uneven for, despite their swords, the two young men were almost overcome by the sheer numbers.

Will had almost given up hope when, holding a lantern high above his head, Elric appeared, leading the Hartslove knights he had persuaded to follow him. Seldom had a sight been so welcome, but it still took too long before the villagers were overcome and secured.

When Gavin and Kamil entered the tapestry room, Ellie did not immediately see them. It was only when Gavin spoke her name that she looked up, and when she realized who was standing in front of her, she thought her heart was going to jump out of her chest.

'Gavin?' It came out in the smallest of whispers. 'Gavin?'

She stumbled, then flew to him. In a moment, she had her arms round his neck. He shut his eyes and for a second they were back at Hartslove, a young couple whose life together was just beginning. The illusion was shattered in a second.

'Very touching,' de Scabious remarked. 'Now, to business.'

Ellie did not notice Kamil until she and Gavin moved together towards the tapestry wall, and the constable himself gave Gavin's companion only a cursory inspection, never thinking for a moment that this could be the hooded man he had met at the quayside. Since both his guests were unarmed and he had dozens of men to call upon, the constable was not worried by his presence. Kamil took his place at Ellie's right side.

'How very convenient of you to turn up today, Master Gavin,' de Scabious began. 'Of course, if King John arrives, your men outside will find themselves in trouble, but I expect you will be gone long before then.' He waited, obviously expecting a reply of some sort, but

Gavin said nothing. De Scabious began to feel a little nervous. He told himself this was ridiculous, since he held all the trump cards. Nevertheless, Gavin did not look like a man about to lose everything.

Ellie felt a shiver of draught on her neck as the tapestry shifted.

'Now,' said de Scabious, 'we did not meet last under the most propitious circumstances, but bygones should be bygones. I am depending on you to get Miss Eleanor to see where her best interests lie. I imagine you know what her best interests are, because you have given yourself quite some time –' the constable tittered, and the serjeant followed his lead – 'to think about them. But I assume you have come here at last because you now fully understand and appreciate that with our new king we find ourselves in a new situation?'

'You can assume nothing,' said Gavin.

'Oh, I think we can,' said de Scabious, rocking. 'The new king –'

'There is no new king.'

'Oh, Master Gavin, not the same old games.'

'I would rather die than play games with you.'

De Scabious's tongue protruded a little. 'Richard is dead,' he said.

Gavin reached for his pouch, which he had made sure to fasten so that he could draw out Richard's seal without help. The constable looked at it stupidly.

'It's Richard's seal,' said Gavin helpfully. 'It comes as proof that he is alive and will shortly be back.'

Ellie held her breath, and in the silence that followed the seal swung gently. The draught from the tapestry was now quite strong, although everything was deathly quiet. Kamil sensed something and Ellie saw the muscles

212

in his face flex. She pressed his arm, warning him not to turn round.

The constable's normally florid face was blotchy. 'So,' he said, 'it's a forgery.'

Gavin raised his eyebrows. 'Can you take that chance?'

De Scabious booted the dogs to one side. 'I don't believe that Richard is alive,' he said, but his stomach felt as if a toad were sitting in it. If only he could boast of the assassin! But even de Scabious knew better than that.

'That is your choice,' said Gavin. 'But it is not a wise choice. Now, let Eleanor, my brother and Old Nurse go. They are of no use to you now, and Richard may be lenient if you send them home without blood being shed. Admit defeat, de Scabious.'

'Never,' the constable shook his head. 'I believe in King John and I will marry that girl.' His voice became as sinister as a snake's. 'And she will agree. I have only to do this –' he snapped his fingers – 'and that stack of hay in the courtyard will go up in flames. Do you know what is behind it, clever Master Gavin? Do you know? Your brother, that fat old woman and – this would especially upset Miss Eleanor – that noisy mare she is so fond of!' The constable was almost dancing. 'Yes! In minutes they will be dead.' He saw Gavin glance at the serjeant's belt and his delight increased. 'The key to their prison is not there!' he purred. 'It is at the bottom of the well.' His purr turned into a snarl. 'Once that hay is alight, nothing will save them.' He crossed his arms. 'Now, Miss Eleanor. You will agree to marry me in front of witnesses. Then we will go upstairs for a little, hmmm, consummation. Then, and only then, might I let Master William and the fat old harridan go wherever they want.

To hell for all I care. It's up to you, Miss Eleanor, entirely up to you.' He held up his hand, his fingers ready. 'Serjeant!'

'Constable?'

'If I snap my fingers, you know what to do?'

'The torches are already lit.'

The soldiers guarding the door drew their swords. The constable smirked. 'Not so clear now, eh, Gavin? Here we are, Miss Eleanor. Come forward at once and make your promises.'

Before Gavin could prevent her, Ellie did step forward. The draught from behind the tapestry drove her on. Surely this was the moment. She seemed to give the constable her hand and his eyes flashed with triumph. Then, using the whole weight of her body, she slapped him across the face. Her blow was so hard and unexpected that he listed heavily sideways, tripped over a chair and fell head first on to the stone hearth, arms akimbo. There was an electrifying split second before, with a mutter that quickly turned into a roar, he heaved himself on to his knees, salty tears springing to his eyes.

Ellie retreated with her head held high. *Now, Will, now*, she prayed. *If you are there, come now*. But nobody came. Instead she had to watch the constable spitting out the blood from his split lip while loosing a cascade of abuse. He began to rise. Ellie began to shake. Where, oh where, was Will? Surely she was not mistaken. He must be behind the tapestry. She must play for more time. With Gavin and Kamil on either side, she addressed her would-be husband, enunciating each word with perfect, chilling clarity and trying to keep his eyes fixed on her.

'Never, never will I marry you, whatever threats you utter and whatever tricks you use. You can kill me.

214

You can do anything. We may all die, but at least we will not be dishonoured. I am not frightened of you, de Scabious. There are worse things than death, and being married to you would be one of them.'

The constable's voice veered wildly upwards. 'Worse things than death, eh?' he screeched, wiping the blood from his chin. 'I'll show you worse. Fire the hay! Fire the hay and burn the fat lardy woman! And burn that mare too. You, by the door, can you not hear? Fire the hay!' The soldier vanished. De Scabious bared his gums like a cornered rat. 'Destroy me, would you, you witch?' he snarled. 'Not a chance. The future belongs to men like me. You and your kind are finished.'

Quite beside himself, he yanked his sword out of its scabbard and thrust it straight at Ellie's heart. Gavin moved quicker than Kamil. In a moment, he span round to use his body as a protective shield. But the weight of de Scabious's lunge cut straight through his mail coat and when the constable triumphantly withdrew his sword, it was covered in blood right up to the hilt.

For a moment, everything seemed to happen in slow motion. Ellie cried out and caught Gavin as he fell to his knees, and they sank to the floor together.

'Ellie,' he whispered, clutching her arm.

His blood soaked into her dress and on to her skin as she rocked him to and fro. Her agony was acute. Will had not come! All was lost. She hugged Gavin to herself and cried his name again and again. He put up his hand to comfort her and it lingered for a second on her neck.

'I have your green jasper,' he breathed, and put his hand on his breast. 'It's here. But Ellie,' he struggled a little and she held him tighter, 'you have kept faith better than I have. And Will too.' A shadow crossed his face. His breath was not coming easily now. Ellie moaned, but Gavin's eyes were clear although his chest was rattling. 'Look at me, Ellie.' He caught her hand and held it to his lips. 'I have always loved you,' he said simply. 'I am glad I can be worthy of you at the end.'

She tried to reply but her voice was only a sob. As she bent down to kiss his lips, he smiled at her, not just with his eyes, but with his whole self, then gave a small sigh and died.

Chaos broke out. De Scabious, half astounded at what he had done, was galvanized into action only when he found Kamil's mouth an inch away from his ear. He blinked. There was something familiar about this man. Kamil said only one word – 'Hosanna!' – and de Scabious erupted.

'You foreign dog,' he howled. 'We made a bargain. You're a traitor. I'll get you for this, you devil,' and he raised his sword.

But before he could bring it down, there was a tremendous ripping sound and the constable reeled backwards as, at last, the tapestry exploded in a monstrous, billowing cloud of heavy yellow dust. Huge and greedy, the dust, like a great, gritty tidal wave, swelled and swallowed everything up, all but blotting out the flames of the fire. In the thick and eerie darkness that followed, all that could be heard was the tight, strangled rasp of people and dogs choking to death. De Scabious, clutching his throat, scrambled and clawed his way to the open door, pushing his gagging and disorientated serjeant straight at Kamil, who chopped his neck with one sharp, killing blow and deftly caught his sword as it flew out of his hand.

Ellie crouched underneath Gavin. His slumped body

protected her and she shut her eyes, only opening them once the dust began to settle. Twisting her head, she saw an extraordinary sight. It was as if the tapestry had come to life. Dozens of ghostly figures were leaping silently through its gaping maw like giant moths, their faces roughly shrouded in strips of cloth. Ellie closed her eyes again. Will was here now, and others besides, but they had come too late. The thought was torture, and Ellie could feel no relief as she stroked Gavin's dead face and clung to his battered body. She could not see how she would ever let it go.

Spluttering and wheezing, their swords falling from their hands, de Scabious's men were petrified. Their masked enemies seemed to have appeared from nowhere, as if born out of the dust itself. Even the air had turned against them, coating their lungs and caking their lips. The more superstitious had only one explanation.

'It's the king. Richard has come to avenge Gavin de Granville.'

Anything seemed possible. As the men tumbled back into the bigger hall, they found the constable goading them on from the safety of the small minstrels' gallery. Every time a Hangem knight surrendered, his venom shrilled forth. 'Fight, you useless bags of offal, fight!' he howled.

But his underlings grew uncertain as cries of 'King Richard! King Richard!' began to drown out the increasingly lonely retaliatory shrieks of 'King John! King John!'

Yet it was not until his own men begin to shake their swords at the minstrels' gallery instead of at their enemies that de Scabious realized with cold terror that he was losing control. Immediately, he turned to flee but it was already too late. The unmistakable sound of boots on the gallery steps sent him into rapid reverse. As the steps grew nearer, their aggressive intent undisguised, he did the only thing possible: he climbed on to the balustrade, sat for a moment, then tipped himself over. For a second his hands snatched at the rail as he hung in mid-air, a strange, insect figure, with skinny legs waving on either side of a bulging paunch. Then he dropped like a stone.

Kamil, who had also wrapped a cloth round his mouth and over whom the dust clung like a felt coat, broke de Scabious's fall. He angled his sword to spit the constable through, but thought better of it. Instead, he drew back and watched the wretched man clamber to his feet, only to be confronted by two of his own servants.

'Move,' the constable barked as his eyes darted hither and thither. The men remained side by side. De Scabious kicked their shins but they did not retreat, only pushed the constable backwards with the points of kitchen knives until he tripped. Sprawled over a body, his dignity outraged and his position ridiculous, he at last found some courage. Seizing the corpse's sword, he clambered to his feet, his head jerking back and forth in his characteristic turkeycock pose. 'Here,' he skipped, thrusting the sword to right and left. 'Here. Come on, then. But King John will get to know. Mark my words.' The servants drew back a little, but still they would not let the constable pass.

Will was fighting in the doorway. He had no idea what had happened in the tapestry room while he had been delayed in the tunnel, and as he finished off his enemy and saw the antics of the constable, he looked quickly around for his brother. There did seem to him to be something familiar about the man who broke the constable's fall, but before he could make his way over, Ellie suddenly appeared, wild-eyed and running and, forgetting everything else, he ran to meet her.

Lying huddled under Gavin's body, she had, at first, been too distraught to move, but something kept pricking the back of her mind, and when it finally pricked hard enough, she leapt up, horrified. Fire! The constable had ordered Old Nurse and Sacramenta to be burnt. Leaping up, she sped through the dust, hardly even seeing Will, who had forgotten that with a cloth mask and his hair incongruously decorated with frayed strands of faded tapestry wool, she would hardly recognize him. As he caught her arm, she fought him.

'Ellie, Ellie, it's me!' He tried not to hurt her and when she cried 'Fire!' he went pale under the dirt. They ran out of the hall together. At the top of the steps Ellie clutched the door frame with relief. Sacramenta was tied to a ring outside the armoury, and Gethin, who had pulled the burning bundles of hay away from the cellar, was busy breaking down the door.

Will led Ellie back into the hall, unbinding his mask.

The constable, still held at bay, could hardly believe his eyes or ears. 'You! You?' He glared with almost childlike incredulity at Will. 'How are you here?'

Wishing that Gavin would appear, Will wiped his face. 'You do not know this tower as well as you think,' he said. 'Now, the question is, what are we to do with you?'

The only defence left to the constable was bluster. 'John is due to arrive any time,' he declared. 'He will have an army, not just a few grubby knights. I should be careful, Master William. You may be master of this tower, but you are not master of the country.'

Will's reply was clear enough. 'Put the constable in

chains,' he ordered, 'and secure him outside. I want everybody to see that his rule here is at an end.'

Kamil, who kept his mask on, stepped forward to obey, and although Will stared, he still did not recognize him. When the constable would not willingly walk, Kamil dragged him out of the door, down the steps and into the courtyard. Finding a set of iron collars lying by the wall, he slipped them over de Scabious's neck and wrists and attached the chains to a ring set into the wall of the well. Then he hesitated for a few minutes, before slipping out through the now unguarded gate and down the hill to the horse lines.

Back in the hall, those soldiers now anxious to disassociate themselves with their former master began to help pile up the bodies with pathetic eagerness. Will moved to help but Ellie shook her head. 'First this,' she said, and her face was like stone.

The dust was no longer floating about the tapestry room, but had covered the walls and floor with a thick dull glaze. The slashed hanging flapped untidily over the tunnel mouth. In the mottled light, picking her way through the blood and grime, Ellie took Will to Gavin. The shock almost floored him. Ellie waited silently as he struggled with himself before she knelt, and, after a moment or two, he knelt heavily beside her.

At first he could do nothing but stare and stare, then, with infinite care, he got up, lifted his brother's body and laid it tenderly in front of the smouldering remains of the fire. A faint glow picked out Gavin's features. In death, his expression was almost radiant. His top lip curled slightly as if he were about to sit up and tease Will, as he had loved to do before disappointment, doubt and injury had cast shadows over both their lives and robbed their childish quarrels of their innocence. Will could no longer bear to look. All he could think was that their last days had been spent in acrimony and jealousy and that when his brother needed his protection he had failed him. He stood, unable to find even one word.

'He died for me, Will,' said Ellie, smoothing and smoothing Gavin's hair. 'And his face . . . I will never forget it. He seemed so happy. It was as if it were the one thing in the world he wanted to do. He looked just as he looked that afternoon when you came back from the crusade.' Her voice, which had been steady, began to waver. 'Just as he should have been able to look on our wedding day.' She was silent for a moment. 'He really loved me, Will,' she said at last, needing to hear herself say it. She looked up, but Will could not look down at her.

'And you loved him?' The words, when they came, were all wrong. Ellie crossed Gavin's arm over his heart and as she did so, she felt the green jasper necklace at his breast. Carefully she slipped her hand through the rents in his tunic and reclaimed it. Then she lifted his head on to her lap. 'Yes, I loved him,' she said simply, 'but I don't think he ever really knew it and perhaps *I* didn't really know it until now.'

Will would not have wanted Ellie to speak anything but the truth. Nevertheless, her words made him stagger a little. The brother with whom he had been through so much was dead. There would be no chance to make amends for all the harsh words now and Will could hardly bear this. But in death, Gavin was still proving a rival and Will found that his fists were clenched. The weight of conflicting feelings rapidly became insupportable and, with a mute gesture of apology, he bent down, touched Gavin lightly on the forehead and walked away. At the door, he turned to look at his brother one last time. Ellie was swaying to and fro, singing a song that Old Nurse had sung in the nursery. Her sweet, clear voice was bleak as a dying bird's, and Will listened until it threatened to overwhelm him, then headed out and into the courtyard. He must find Hosanna. Only in his horse was there a chance of comfort now.

It was already difficult to see clearly, for although the snow had given up, the clouds still hung low, blotting out the sun. Evening came early. The Hartslove men were making themselves at home, knowing they would be going nowhere tonight. Will breathed slowly, drawing the air right down into his clogged lungs. The constable was clanking his chains but Will hardly saw him. Old Nurse was now free and she sat, a mountain of tired flesh, on an untidy pile of the same hay that the constable had intended would form her funeral pyre. She was sharing ale and bread with Elric.

Will hurried over and Old Nurse tried to get to her feet. 'Ellie's safe, Old Nurse,' he said. 'She's with –' He stopped, not knowing if she knew already that Gavin was dead. He spread his hands.

'I do know, dearie,' the old lady said quietly. 'It is very hard to bear.' She turned away for a second. 'But this young man –' she turned back and pinched Elric's cheek, shaking her chins – 'reminds me of you and Gavin when you were both younger. He crawled along the tunnel to that terrible cellar and when the hay was lit, he started to pull away the stones to see if he could get me out in case it took too long to break through the door. Look at his hands!' She caught one and showed Will a set of bloody fingers. 'He could have been killed.'

Elric tried to pull away. This enormous woman who kept stroking him and calling him 'dearie' was embarrassing. He slipped out of her grasp as she drank some more ale and tugged at Will. 'Shall we go to the horses?' he asked. Will shrugged at Old Nurse and allowed himself to be pulled along. Elric chattered as he looked about for Kamil. 'Somebody has let my da and his friends out now,' he said. 'After your men tied them up, I don't think I can go home. He'll beat me senseless. Careful now!' They both slithered a little on the slushy ground. 'I wanted to follow you into the tapestry room, but I had no weapon.' The boy's voice still reflected his keen disappointment. 'But,' he added cheerfully, 'I went down the tunnel. It was all smoky but I found that Old Nurse. The constable wanted to roast her to death.' Elric stopped in his tracks. 'And I thought hanging was bad,' he said. He shook his head and began to look around the courtyard again. 'I can't see the foreign man, but perhaps that's just because it's getting dark. He must be here somewhere.'

Will was trying to listen but his head was already too full, and suddenly, a roar of shouting and stamping from the other side of the wall began to drown out the boy's chatter. One of de Scabious's soldiers rushed to Will. 'Shall I open the gates?' he asked nervously, anxious to please anybody who might turn out to be his master. 'I think the rest of your men want to come in.'

Will pushed Elric to one side for a moment. Desperate as he was to find out if Hosanna really was still alive, Gavin's death meant he must take charge. 'Climb up on to the top of the wall,' he ordered the soldier, 'and tell me what you can see.' The soldier, glad to impress, climbed quickly.

Elric crept back. 'I didn't make it up about your horse,' he said.

'I hope not,' said Will, straining to hear what the soldier was telling him, 'because if you did, I will find it hard to speak to you again.'

'There's banners,' came the voice from above. 'But it's difficult to make them out in this light. There are a lot of people. There are two standards flying. One is yours, I think, and the other – well – I can't make it out. There is no fighting, though. They must be friendly.'

'Come down,' Will called back, 'and throw open the gates.' He gestured to other soldiers milling around. 'Stick with me,' he said to Elric, 'or you'll get run down.'

A trumpet sounded outside and people gradually fell quiet, all except for de Scabious, who strained at his collar and used vocabulary rivalling that of Old Nurse. From her throne of hay, she was momentarily tempted to reply in kind, but Gavin's death dented her heart too much.

To Will's astonishment and relief, first through the gate, after the Hartslove standard bearer, was Hal. He was riding a scruffy pony and by his side was Prince John. When Hal pointed Will out, two expressions fought for dominance over John's face. One was arrogance and the other was shame. Will did not move, but Hal leapt off and took hold of the bridle of John's horse. The prince was going to speak. Before he could open his mouth, however, the constable's invective morphed into squeals of delight.

'I knew it, I knew it, I knew it!' He bobbed and bowed as his restraints allowed. 'The king is here. What did I tell all you traitors?'

But John seemed unimpressed by the constable's

ecstasies. He fiddled with his reins. 'I am glad to be here today,' he said, with a smile that deceived nobody, 'to bring you some good news. This squire –' he flicked his hand towards Hal in a gesture that he hoped was suitably judged as a polite but not subservient acknowledgement. 'This squire, who was disgracefully captured by thugs on the coast road, was eventually brought before me. And he turned out to be the bearer of good news. My brother, Richard, though a prisoner, is very much alive. The squire assures me that I will find the Count of Hartslove with Richard's seal and a quite unmistakable message that he is returning. Why Richard did not send the seal to me is a mystery, but that's brothers for you.' He gave a small grimace. 'I have since received a letter from the emperor in Germany. He now has my brother and is demanding a ransom.'

At this, there was a loud clanking noise as de Scabious collapsed. He was utterly betrayed, betrayed on every side. He tried to catch John's eye, but the prince would not look at him. 'Over the past few months,' John continued blandly, 'I have been badly misinformed. Terrible as it seems, there are people in the kingdom who wanted Richard to be dead and I set too much store by what they told me.' He glared round as if to identify the culprits and warmed to his theme. 'I have always wanted only what is best for this country,' he said, a tinge of bitterness colouring the edge of his words. 'I am not like my brother, Richard. I know this place. England cannot afford only to be milked dry for the crusade. We must make him realize that. But nor can the country afford to be ruined by civil wars. Our father, Henry of blessed memory, taught us that, for it was his life's work to create unity where there had been disunity. If I have been premature in claiming the throne of England, it has been only because I do not wish our father's legacy to fall into ruin. Believe me, that has been my only concern.' He dared somebody to challenge this but nobody did. 'If peace and unity is your concern too, we should, in this courtyard here and now, agree that each of us has acted as we felt best for the greater good over these last difficult months. There should be no recriminations from anybody against anybody else. If we are all agreed, we will go forward together and in peace.'

He tried to wrest his horse's rein from Hal, but Hal hung on for a moment yet. 'Oh yes,' said John, forcing himself to smile, 'and long live King Richard.' Hal let go.

However, John was not to escape so easily. Ellie was standing on the steps outside the great hall. The front of her dress was covered in blood, but though her face was dirty and her hair dishevelled, she held herself like an empress. The crowd parted to let her through. She walked slowly, stopped briefly to embrace Old Nurse, then stood right in front of John. He shrank before her unforgiving gaze.

'It is all very well to talk of unity,' she said, raising her voice so that everybody could hear, 'but Gavin de Granville, Count of Hartslove, a better man than most here –' she dared anybody to contradict – 'has died while you have been playing about with our loyalties. Not only that, but this man,' she pointed to de Scabious, 'has fired a castle and caused the death of a valuable horse.' Her voice wavered slightly but her bearing remained regal. 'I demand that Constable de Scabious remains under lock and key until the king decides what is to be done with him.'

'I am sorry to learn of the count's death,' said John,

flinching a little. Then he recovered himself. 'Perhaps the constable deserves death himself. Shall we hang him here and now?'

The girl gave the prince a look of utter disdain. 'A prince should dispense justice not lynchings,' she said. 'Particularly a prince with pretensions to kingship.'

Will held his breath. John, well known for sudden changes of mood, would surely not stand for that. But the prince looked uncharacteristically humble. He dismounted, approached Ellie on foot and took her hand. 'I am truly sorry about Gavin,' he said, and his sorrow was, to his surprise, genuine. 'Any part I played in causing his death I regret. He was a fine knight. I cannot bring him back, but, as the guardian of the realm while Richard is away, I can do one thing, of which I am sure both the Count of Hartslove and Richard would approve.' He led Ellie back up the steps. 'On behalf of my brother, King Richard,' he said, and his lips only twitched once as he said the king's name, 'I grant Eleanor Theodora de Barre permission to marry whomsoever she pleases and to bestow her estates as she chooses. She is nobody's ward, but her own mistress, and, also on King Richard's behalf, I grant the same privilege to any daughters she has.'

Ellie gave a wan smile. 'I am not ungrateful,' she said, 'it's just that it's a bit late.'

This was the last straw for de Scabious, who had clambered, as far as his shackles would allow, on to the wall of the well and was now precariously balanced as if he were a frog. Unable to help themselves, people began to laugh. The constable grew more and more agitated until, in the end, the inevitable happened. He lost his footing, teetered on the brink, and finally toppled clean into the well itself. Jerked up short by the chains on his neck and arms, he dangled above the drop, his face a nasty shade of purple.

With an alacrity that belied her age and condition, Old Nurse heaved herself to her feet. Summoning a man from the crowd, she pointed to some loose stones and bid him pick them up for her. Then she bent over the well until she was directly above the constable and, almost absent-mindedly, dropped the stones, one by one, so that they bounced from his head and into the echoing depths. It was a long wait before any faint splash, and the constable's skinny legs peddled furiously as tears of self-pity streamed down his cheeks. By the time he was hauled back from the abyss his pompous oaths were reduced to faint quaverings, and when John ordered Will to oversee the transfer of the prisoner into the cart that would transport him south for trial, the constable resembled nothing so much as a deflated pig's bladder.

Ellie did not watch her would-be husband's final humiliation. She busied herself arranging for Gavin's body to be laid on a trestle with due dignity. He would be buried at Hartslove, not here. Afterwards she made her way through the general melee until she reached the gate. It felt strange walking through it unchallenged. Men moved out of her way at once, in awe of this proud but melancholy figure who had shamed a prince and got away with it.

She walked down the hill and stumbled through the Hartslove tents, now largely deserted in favour of the Hangem courtyard, and at last allowed tears to blind her as much as the dusk. Careless of her footing, she tripped, and as she put out her hand to save herself, she dropped the broken green jasper necklace she had been clinging to since taking it from Gavin's tunic. It was impossible to judge where it had landed and her despair was so great she did not see the shadow in the dark until a voice in an accent Ellie had never heard before asked softly: 'This was between the horse's hooves. Is it what you are looking for?'

Two hands gently took hers and placed the necklace safely between them. The hands tried to withdraw but Ellie kept hold. 'Who are you?' she whispered, but she got no answer. Then, from above her head came a sigh. It was too rich to be human. Ellie let go of the hands and patted the ground with her fingers until she met a horse's leg. She followed the leg up, tracing its delicate veins, until she reached the slope of a shoulder. Light as gossamer, her fingers curved round, searching and searching for things she could not believe she would find. But there they were. Quite unmistakable. Two wounds that Ellie did not need to see to recognize. Now she was on her feet.

'Hosanna?' she whispered as her fingers stroked his scars over and over. 'Hosanna? Is it really you?' Her arms were round his neck and when she felt the answering vibrato from deep within his chest, she had her reply. Hosanna stood like a rock as Ellie buried herself against him and drowned her sobs in the shrouding warmth of his mane. Eventually, she raised her head and exclaimed quietly, 'Oh, I'm so selfish. I must find Will!' But she could not leave Hosanna just yet. She put up her hand to touch his white star and found the other hand there also. 'Please tell me who you are,' she begged.

'It doesn't matter who I am,' came the reply. 'Just take the red horse back to his master.'

Ellie caught her breath. 'I think I know who you are,' she whispered. 'If you call Hosanna the red horse, you must be the Saracen man that Will sometimes talks about. You are Kamil from the crusade.' Sudden understanding flooded her mind. 'The constable told us Hosanna was dead, but somehow he must have given him to you. You must have had him all this time. Oh, if only we had known! Now we must find Will. Oh please, quickly, it's so important, for he has been so unhappy.'

Kamil's voice was barely audible. 'I think that will not be necessary,' he said.

Ellie looked up, saw a light bobbing towards her and heard a piping voice bidding Will not to be such a doubting Thomas. She felt the green jasper in her palm and called out, 'Will! Will!'

'Ellie!' His voice was full of anxiety and longing.

'Here,' she cried. 'Come here. It's all right. Hosanna –'

But her voice was no match for Elric's. 'I told you, I told you,' he sang out, and suddenly they were there, Elric holding up the light, Will speechless and Hosanna whickering his greeting over and over again.

In the flurry of arms, exclamations and questions, it was Hosanna who alerted them to the fact that Kamil was loping away into the night. Will grabbed the torch and ran after him. 'Kamil,' he called. 'Kamil, don't go!'

Kamil stopped. 'I have done my duty,' he said to Will. 'Now it is time to return to my own land. I cannot stay any longer.'

But Will would have none of it. 'You must stay,' he said. 'I don't know how you came here. I know Elric said – but in all the commotion I didn't – and Gavin never had time – and Elric just dragged me out here before –' Will knew he was gabbling, but at least Kamil was still standing there.

He looked at Will. 'You don't know,' he said quietly.

'I am your enemy. I wanted to ride the red horse away this evening. I wanted to break my promise to the girl Marissa.'

'You met Marissa?'

'It is a long story,' said Kamil. 'And I don't know it all. But yes, I met Marissa. You will find out that she saved the red horse's life when I could not, and that I only agreed to come here with your brother because if you died, I could take the red horse away. But your brother died and not you. Nonetheless, I thought maybe –' Kamil's voice tailed off.

'But you couldn't take Hosanna because it didn't seem right?' Will hardly needed to say it. 'That is what Hosanna does to us, Kamil. I don't understand it, perhaps nobody does, but I do understand one thing, that different as we are, enemies even sometimes, you feel the same as I do when Hosanna is near.' He tentatively touched Kamil's arm. 'Please come back with us to Hartslove,' he said. 'I must bury my brother and I would like you to be there.'

'I can't,' said Kamil. 'Hosanna may unite us in some things, but I am still not your friend.'

'You are tonight,' said Will. He could feel Kamil's reluctance as if it were a physical thing. He waited patiently. 'I owe you something for your bravery today, Kamil. In the name of honour, not sentiment, and in the name of Hosanna, I ask you to come home with me.' Kamil bent his head. 'There is a place at the hearth for you at Hartslove,' Will said gently, and walked back to the tents. He could do no more.

Kamil heard the words and when he looked up, by the light of the torch, Hosanna's star shone like a homing beacon.

15

After a night spent mourning the gallantry of the Hartslove dead and celebrating the stories of the living, Prince John and Will made an uneasy peace. They agreed to meet in a fortnight to discuss the collection of Richard's ransom. It would be a huge undertaking but John could do little except appear keen to get started. 'Once it is collected, I will supervise the delivery of it myself,' Will told him, and John made suitably grateful noises before gathering his forces together and leaving. Will and Hal watched him go.

'I think he will do his duty,' Hal said rather unexpectedly. His expression, like Will's, was graver than it had once been and he was reluctant to tell anybody all that had happened to him while in the clutches of the mercenaries. 'They treated me badly,' he said, and a spasm crossed his face. 'But the day I was brought before John as a lying traitor because I said Richard was alive, the letter from the emperor arrived. It was strange. John didn't seem angry. It was almost as if he were expecting it. He's an odd man, whose ambitions test his loyalties. I dread to think what will happen if he ever does become king.'

Will shook his head. 'If he saved you from death at the

hands of those thugs, I at least owe him something,' he replied. 'Now, Hal, send for the Hangem villagers. We'd better make things right with them.'

Most of the villagers appeared, however reluctantly, and their number included a scowling Peter the cowherd. From now on, Will told them, the village of Hangem was to be renamed Granville and would be under the protection of himself as Earl of Ravensgarth, at least until King Richard returned. The villagers did not cheer – one master was much like another in their experience – but when soldiers were sent to chop all the gibbets into firewood they began to look a little more optimistic. The earl, they muttered to each other, seemed more decent than most, although you could never really tell.

Will made no further speeches. He asked only that they should continue to build their church and pray for those who had perished. As the villagers dispersed, he drew Peter to one side and asked if Elric might come to work as a squire in his household. The offer was a good one, and Peter was lucky not to meet the same fate as the constable, but the man was surly. He had seen too many knights come and go to have much faith in any of them. Moreover, when Elric was far away, drinking fine wine and eating rich food with Will, would he remember his parents, eking out a subsistence living from the stony soil? He shuffled his feet.

Will tried to be good-natured. 'Elric has proven himself to be both courageous and steadfast,' he said. 'England needs him – I need him. We have freed the prisoners here, but King Richard is still captive and we will live in dangerous times until we can ransom him home. Since my brother is dead –' Will's jaw tightened – 'I shall be basing my household at Hartslove in future rather than in my lands to the west. There will, of course, be generous rewards for those Hartslove squires and knights who fulfil their service to me with loyalty.'

His earnest, honest gaze made it hard for Peter to carry on scowling. Nevertheless, he was not going to give in easily. 'The boy didn't show much loyalty to me,' he muttered, and Will saw from whom Elric had inherited his occasional obstinacy.

'He was loyal where he felt loyalty was due,' he responded. Then he changed tack. 'Do you love your son, Peter?' he asked.

'Of course.'

'Then tell him to come with me.'

But it was not Peter who answered, it was Morwenna. She had come up to the tower, for laundry always has to be done. 'We must let him go, Peter,' she said, looking nervously at her husband.

Peter growled at her. 'You weren't so keen when we talked of sending him to the constable.'

Morwenna smiled and once again looked a little like the girl Peter had married. 'Look at the bonfire where the gibbet once stood,' she said, 'and tell me he will not be better off with this man here.'

Peter growled some more, but it was clear that the matter was settled.

The tower was not difficult to secure and Will wisely left a garrison of soldiers, for there were understandable tensions between the Hartslove knights and those who had been in the constable's pay. But he himself could not wait. He needed to go home.

It was a sad procession that wound down the track. In the first wagon sat Old Nurse, singing psalms and occasional nursery rhymes, her sea-deep voice intoning the ancient melodies to the steady shuffle of the horses' hooves. The villages through which the procession passed, when asked for hospitality, gave it gladly, but there was no dallying. Although news of King Richard was spreading, danger still hovered. John may have been caught out and the constable taken prisoner, but the prince still harboured ambitions and de Scabious was not the only villain in England. Until Richard returned, nothing was certain. From the corner of his eye, Will watched Kamil on Sacramenta and Ellie steadying Gavin's coffin over the bumps. He himself could barely look at the wooden box. The wounding words he had tossed so carelessly over his shoulder as the smoke rose above Hartslove's keep beat in his head and drove a deep furrow down between his eyes. Years later, the furrow was still there and Will never forgot why.

Ellie had not shrunk from overseeing the process of embalming, although it was the first time such a thing had been asked of her, and just before the coffin lid was nailed down, she had slipped into Gavin's hand the little wooden dog he had given her years before. 'For company,' she had whispered. The thought of the dog, nestling in Gavin's folded fingers, comforted her. She too watched Kamil, and noted how well he and the mare suited each other.

Will had offered Hosanna for the ride back to Hartslove, but Kamil had turned the offer down. 'It's better I don't,' he had said shortly, without rancour but not without effort. Ellie could see that although he knew in his head that Hosanna could not be his, his heart still did not want to believe it. During the journey home, she puzzled over how to smooth away the jangled edges of this aloof, touchy man, who, for all his eastern exoticism and self-contained confidence, seemed a little lost. Now she decided. She would give him Sacramenta to keep. The mare was not Hosanna, but, looking at the easy way they swung along the track together, she might provide at least a little solace for his sore heart.

From the back of the procession Elric's voice sang through. He had proven something of a handful, telling Hal firmly before they left Hangem – it would be a long time before it was easy to call it Granville – that although he had scarcely been on so much as a pony before, he wanted 'a destrier, a proper warhorse, one like Hosanna'. Hal had laughed and pitched Elric into the saddle of a large skewbald. It amused him to see the boy's smile soon become a little strained as, for large parts of the journey, instead of Elric being in control of his mount, it was in control of him. From the happy familiarity of Dargent's back, Hal nudged Gethin, who was thrilled at being taken into his confidence. 'Just watch the child,' Hal said, 'but let him learn a lesson or two. He'll be a sorer but wiser boy by journey's end.'

Spring was breaking out everywhere and they made good time. After two days, Will ordered Hal, Gethin and Elric on ahead to alert the Hartslove household that they were on their way. Food and drink for horses and people were to be plentifully supplied. The abbey was to send honey, and the abbot and a few monks were to come to conduct the offices of the dead.

'Tell them to dig Gavin's grave under the old chestnut tree,' said Ellie to Hal. 'Tell them to dig it very deep, so that it will never be disturbed, not for a thousand years or more.' Will nodded his agreement.

By the time they got home, Alan Shortspur had spurred

the castle labourers to greater and greater efforts. Not only was the Hartslove standard flying high, but the castle keep and stables were almost fully restored. Marie was busy organizing the kitchens while Marissa fussed about, demanding a thicker bed and fresher hay for Hosanna. She had the ruby brooch tucked back in her belt.

Everybody turned out to see the procession arrive. Many knelt and crossed themselves. When they drew near, Ellie got out of the hearse and walked slowly behind it until the horses crossed the moat and drew to a halt. Hal and Gethin were waiting and together with Will and Kamil they carried the coffin carefully up the steps and into the great hall, where Alan had laid trestles to receive it. Marie was white and silent, and Marissa, who had rushed forward to welcome Will, found herself courteously but firmly pushed to one side as Will, his lips tightly pressed together, headed back into the courtyard.

It was the strangest day of Ellie's life. Half of her could hardly believe she was back, while the other half felt as if it were still her wedding day. There was the fireplace in front of which Gavin had given her the green jasper necklace. There were the empty chairs of Sir Thomas and Lady de Granville. There was Will's wolfhound still sniffing about, hoping for a bone. She found Old Nurse beside her. 'Come, dearie,' the old lady took Ellie's hand and sat her down. The day outside was warm, but because the hangings had not yet been replaced, the great hall was damp enough for Alan to have ordered a big blaze. Ellie was glad of it. She could see how badly the roof had been damaged from the new, pale-coloured beams that now straddled the ceiling and cast bright shadows. Drawing closer to the fire, she huddled into Old Nurse's arms. The future was all around her, but she was not ready for it yet.

Long, thick candles had been lit and placed at the four corners of Gavin's coffin. Drifting in from outside, the voices of the chanting monks grew louder. Ellie stood up as they filed slowly past her, their faces shadowed by their cowls.

Marie, holding early primroses, followed behind, blinded by her tears. Ellie felt a stab of irritation, followed immediately by a stab of pity. Of course Marie was sad. Hal had told her how carefully and selflessly she had nursed Gavin. Now she had lost both her patient and her guardian.

'Go to her,' murmured Old Nurse, and was proud when Ellie obeyed without question.

'Come, Marie,' the girl said. 'Lay your flowers on the coffin.'

The petals shivered in the candlelight and in their beauty Marie found courage. 'I'm very glad to see you back,' she whispered to Ellie. 'You have been much missed.' Then she went to sit quietly near the door. Here Hal found her, and, after introducing Elric, went back to the stables, full of the sad sweetness of her smile.

Marissa stood at the side of the hall, fingering the brooch. Ever since she had learnt that Will was safe and reunited with his horse, she wanted, above everything, to confirm that his feelings for her were as strong as hers for him. However, now that he was here, she was nervous. Perhaps Kamil had not bothered to tell him about the dramatic rescue from the moat. Perhaps Gavin never had the chance. But her part in that must surely make Will love her. Yet now, here was Ellie back again. Marissa knew she should be glad that Ellie had been rescued, but she was not. Nor was she glad to see Kamil, and wondered if Will knew how much the foreigner coveted his horse. She would warn him. Watching Ellie help Marie put the primroses on Gavin's coffin, she pursed her lips. Then, like a miracle, she heard a shout. At last! Will was calling for her! Forgetting her limp, she flew out and, not even needing to think, headed straight for Hosanna's stable. The horse was standing with his trappings still on and Marissa flung her arms straight round his neck.

Will laughed. 'To think how fearful you were when you first came here,' he said.

Marissa raised her head and at once saw Kamil in the corner. Why did he have to be here? She glared at him. 'I am not so fearful now, but I expect Kamil has told you that I'm not much good as a rider and how we only met because he had to help me.'

Will half smiled, half frowned at her tone. 'He has told me only that you saved Hosanna from drowning. I shall always be in your debt, Marissa.'

She took a deep breath.

Hal came to take off Hosanna's bridle. 'I'll make him comfortable now,' he said, and Elric popped up from under his arm.

'I'll help,' he said, excited by everything he saw.

Hal laughed. 'Come on, then, I'll show you how.'

Will left the stable, tucking Marissa's arm into his own. She was floating. 'I meant what I said about always being in your debt,' he said. 'If Hosanna had drowned, well . . .' They walked in silence until he felt able to continue. 'This afternoon,' he said, 'we are going to bury my brother. You and I are the same now, both without

239

parents – except you are luckier in one respect because you have a sister. Gavin and I parted on bad terms, Marissa. That is a terrible thing. The worst. Make sure you never part from Marie like that for you may never get a chance to make it up. But what I really wanted to say is that I'm going to make Hartslove my base now and that you and Marie will be my family just as you were Gavin's. You are both brave, like Elric, the boy you have just seen with Hal, and brave people are in short supply. King Richard has not yet returned, and who knows what may happen before he does. I will need you.'

Marissa beamed. Keeping hold of his arm, she asked about the escape from the tower, and filled her face with sympathy, not all of it manufactured, when Will told her how he, Ellie and Old Nurse had believed Hosanna to be dead and how Gavin had been killed by de Scabious. He sat down on the edge of the horse trough, and turned his face to the sun as words flooded out about his father, about the crusade, about his boyhood and especially about his brother. Over and over again he told Marissa how Gavin had saved Ellie, as if by telling and retelling the story, he could assuage the pain in his soul. That he had turned out right about Richard, and Gavin wrong, was no comfort. Gavin had done as he saw fit. A man could do no more.

'I wish you had known Hartslove as it was when my father was alive,' he said eventually, getting up. 'But I hope you and Marie will come to like it here. I will do anything I can to make you feel you belong.'

Marissa hesitated only for a moment, then brought out the ruby brooch. The look on Will's face made her hurry to speak before he did. 'If you hadn't given me this brooch,' she said, 'Hosanna would have drowned. I have hardly taken it off since you told me to keep it, and, you know, it was the brooch's stem that helped me to cut Hosanna free.' Will took the brooch and held it, not knowing what to say. But Marissa did. 'Will you pin it on properly, now you are home? After Hosanna and you, it is the thing I love best in the world. It really makes me believe that I belong.' She said nothing more, but took his hand.

She chose her moment well, for as Will, not knowing what else to do, pushed the pin where she showed him, Ellie emerged from the small door at the bottom of the keep, intent on collecting her thoughts as the final preparations were made for Gavin's burial. Will had his back to her and it was not so much the sight of the brooch as the triumphant smile on Marissa's face that brought Ellie up short. Something pricked behind her eyes. She frowned a little, then went to Hosanna's stable, praying that the horse would be alone.

But he was not. Elric was brushing away, untangling his mane, while Kamil leant against the partition. Ellie would have retreated but Hosanna had already seen her and stretched out his head to greet her. He nibbled at her hand until she opened it and showed him the green jasper necklace she was holding tight.

'It's broken, Hosanna,' she said flatly, and slid down into the straw. Elric finished his chores and went away but Kamil remained, watching. Eventually he bent down, took the necklace from Ellie's hand and drew a small knife from his pocket. Ellie closed her eyes. She had dreamt of coming home, but it was not as she expected. She could not find her proper place any more. She was neither bride nor widow nor mistress. Even the servants had grown used to asking Marie about domestic arrangements and did not come near her. And now the ruby brooch was gone for good. Ellie had been through too much to care about jewels, but somehow the loss of that brooch, her wedding brooch, hurt her. She felt that Gavin, as well as herself, had somehow been walked over. The straw shifted as Hosanna lay down, luxuriating in the strengthening sunshine that dappled his side through cracks in the wooden roof. Kamil spoke to him in Arabic.

'What did you say?' asked Ellie, grateful to have something to interrupt her own thoughts.

'I was reminding the red horse of other days, when the sun shone hot in the desert,' replied Kamil. His eyes saw far beyond the stable wall before he bent his head back to his work.

'Tell me,' prompted Ellie.

Kamil held back at first, for Hosanna was the only confidant he wanted, but Ellie's troubled face touched him. As she settled herself against the red horse, allowing the warmth of his body to ease her, Kamil's low, musical voice lulled her half to sleep. He told of Saladin, of how he had been taken under his wing and treated as a son. He described the glory of the desert flowers and the bitter beauty of the mountains and finally he talked of his own family, torn from him when he was a child. There was no direct mention of the crusade – Kamil did not think war was a fit subject for a girl – and when he was finally quiet, he crouched down and Hosanna's skin quivered against his caressing hand.

Kamil wondered at himself, that he had exposed his secrets. He looked defensively at Ellie and found himself scrutinized by a pair of eyes so candid and thoughtful that it was a struggle to break away. He was both sorry and relieved when a shouted summons broke through the silence. The monks were ready. It was time.

Ellie stood, dredging up last reserves of courage, and Kamil, stepping back, closed his heart again. 'Here, it is mended,' he said, holding out her necklace. But he was gone before she could ask him to help her put it on.

Will was standing beside his brother's coffin. When everybody was assembled, he gave the signal and he and four knights picked up their sorry burden to begin the long walk down to the burial place. The monks processed in front, their chant rising above the slow tread of the coffin bearers as they crossed the drawbridge. Ellie followed behind, her hands clasped in front of her. Behind her came Old Nurse, then Marie and Marissa and after them all the Hartslove household, their heads bowed, with Elric in their midst. Kamil watched from the top of the keep.

The afternoon saw the first truly clear sky of the year and the valley was a brilliant patchwork of vivid greens. The squat buds of the chestnut tree were bursting and the young leaves vied with each other for their place in the sun. The gravediggers had dug very deep and long ropes were needed to ease Gavin into his last resting place. Ellie knelt as the coffin was lowered. She gathered leaves from round about her and fluttered them like wedding confetti silently into the grave. She remained kneeling until the monks had finished their prayers and gentle hands eased her away so that the gravediggers could finish their work. Only then did she notice Will standing quite alone. His hands were shaking and holding something as if he could never let it go. Ellie took a deep breath and went over to him.

'Will,' she said, 'will you help me?' He looked at her,

uncomprehending, as she showed him the green jasper necklace. 'It's mended,' she said. 'Kamil fixed it. I want to wear it. Will you fasten it?'

Will lifted his hands and Ellie saw a small skin bag. Wordlessly, he showed her that it contained a ring made of Hosanna's hair and a piece of parchment. 'Can I read it?' she asked.

He nodded. 'Marie wrote it for me. It says "For God, the king and Hosanna". It was our battle cry on crusade, Ellie, and I didn't know what else to put.'

'It's perfect,' she said. They walked towards the grave together and Ellie watched as Will dropped his gift into the earth. 'Gavin is everywhere around here,' she said. 'In the jousting field, by the moat, near the horse trough. We'll never forget him.' She waited for a moment, then handed Will the necklace.

'Green jasper for faith,' he said as he closed the clasp. 'Who will you put your faith in now, Ellie?'

'Myself,' she replied decidedly. 'John has made me free to choose how I live and who I marry, if I should ever choose to do so.'

'And will you choose?'

'I don't know, Will. But I would like to choose to live here, for the moment, at least.'

'This is your home just as it is mine, although it is not the home it once was.'

They began to walk back to the castle. When they got closer, they lingered outside for a while, thinking of Gavin and watching the people going to and fro. Elric trotted behind Hal, who was talking quietly to Marie.

'I shall ask Richard to knight Hal,' said Will. 'He deserves it. And when it happens, I shall give him a castle in my lands at Ravensgarth. I'll keep Elric as my squire.

After Hal has finished training him, he'll do a fine job. What do you think?'

Ellie nodded. But her attention was taken by the figure on top of the keep looking east. 'And Kamil?' she asked. 'What will happen to him?'

But Will did not look at Kamil. He could not stop looking at Ellie. Her face betrayed a longing he had never seen before. 'Ellie . . .' he began, and his tone was full of warning.

She looked at him with surprise and then some fury as the reasons for his concern struck home. 'Do you think girls think about nothing but men and marriage?' she demanded, her eyes accusing.

'Well, no –'

'Kamil was describing the desert to me,' she said. 'I thought I might like to see it for myself one day.'

Will was completely silenced by this. Ellie turned to leave him and saw Marissa hanging back, well within earshot, the ruby brooch blazing on her shoulder. 'If you want a wife, I see one ready and waiting.'

Now it was Will's turn to be angry. 'Don't be so unkind,' he said, and he made Ellie face him. 'Marissa's just a child – a brave child, but just a child. There are lots of things she doesn't understand, things I would never have to explain to you. She knows nothing, really. How could she? She's only just arrived.'

'She looks settled enough to show off my wedding brooch. It should have gone into Gavin's grave.'

Will flinched but he kept himself steady. There must be no misunderstanding here. 'She had it for safekeeping after it dropped when you were abducted,' he said. 'She used it to save Hosanna from the moat. I didn't mean to give it to her, but I felt I couldn't take it back. I thought you would understand, since without her Hosanna would have died. I felt that in some way she deserved it.'

His voice carried in the clear day and before he had even finished, Marissa was running towards them. She was fumbling with the brooch, ripping it off and pushing it at him. 'Marissa!' Will was exasperated. This was Gavin's funeral and no time for childish tantrums. 'Don't be silly. The brooch is yours. It comes with my gratitude.'

'Gratitude? I don't want gratitude.' Marissa flung the brooch to the ground.

Will caught it. 'How dare you,' he said. 'This is Hosanna's brooch.' Then, more gently, 'Can't you see how it should join us all together, not push us apart?' Marissa was crying now and Will put his hands on her shoulders. 'Marissa,' he said, 'you are making a fool of yourself and on this day of all days. Can't you see that?'

'I only see that I will always be on the outside.'

A loud clattering made them all look up. The Hartslove warhorses were galloping over the drawbridge, this time not driven by fear of fire, but by the overwhelming desire to run free and roll the winter off their backs. Will drew Ellie and Marissa to one side as Hal, Elric and a dozen others rode with the horses to guard them. Greys, blacks, roans, skewbalds and bays, they poured out, tossing their manes in the breeze. Even the old horses bucked and kicked in their delight. Hosanna and Sacramenta brought up the rear. They paused when Ellie called their names, circling the three figures several times, their tails like banners. Then they streamed off, their hooves skimming past the newly dug grave as they made for the river.

'Those two look like rubies themselves,' said Ellie, and

246

the moment was suddenly very full. Before it could pass, she took the brooch from Will and deftly pinned it back to Marissa's bodice herself. Will made an exclamation and walked away.

Ellie watched him drift after the horses, his head bowed, and sighed. Then she turned back to Marissa. 'This is Hosanna's gift,' she said, 'and you should wear it with pride. You are not on the outside here. How could you be? We all know that we owe Hosanna's life to you. You and Marie are the start of something new at Hartslove. Don't let's ruin it with silly jealousies and pointless hankerings after things that can never be.'

'I'll love Will always,' said Marissa defiantly, but she left the jewel where Ellie had placed it.

'Love Will, by all means,' said Ellie, 'but if you let love make you angry and miserable, you will lose everything. As for Hosanna's brooch, well, Will's right. You do deserve it. I can't help feeling something when I look at it, Marissa, but that feeling, if we both try, need not always be as it is now.'

The younger girl looked after Will, but she knew that she would never find what she hoped for in his eyes. She left Ellie and as she crossed the drawbridge, she glanced into the moat's still waters, then down the hill to the grazing horses. When she eventually went back through the castle gate, she sat in Hosanna's empty stable for a very long time.

Ellie caught up with Will. 'Green jasper,' she said wistfully. 'Gavin gave it, the constable broke it, Hosanna found it, Kamil mended it and you refastened it. What does it all mean, Will?'

He shook his head. 'I don't know, Ellie. Perhaps it means that faith is the only thing that lasts.' She knelt down, crumbling the earth and he knelt beside her. 'I must go and help organize Richard's ransom gold,' he said. 'I have told John that I will take it to Germany. It must be collected quickly for we need to see our king back on English soil.'

Ellie was quite still. 'When the ransom is ready,' she said, 'I will go with you.' Something flickered in Will's heart. 'You can't stop me,' Ellie said. 'Gavin paid a high price for my freedom.'

'I don't want to stop you,' Will replied. They got up and stood briefly silhouetted together in the afternoon sun.

Then Ellie turned away and walked back, alone, to Gavin's graveside, her necklace softly glowing against her neck. 'Green jasper for faith, Gavin,' she whispered. 'I shan't forget.' And as if in answer, from over the valley, the abbey bell tolled.